Going Gone

Book Two of
The Irish End Game Series

Susan Kiernan-Lewis

Susan Kiernan-Lewis

San Marco Press

Copyright 2013

ACKNOWLEDGMENTS

First, I want to thank my editor, Elizabeth White, for her spot-on insight and advice in the editing of *Going Gone*. It helps immensely when dealing with continuity, facts (even when I deliberately switch them all around) and the mechanics of writing when you have someone in your corner as smart and experienced as Elizabeth.

Thanks also to my critique group, *The Serivilous Panerians* including Cheri Roman, Cynthia Enuton, Tracie Roberts, Mark Vance and Rai Yates. You guys keep me grounded and save me from an awful lot of egg on my face.

Susan Kiernan-Lewis

Chapter One

Mike Donovan looked up from the drawings in front of him on the makeshift wooden desk, his reading glasses perched on his long, very un-Irish nose. His sister, Fiona stood in the opening of the lean-to, an empty cookpot resting on one hip, watching him. He sighed and removed his glasses, tossing them down on the desk.

"We've got a problem," she said, pursing her lips as if she'd just tasted a lemon.

"Whatever it is, Fi," he said, "couldn't you have softened the blow with a cuppa?"

"It's Gavin," Fi said, jerking her head to indicate the direction of Mike's son. "And young John."

He looked up with interest. "John?" he said, frowning. "What trouble has Gavin gotten the boy into now?"

Gavin was a good lad, and immensely helpful as an extra hand, but he lacked the judgment that would enable any sane body to call him mature. The fact that he had taken Sarah's boy, John, under his wing as the little brother he never had was rarely to anyone's benefit.

"Their roughhousing knocked the chicken stew in the dirt. It's only fit for the hogs now."

"None of it could be saved?" Mike stood up. Wasting food was a serious offence. Probably would have been even before The Crisis, but now it could mean the difference between life and death. And there were none of them that didn't know that to the very marrow of their bones. "Where are they?"

"Waiting for you. In the barn."

"Shite." Mike stood to his full height then ducked to avoid hitting the short lean-to's ceiling. His hand rested on the belt around his waist.

"You'll not beat them?" Fiona asked. She stepped out of his way, as if half expecting him to bowl her over in his eagerness to reprimand the boys.

"Gavin's too old," he said tiredly. He glanced at his sister, whose eyes snapped with irritation over the ruined stew.

"And little John?" she said. She stared him down, challenging him. He knew what she was thinking. Sarah's boy. You wouldn't dare.

"Tell Gavin to take the night watch on the south pasture," he said. He knew he had to send him mounted. No sense in sending the daft bugger on foot—although Mike was sorely tempted to do it—in case he needed to sound the alarm. "But he's wasted enough food for one day. He can do it on an empty stomach."

"And John?" Fiona repeated, more gently this time.

"He knows what's coming," Mike said gruffly. "Tell Gavin to go. I'll be on my way directly." He could see his answer satisfied her, which annoyed him. "And maybe you can find something in the way of replacing the meal we'll be needing in a few hours?" he added acerbically.

She nodded and hurried off toward the barn.

Shite. Mike took a moment to look over the edge of the camp to where David and Sarah's cottage sat. He hated that they refused to join the community. But they let John come as much as they could spare him. And they knew the rules as well as he did. Even so, he didn't relish telling the American soccer mom, who only countenanced "time-outs" and lengthy written exercises as punishments, that he was about to beat the pants off her boy with a leather belt.

***

David and Sarah arrived at Donovan's community late in the afternoon. A skinned rabbit was carefully wrapped and stashed in a hamper sitting on Sarah's knee. Every time Sarah came to the camp she was surprised at how much had been built to make it the little bustling community that it was.

The first person she saw was Fiona Donovan. "Hey, Fi," Sarah said, hopping down from the cart. "Brought ya a bunny for your crock pot."

"Sure, I'll never understand your American humor," Fiona said, taking the meat from her and giving her a hug.

"John in shouting distance?" Sarah asked, looking around the settlement. A large campfire anchored the middle of the camp, with recently constructed huts, tents and bedrolls fanning out around it.

"Oh, he's around here somewhere," Fiona said. "Good afternoon to you, David," she said, as David jumped down from the cart seat. "You'll be wanting to put the animals up in the barn. Just leave the cart where it is."

David unharnessed the pony and led him away from the center of camp. Fiona and Sarah walked over to the large black pot hanging from a hook over the fire ringed in stones.

"Mmm-mm. Smells good." Sarah peered in the pot.

"If you lived here," Fiona said, leaning over to pick up a steaming kettle of water, "you'd eat with us every night."

"We're doing fine over there."

"Who said you weren't?" Fiona said, pouring boiling water into a large, chipped teapot. "It's not just about protection or getting enough to eat. It's about fellowship, Sarah."

"I know, and I agree with you." Sarah continued to crane her neck, searching.

Fiona handed her a cup of tea.

"Hey, Mom. Looking for me?"

Sarah turned to see John who had materialized at her elbow. She had recently learned not to hug him—at least not in public. Her smile dissolved when she looked more closely at him. "John, what happened to you?" She reached out to him.

"Nothing happened to me," he said, pulling away from her grasp. "Stop it."

His eyes were red and his face tear-streaked. Sarah knew it took a lot to get tears from her boy. She looked at Fiona and was rewarded with a hasty glance away. "What happened, Fi?"

"Nothing, Mom," John said. "Why can't you leave it alone?" He turned on his heel and bolted away from her.

Sarah watched him go, her mouth open, then turned back to her friend. "You're not going to tell me?"

"Not if the lad doesn't want me to. Drink your tea."

Sarah turned in the direction John had gone and forced herself to let it go. He was all in one piece. That was the main thing. Whatever had happened, he didn't want to share it with her. She had to admit that had started to happen more and more. On top of everything else, she thought miserably, I'm losing my little boy, too.

She sipped her tea, letting the heat slip down her throat and soothe her. A young woman approached and spooned up a bowl of soup. Sarah couldn't help notice how outlandish the woman, Caitlin's, outfit was. Dressed in skintight leggings with a low-cut top, she looked like she was dressed for a night of clubbing, not eating stew by a campfire. The girl made a dramatic show of looking at Sarah from head to toe before sneering and turning away.

"What the heck is her problem?"

Fiona sighed. "Well, Caitlin is a special case, there's no mistake. But still, you can't be too surprised not to have people waving flags when you show up, what with you so standoffish and all."

"Standoffish? Are you serious?"

"Sarah, we've talked about this before. You and your David setting up in Deidre and Seamus's old cottage far outside our walls—"

"First, Fiona, you don't have walls, and second, you know we took their cottage because it's hidden from the road. We're safer there."

"There's nothing safer than numbers," a voice boomed out, making Sarah spill her tea on her jeans. Mike Donovan definitely had a big way about him, not the least of which was his voice. Using it now, while he was still a good twenty yards away, her first thought was incredulity that he had heard enough of their conversation to enter into it.

"Hey, Mike," she said. "Still banging on that drum, are you?"

"Sure, and I'll be banging on it until you and David come to your senses and move out of the McClenny place and over here with us."

Mike squatted down next to the two women and Sarah couldn't help but think it wasn't an easy feat with his long legs. "You doing alright, Sarah?" His eyes pierced hers in anything but a casual inquiry and his directness made Sarah catch her breath.

"We're doing good, Mike," she said, smiling at him. "We're hanging in there."

The look he gave her said that was not the question he had asked. Before she had the chance to divert him along safer lines, a commotion behind him in the direction of the stables did it for her. She looked past him to see David and John walking quickly toward them. John was trying to talk to David and was running along beside him. David was walking, his chin high and confrontational, his fists clenched at his sides,

"I want a word with you, Donovan," he said abruptly as he approached the group.

Mike stood up slowly and turned to face him. Sarah saw him rest his hands on his hips in a gesture of calm and insouciance. She stood up too.

"Woodson," Mike said calmly.

"It's none of your business," John said hotly to his father. "It's my business and I've taken care of it."

David ignored him, his eyes drilling into Mike Donovan. "Some of the guys at the stable mentioned to me that you beat my son today?"

Sarah gasped and couldn't help looking at Mike and then John.

"It's none of your business!" John said, jerking his father by the sleeve to get his attention. "I screwed up."

"I asked you a question, Donovan," David said, clenching and unclenching his fists.

"That's right," Mike said. "John knows the rules. He broke 'em. He was punished for it."

"You…you struck him?" Sarah asked, looking at John with the streaks of dirty tears down his face.

Mike turned to her. "I gave him a hiding, same as I'd do to anyone if through horseplay and uncaring they deprived the community out of hard-earned food." He turned back to David. "You think this is a game, Woodson? You think we're camping out here? This is life and death, man."

"You arrogant bastard," David said. "You got your own private dictatorship here, don't you? Donovan's Kingdom."

"No, Dad," John said walking over to Mike and standing in front of him. "It's not like that. I was wrong. It's the rule. We gotta have rules. Especially now."

Sarah gritted her teeth and took a long breath to keep control of her emotions, but she saw David lose his own as his face contorted into a mask of fury and intent.

Just when she knew he was about to launch himself at Mike, the earth rumbled beneath their feet and a roar of thunderous noise bombarded the camp, building to an excruciating pitch until the noise obliterated everything.

Chapter Two

From the pieces of knapsack and useless bits of metal trinkets found embedded in the surrounding oak trees, they guessed he had been a peddler.

The sound of the explosion had sent half the camp running toward the south entrance. Mothers ran screaming the names of their children, the unbearable sounds of terror ratcheting higher with every step.

Mike reached the area with the first wave of the panicked. He stepped carefully into the brand new clearing, which was smoking and foul smelling. "Head count!" he shouted, looking around with pounding heart. It wasn't one of their watch sites—in fact, everyone knew it was strictly off-limits—but that didn't mean it wasn't a place a bored child wouldn't wander off to. He listened to the voices, tremulous and tearful, angry and confrontational, as they reeled off their names in the order that had been decided. Each head of household called out his surname and the phrase "all accounted for" to indicate the whereabouts of each member of his family was known.

When Donovan announced his own name, with only Gavin to account for, it occurred to him like the feel of a deadly asp slithering into his sleeping bag that he did not know where his son was.

The Woodsons were at his elbow within minutes. Not formally a part of the group, they remained silent as they surveyed the damage. "Who set it off?" Sarah asked.

Donovan held up a hand to her, demanding silence as he listened to the members of his group call out their names to assure him as they did that their community remained intact.

As he listened, his eyes scanned the trees and the smoking hole before him where the landmine had been triggered, and he registered that the birds had stopped singing, the camp dogs had stopped barking.

Death has a habit of stalling everything about normal daily life, he thought bitterly.

"Da? You okay over there?"

He gave a shuddering sigh at the sound of his son's voice, calling to him from across the camp. Without looking at him, he raised his hand to indicate Gavin was to return to his watch.

By this time, the crowd had stopped calling out their names and were, instead, jostling babies, pulling children back from the lip of the smoking pit, and kicking at the rim and surrounding area with boot toes and sticks.

One woman's shrill voice pierced the din of noise above the others. "God have mercy, Mike, are there any more here?"

Donovan turned to look at David, who stood grimly by his side.

David shook his head without looking at Donovan.

"No, Maeve," Mike called to the woman. "Just the usual areas. You all know them."

"Well, what made it go off, then?" another man called out. "Were we being attacked, or should we be looking to pick pieces of raw mutton off the trees?"

Mike registered the angry voice, soon joined by others, and he resisted the urge to look at David—the man responsible for the smoking hole and the slowly building hysteria in his community.

"Go back to camp," he said tiredly, trying to sound commanding. "I'll investigate and make a full report at dinner."

Now he did turn to David who, maddeningly, didn't appear to show any responsibility for what had happened. If anything, he looked as if he had a mind to resume the fight with Mike over John's whipping. Steeling himself to stay calm and not react, Mike glanced at Sarah. "Take John back to camp," he said. When she hesitated, looking instead to David, Mike added an edge to his voice. "*Now*," he said. Without a word, she grabbed her son's hand and tugged him away from the two men.

Mike stood with his hands on his hips looking at the destruction. "I want the rest of the landmines dismantled," he said icily. "If you want to ring them around your own cottage, you're welcome to."

"That's not what your group said three months ago when we buried these."

"Three months ago we were bulldozed by your paranoia."

"I'm not sure anyone would believe *you* were bulldozed, Donovan. Fact is, you were outvoted. Your group wanted the security. Just because some degenerate gypsy or wandering tinker crept up on the camp and got himself blown up doesn't mean the mines aren't still a good idea."

"Just get rid of them."

"We haven't had an incident in six months and now you think you're living in Brigadoon?" David looked at him with disgust. "How do you know this guy, whoever he is, wasn't the advance guard of an attack? How do you know the landmine didn't send the message to his gang that we aren't ripe for the picking?"

Donovan strode over to a nearby ash tree and pried out a metal button with flowers stamped on it. He came back to Woodson and threw it at him, watching it ping off the man's chest. "This guy was a peddler," he said heatedly. "He wasn't the *advance man* on anything except maybe in his plan to trade a few buttons for a hot meal tonight."

David shrugged. "For all you know."

"Yeah, for all I know. But I'm in charge and I'm telling you to remove them." He turned to look at the smoking hole again.

"It makes me sick to think I let you talk me into them in the first place."

"Maybe you were more concerned about protection a few months back."

"We have security measures."

"A few pits with sharpened stakes in them? A couple of tree snares? Three teenage boys rotating watch on the perimeter?" David jabbed a finger in the direction of the hole. "*This* is the only thing that protects you at the end of the day. Telling everyone under no uncertain terms that you'll kill first and ask questions later. *This* is what keeps the murdering thieves and opportunists moving past your place to the next poor sod."

"Maybe," Donovan muttered. "But right now we just killed the next poor sod and I'm not convinced the price was worth it. Dig up the other two. *Today*." He turned on his heel and left Woodson standing alone in the peaceful glade, the chirping of the birds in the trees once more resuming.

John and Sarah trudged back from the explosion site to stand next to their pony cart in the center of camp and wait for David. They felt the hostile stares and grumblings as they walked. It was clear whom the camp was blaming for the disturbance.

"Mr. Donovan's gonna make Dad dismantle the other bombs," John said, swinging up to sit in the driver's seat. "He thinks they're dangerous."

"They *are* dangerous," Sarah said, watching the opening to the grove where Mike and her husband still conferred, hidden from view. "But necessary. Like having a loaded weapon. Very dangerous, but thank God for it when you need it."

"Yeah. Dad says you can always accomplish more with a kind word and a rifle than you can with just a kind word."

"How very Irish-sounding of him." Sarah smiled, trying to lighten the mood.

"Who do you think got blown up?" John asked, looking at his hands.

Sarah felt her heart clutch. Lately the child was always so sure of himself, it surprised her when he reverted back to being the young boy he really was. She reached out to take his hand. "I don't know, angel," she said. "Some poor soul, I suppose."

"Dad says we have to strike first if we want to be safe."

"Well, I think he's right. This world we live in isn't like Jacksonville during a hurricane warning or something. There are truly treacherous people out there…" She turned to wave to the countryside beyond the borders of the little camp. "It's a lawless time right now. Until we can get everything back up."

"I know, Mom, but doesn't that make us lawless too? I mean, hiding bombs for innocent people to walk on?"

"John, I know this sounds harsh, and I don't want to scare you, but you don't know when the bad people will come. You have to be ready. You have to strike first."

"That's what Dad says too."

Sarah realized that the time John spent in the community away from his family was having an effect on him. He was pulling away from her and David, toward their way of thinking.

"Fiona says we're like isolationists or something," John mumbled.

"Fiona said that?"

"Don't be mad at her, Mom. She's just saying what a lot of people are saying, only nicer."

"I see." Sarah turned away from him as she caught a glimpse of Mike striding back into the camp without David. "People blame us for what happened."

"Well, it *is* our fault. Being Americans and all."

"Maybe." Sarah patted his knee. "Chill here for a bit, John? I need to go have a word with Mr. Donovan."

Mike saw her heading his way and knew he should've expected it. She wasn't used to being ordered about, least ways by him. Come to that, he wasn't used to doing it. It surprised him how easy it came and, truth be told, how he'd actually enjoyed

15

doing it. No, safety in numbers or not, he had to admit there was some benefit to having her live out of reach.

"Mike, hold up, please," she said as she trotted beside him.

"Sarah," he said, not breaking his stride.

"Are you having David dig up the other landmines?"

"I am."

"Do you think that's wise?"

"Why else would I be doing it?"

She grabbed him by the sleeve and forced him to stop. "There are threats everywhere, Mike."

"So you say."

"How can you possibly doubt it? After what happened last year? After what nearly happened to Gavin? To…to me?"

Mike looked down into her face and remembered the fear and desperation of those bad days. He remembered her agony when she thought she had lost her son and her husband, and he knew why she couldn't feel safe. He lifted a hand and touched her shoulder lightly.

"We can't live in anticipation of the worst happening," he said gently.

She watched his eyes, as if he would say more. As if that wasn't enough. As if that argument wasn't just too obviously weak to stand on its own.

"That's exactly what we have to live in anticipation of," she said finally. "All the time. Or risk being caught off guard. That's what these new times require, Mike."

He dropped his hand, like it had suddenly become too heavy for him to lift. "Not here, they don't," he said, turning to leave her where she stood by the center cook fire.

Caitlin stood in the veiled opening of her tent and watched as Mike put his hand on the American's shoulder. She saw his glance, just for the barest of moments, leave the woman's eyes as she spoke and drop to her mouth. The fury she felt when he did that pulsed through her like a tidal wave surging over a seawall. Caitlin knew he fancied the Yank. Everyone in camp who wasn't either blind or half-witted knew it. That he could be so bold with her—and her with her own husband not twenty yards away! — made Caitlin want to rip his ruddy, handsome face with her fingernails. Though she'd yet to catch them, she was sure the two were already rutting: *they must be! And catch them she would, of that you can be certain*, she thought, squatting and stabbing the ground mindlessly with the broken fork she'd been holding in her hands.

She definitely bloody *would*.

Susan Kiernan-Lewis

Chapter Three

In the months and years to come, Sarah would always remember that crisp, bright fall day as one of the prettiest she'd ever experienced since coming to Ireland. The memory would do little to console her during the terrible days ahead.

She and David and John had left the camp as dusk fell. David refused to stay—and no one begged them to change their minds. In the back of the little pony cart sat the two rusting landmines David had removed from the perimeter of the camp. He'd intended to replant them around their own cottage, but had to admit they didn't look functional anymore—if they ever had been. Mike insisted he take them away, and so they rattled and jostled in the back of the pony trap until he could dump them at the edge of the little pond on the outskirts of Deirdre and Seamus's property. In the morning, he would row out to the middle of the pond and drop them in.

John had been silent on the ride back to their cottage. Sarah knew he wanted to be with his parents, but that he was torn. She made it easy on him by insisting he come home with them. She offered an early release to him by allowing him to return the next day after breakfast if his chores were done.

After leaving the undetonated bombs by the pond, they'd trudged home, tired and hungry in the dark. Sarah knew they had been viewed as bad mannered and foolish to leave after dark, but there wasn't anything for it.

They were no longer welcome in Donovan's Lot.

David drove the cart to the front of the cottage, where Sarah and John hopped out. Someone had tossed the dead rabbit into the back of the cart—dramatic proof in these hungry times of how reviled they had become. She ushered her tired boy into the house while David led the ponies to the barn, where he would untack and feed them.

After a quick swipe with a soapy washcloth, she bundled John off to bed. There was enough light by the full moon, so she didn't bother wasting precious oil by lighting the lamps. She lit one candle and set it by the bedside and waited for David. She heard him come in and wash up briefly before coming into the bedroom and sagging onto the bed. It had been a demoralizing, sapping day for all of them. As bold and sure as David sounded when arguing with Mike—or even the whole camp, as it had felt when so many people approached them later with recriminations for their part in the peddler's death, indeed the origin of The Crisis, itself—Sarah knew he had doubts.

It's true, she thought, tiredly. *If they want to lay the blame for this at the Americans' feet, they're probably right.* While the few facts they had about why all the electronics failed and all the cars refused to move seem to point in the direction of a retaliation attempt against the Americans for something that happened in the Middle East, it was still hard for a middle class family of three to carry the can for a whole nation in the face of such righteous anger.

When you're the head dog, the other dogs in the harness—so-called friends or not—are not going to soon forget the poor scenery they suffered through along the way. It didn't matter that Ireland and the US were friends (or at least they used to be.) It didn't matter how many people in the US were Irish-descendants. In the end, it only mattered that the US had been the target that allowed its closest friends (at least those friends standing too close) to take the hit for them.

And David and Sarah were the face of that now-hated target.

"Pretty crappy day," David said, as he sought a comfortable position in the bed. "John okay?"

"He's fine," Sarah said, feeling the weariness of the day sink into her bones with the realization that she never got her dinner. "Did you eat?"

David gave a half-laugh that relayed no mirth.

Sarah put a hand on his shoulder. "We need to mend our fences with the community, David. They're all we have. We can't cut off ties with them. We need them."

"For what? In what possible way do we need them?" David wrenched the covers over his shoulders and turned from her. She knew the questions weren't an invitation to conversation. It was just as well. She was so tired as it was she could have wept.

The next morning crept up on them. Accustomed to the mornings being cold and wet during this time of year, David and Sarah had gotten in the habit of rising late and allowing the fog and mist to burn off before starting their chores. Sarah would get the cook stove going for their morning tea, and if there was any food in the house she would cobble together a kind of breakfast. Most mornings she would make dough in hopes that she'd have bread to serve for dinner. Her inexperience combined with the continual dampness in the air usually prevented the dough from rising, resulting in an unsatisfyingly unleavened and very dense bread that nobody enjoyed, but all ate.

John's chores involved keeping the firewood box in the kitchen full of kindling—for which he didn't have to use a hatchet or an axe to Sarah's relief—and to feed the animals—the two ponies, the dog, the lone goat and the flock of chickens that essentially sustained them when the summer garden's harvest ran out. Sarah noticed that the box was full of kindling but they were running low on firewood. She stood in the kitchen door that opened up to the back pasture, where she saw David already chopping wood. He looked intense, single-minded and determined. A wave of sadness passed through her as she watched him. He'd had such a different life "back home." An associate professor at a small university in Jacksonville, Florida, he had been beloved by his students and enjoyed a rich and stimulating life of the mind.

She watched him attack the wood stump, his arms rippling with the muscles he'd created through their new life, and wondered what he thought of these days. Did he still worry out knotty philosophical problems as he toiled and physically labored? Did he miss beyond endurance his world in the classroom? His kingdom of academia? No wonder he let Mike get to him. Sarah couldn't help glancing in the direction of the community. Mike's plantation was real, his rule unassailable and tangible. His authority unimpeachable.

No wonder David flinched under his influence. Back in his world, Mike Donovan would be cutting David's lawn for him.

Sarah squinted against the horizon to catch a glimpse of John. She could tell by where the sun was that it wasn't early, though still well before eight in the morning. She glanced again at the box full of kindling. It was very possible the boy had rushed through his chores before his parents were even out of bed, saddled his pony and left for Donovan's camp. He was drawn to the man—and his tented kingdom—like a boy was drawn to adventure.

She withdrew into the kitchen and began pounding the dough that, hopefully, would transform into a loaf of bread in eight short hours. As she was covering the bowl of dough with one of Deirdre's kitchen towels, she turned to see her husband standing in the doorway, his arms full of cut firewood. He was staring at her with an expression of unutterable sadness.

"David? You okay?"

He grunted and dumped the wood into the flat basket next to the cook stove. "I think John's already gone off."

"I was wondering about that. You didn't see him before he left?"

David didn't answer, and when Sarah looked up from tucking the bowl of dough against the wall on the kitchen counter she saw that he appeared to be examining her thoughtfully.

"What is it?"

"You know he's in love with you," David said flatly.

Her face must have relayed her thoughts, because he spoke before she could. "And do us both a favor and don't say *who*?"

"Well, I think you're imagining that," she said, wiping her hands on her apron and breaking eye contact with him.

"Yeah, right. How can I blame him? I just don't need to see it on a daily basis."

She faced him. "Look, David, I can't say what is or isn't going on in Mike Donovan's head, but as long as it isn't in mine, what difference does it make?"

"Yeah, right," he said again. "He's already taken my son."

"Don't even say that! If you're talking about the…about Mike spanking John, I hate it too, but I understand it. These are different times, hard times."

"It takes a village?" David said sarcastically, and Sarah suddenly realized it wasn't a part of him she had ever seen much. Except lately.

"The concept of everyone having your back in a community is as old as time," Sarah said, wondering why he was putting her in the position of defending the community. "Mike didn't invent it." She turned to pour his tea into a large earthenware mug.

"Are you making an appeal to move in with them?"

"You know I'm not."

She set his tea out on the table in front of him, but he turned after a moment and walked out of the kitchen.

The rest of the day was a quiet one between them, and Sarah would have cause to remember that, too. The fog had burned off and revealed a beautiful fall day, crisp and clear, the sky a blue so vivid she wished she had watercolors to capture it. Even the sun struggled out for several hours in the afternoon and Sarah wondered what John was doing with the fine day. *Was he swimming with Gavin in the pond? Was he fishing? Was Mike showing him how to use the new hand-carved tools some of the men were making?* She thought of Fiona and was grateful for the affection and warmth she knew she directed at John.

It was just as she was pulling the pan of baked bread from the oven and feeling the thrill of a job well done—it had risen beautifully! —that she heard the noise from the road that zigzagged covertly up the hill above their cottage. She set the bread on the rack on the counter and went to the kitchen window, turning back a corner of the curtain she often thought of poor Deirdre hand-sewing as a young bride. The forecourt was empty and she tried to recreate in her mind the sound she thought she had heard.

Situated as it was down a twisting hill covered and camouflaged by rampant ivy and scrub brush that prevented an easy view of the little cottage tucked away at the bottom like a jewel, the idea that casual travelers or wayfarers would happen upon the cottage was not readily believable. It was half the reason she and David decided to move into it.

Had she imagined the noise?

Having learned the hard way on more than one occasion the merit in taking action based on the safest course rather than a philosophy of *what were the odds?* Sarah stepped out of view from the window and dug out the loaded Glock pistol from a kitchen drawer. She had been standing in this very cottage the day three murdering gypsy ruffians had attacked her, though then she'd been armed with only a rolling pin.

She held her breath and waited. Complete silence answered her. A stab of growing unease punctured her chest and begin to creep its way toward her throat. David had been working on the fence in the south pasture—the one closest to the house. The faraway ringing sound of his hammer against the metal studs of the wooden fence could be heard from the kitchen...or should be.

There shouldn't be complete silence.

It had been many months since she had handled the gun, and she felt her nerves jump as she quickly checked the clip to make sure it was loaded. Her hands were moist and she took a moment to wipe them, one by one, on her apron. She edged over to the back door and peered out, taking care not to show herself in the window in the door.

There were four of them. Three men were standing by David at the furthest corner of the pasture fence line, his tools lying discarded at his feet. He had his hands up as if to disarm them with his vulnerability. Sarah's heart jumped when she saw him, saw them. From this distance, it was no wonder she hadn't heard them, although she could see they were conversing. When one of the men raised the butt of his rifle to David's face, he almost looked like he was pantomiming until he brought it crashing down, causing David's head to snap back before he fell against the fence.

Sucking in a horrified breath, Sarah flung open the kitchen door and was down the back steps and into the pasture, door banging shut behind her. She wasn't the only one who heard it. As she ran, the gun she held in both hands pointing at the group of men in front of her, the tip of it bouncing up and down, she heard only her breath coming in jagged rasps and pants. She could see David on the ground.

He wasn't moving.

She saw them turn—all three of them—to face her. The closer she got, she could see by their clothing that they were not Irish. They were not starving either. The man with the rifle pointed it at her and she slowed her steps to allow a steadier aim. Seamus had killed three men the last time they'd been attacked at this cottage because the blackguards hadn't thought him capable of it. She wasn't sure she was fostering the same assumption of incompetence this time.

She moved nearer to them, and caught glimpses of her husband on the ground. He was moving and groaning, thank God. She forced herself not to look at him and aimed the barrel of her Glock at the man with the rifle. She was surprised to see how normal he looked. He wore jeans and a tee shirt with running shoes. He looked like he had somehow avoided the last hard year of no food, no petrol, and fear. Unlike almost everybody else she had seen since The Crisis, he didn't look uncomfortable or needy.

He smiled at her in what looked, perversely, likely a genuinely warm greeting. "Well, hello, hello," he said, his voice smooth and controlled.

He was English.

"This little plum was worth stopping for, eh, boys? Fine round arse on her. Won't Denny love trying *her* on for size? Are you American, then, too, luv?" he asked as he casually swept the barrel of his rifle so that it pointed at David on the ground.

Sarah glanced at the other two men to satisfy her initial assessment that they were the underlings and this young man—he couldn't be twenty-five—was the one in control.

"All of you bugger off," she said breathlessly, feeling her arms start to shake from the exertion of holding the heavy gun out in front of her.

The three men erupted into laughter, truly delighted.

"Blimey! She's like Wonder-fuckin'-woman!"

The other two men crowed loudly at their leader's humor and repeated the phrase to heightened bouts of laughter.

"David!" she called out. Out of the corner of her eye she could see he was stirring, trying to sit up, but his face was splattered with blood. He appeared dazed and shook his head, trying to clear it. "I mean it, You bastards better head out. I will shoot you!"

"Nah, you won't, darlin'," the leader of the group said, nudging David's face with the barrel of his rifle. "I must say, I don't like people pointing guns at me. Oy, Jimmy, sit the Yank up there by the fence."

Sarah watched as the two men grabbed David by the arms and dragged him to a sitting position and propped him up by the fence. She could see he was struggling to come to his senses.

If only their positions were reversed! Should I just start shooting? The bastard was holding his gun right to David's head. Would he have time to shoot him before I—

"Oy, chickie, here's the deal," the leader said, grinning a smile of very white, very straight teeth. "Give me your gun or I'll blow his fuckin' head off."

She could see David shaking his head. He might be trying to clear his head, he might just be addled, but she felt sure he was telling her not to give it up.

The Englishman slammed the nose of his rifle into David's temple and David groaned, but he didn't topple over.

"Give me the gun or I shoot the bastard!" the Englishman yelled.

Sarah later would believe that a part of her didn't understand the words or comprehend the meaning. A part of her was only terrorized and harboring some belief that this creature would not kill her or her husband—even in this terrible new world. But right at that very moment she only knew, if it meant her own death, she couldn't just let them kill the man she loved, the father to her child…her David. And so she dropped her arms —her heavy, tremulous arms, with their weighty purchase—and let the gun fall into the grassy dirt at her feet.

She never even heard the monster's grunt of satisfaction over the sound of the gun blast that blew the top of her husband's head off.

Susan Kiernan-Lewis

Chapter Four

The sounds of gunshots were unusual these days, and it didn't take long for reports of the noise to make the rounds in Donovan's small community of fifty people. He, himself, had heard the single gunshot as he was coming out of the stable, leading a horse on either side. He must have tensed, because one of the horses shied and had to be calmed. Although it was impossible to tell which direction the sound came from, instinctively he looked toward the Woodson cottage. He noticed his sister-in-law, Caitlin, standing by her tent watching him and he nodded curtly toward her in greeting. Gavin came running from across the central camp cook fire.

"Da! Did you hear that? Sounds like it came from over near the Woodsons'. Me and Danny'll check it out, eh?"

Mike handed the horses off to a young teenage girl who materialized on his left. "Take these two, Nuala," he said to her. "Put 'em in the paddock for now."

"Not the south pasture, Mr. Donovan?"

The girl was earnest and hardworking, Donovan knew. Pretty, too, but she didn't seem to realize it.

"Not just yet. Go on now." He turned to Gavin, who was standing in front of him bouncing on the balls of his feet.

"Where's young John?" he asked.

Gavin pointed to the other side of the cook fire. "Fiona's got him plucking chickens," he said.

Donovan followed his glance and saw that John was, indeed, standing with Fiona, a pile of feathers at his feet. But he was looking in the direction of his home.

"Send him to me," Donovan said. "And you go. But mind! Be sneaky about it. If there's trouble over there, I want information not grandstanding."

Gavin was off before Mike had finished speaking. He watched him grab John by the shoulder and point to Donovan before sprinting off in the direction of the house. Mike saw John struggle between the desire to follow Gavin and obey the order to come to Mike. He turned and trotted over to Donovan.

"You hear a gunshot?" Mike asked him.

"Yes, sir. Over at our place."

"We don't know that. Gavin's off to check on it and I'll be needing you to stay here until we know what's going on."

"But, I…" John was clearly moments from tearing out after Gavin and Mike couldn't help but think it a blessing that just the day before he'd the opportunity to impress upon the boy that he was to be obeyed at all times. If young John's backside hadn't still been smarting from his recent shellacking—and Mike had no doubt that it was—he might have been tempted to ignore Mike's wishes. As it was, he looked in frustration in the direction of his house.

"Go on, now," Mike said. "Finish your chores. Gavin'll be back in a tick if there's anything to report."

Mike watched John trudge back to the campfire, where Fiona waited for him. She gave Mike a questioning look but he merely shrugged.

They'd find out soon enough.

***

Sarah sat in the back of the wooden cart, her hands tied in front of her, a gag in her mouth, her head leaning and banging against the rough wood sides of the bouncing cart as it jostled over the once-smooth country roads. The time between David being shot and her placement in the cart felt like a sequence in a dream. She didn't remember how she got here, if she walked or was carried. She didn't remember if the men spoke to her after they'd killed David, or laughed, or just turned away from the carnage. She didn't know how long she had been sitting in the cart or how long it had been traveling down the long, bumpy road.

Three women huddled with her in the bottom of the wooden cart but Sarah didn't look at them. The smell of vomit, and worse, pooled on the floor, and with her mouth bound she was forced to breathe every vile gust through her nose. One of the women, a girl it sounded like, was crying softly, almost noiselessly.

The sound began to push the image of David to the forefront of her mind and she fought to sink back into her numb state. She couldn't think of him. She couldn't remember her last vision of him. Dear God, she would go mad. She couldn't remember any of it right now. Later. She would remember it later.

She tried to tell herself, as the cart lurched down the road, that none of this was real.

How? How could it have happened? The cottage was hidden from the road, was virtually invisible.

As she fought to keep the images and thoughts from overwhelming her, she looked back at the cottage from where she sat in the cart. A heavy tarp was thrown over the top, but afforded a wedge of a window to the outside world. She thought, inanely, of the lone cooling loaf of bread on the counter in her kitchen at the same moment that she saw the long telltale smoke from their chimney and her cook stove heralding the way to their sanctuary.

Donovan didn't believe he had ever been more exhausted in his life.

It was well past dark as he packed his saddlebags and gave out his last orders. Fiona and Gavin stood in the stables, silent as mutes, watching him secure his bedroll on the saddle.

"Why can't I come with you?" Gavin asked the question without conviction. Donovan knew he didn't have to explain why Gavin needed to stay.

Fiona was another matter.

"We need you here," she said fiercely. "Send someone else after her."

Donovan tugged down the stirrups on the saddle and turned to her. "I can't." He glanced at Gavin and held his arms out. The boy came into them and Gavin held him close and long. *This was something little John would never be able to do again*, he thought. He'd never again know the warm and secure feel of his loving father's arms around him. The least Mike could do was make sure the lad got his mother back.

Like that's the reason I'm going.

He released Gavin and clapped a hand on his shoulder. "Watch over the camp, but err on the side of caution. Take no chances. No heroics. If someone comes, gather everyone together and hide in the caves like we practiced, you hear?"

Gavin nodded solemnly. "I'll take care of the place."

"I know you will, son." Donovan gave Gavin's shoulder one last squeeze and the boy turned and slipped out of the stable. He glanced at Fiona. "Who would you have me send, then?"

Fiona rubbed the chill of the autumn night from her arms as she looked wildly around the stable as if trying to find someone else. "I don't know," she said finally. She looked at him quickly. "And I love her, too, mind. It's just, we can't afford to lose you."

"You won't lose me."

"I'm sure that's what David said too," Fiona said tartly.

The exhaustion pierced Donovan and his shoulders sagged with the weight of it. It was nearly impossible to believe that David was gone. When Gavin had come running back with the terrible news, Mike had gone himself to see. The sight had nearly made him sick.

From what he could see by the boot prints in the damp earth by David's body, there had been two of them—and Sarah. He could tell that Sarah had been dragged away. He followed the tracks to signs of a heavy cart moving due east from the Woodson cottage. Whoever they were, they were traveling loaded and slow. He should have no trouble in overtaking them.

He mounted and leaned down to pat his sister on the shoulder. "Take special care of young John." The boy had been devastated, naturally. His tears—and his bravery—had nearly broken Mike's heart. "Tell him I'll bring his mother home. He'll believe it because I will." As Mike spoke, he felt his throat closing up again and he knew he was telegraphing his emotions to Fi.

Yes, it had been horrifying to find David—*the man had been so vital and alive just a few hours before!* Yes, it had been upsetting for the whole community to be reminded that such horrors could still happen. But the real agony? The gut-wrenching, bone-watering agony that Mike struggled not to let overwhelm him?

They'd taken Sarah.

They had her, whoever they were. They must have her bound and probably hurt, because there was no way Sarah wouldn't put up a fight not to be taken from her son.

Just the thought of her, hurt, helpless and heartbroken herself, made Mike put his heels to his horse's flank, exhaustion be damned.

Susan Kiernan-Lewis

Chapter Five

The cart moved relentlessly forward for hours. Sarah didn't notice if it stopped, though later she would realized it must have in order for the men to relieve themselves on the side of the road. Two of the women she shared the back of the cart with soiled themselves and seemed not to notice or care. When Sarah began to emerge from her self-induced dreamlike state, she was aware that it was nearly dawn. They had driven all night. Or, if they stopped, she had no memory of it.

It was her own need to empty her bladder that tugged her back to reality. When she found herself looking around the cart interior, she saw a pair of bright brown eyes watching her.

"If you need to use the loo," the voice whispered in an English accent, "you just knock on the seat behind you. They'll stop because they don't want to have to clean up any messes."

Sarah stared at her and licked her lips. Someone had pulled her gag down and it hung like a decorative scarf at her neck. She glanced at the other two women, who clearly could have benefited from that information earlier. They hugged each other tightly, their eyes sealed shut. Sarah assumed they had been taken together. She looked back at the woman with the big brown eyes.

"Why?" she croaked. As soon as she spoke the word, she was sorry. The last thing she wanted to do was talk about or think about what had happened, let alone what *was* happening. Immediately she held up her hand, palm out, and shook her head. "No," she whispered.

But it was too late. The image of David came roaring back, blotting out every other sight or thought or sound. Sarah covered her face with her hands and a terrible, keening moan erupted from her throat. David all crumpled up and bloody, his eyes not seeing the sky or the ground. Her handsome husband. His wit, his crinkling blue eyes that saw everything so clearly. *Dear God, how could it be possible? After everything they'd been through. After all the close calls, all the sacrifices…how was it possible to lose him now?*

"Do you need to go?" the voice whispered again.

Sarah pulled her hands from her face. Her wrists chafed badly where they were tied but she didn't care. She looked at the woman, who looked almost friendly.

"Why?" she asked again, this time with resignation.

"I overheard them talking," the woman said, scooting closer to Sarah. "They're hoping to ransom us to our families."

Sarah looked at her like she was mad.

"We just need to sit tight," the woman said, smiling shyly. "Not do anything to get us hurt in the meantime."

"I have no family." The pit of her stomach roiled as she thought of her husband lying in his own gore in their south pasture. A flashing image of John came to her and she felt a moment's dread that these monsters might have visited Donovan's place, but no, there was just the four women in the cart.

"Well, then whoever wants you returned, pet," the woman said. "I'm Angie by the way."

Sarah could see that Angie's bonds were looser than her own. As she watched, the woman constantly moved her wrists and tugged at the fibers of the rope that bound her.

"Sarah," Sarah said tiredly. *Could it be that simple? Ransom?* "How do they know where to go to find our families?"

Angie shrugged. "I'm just telling what I heard 'em say."

Sarah nodded and then reached up and tapped firmly on the wooden bench over her head to get her captors' attention. She felt the cart slow and then stop. The tarp over the top of the cart, which had given them the impression of a snug little cave, was wrenched off, exposing them all to the wind and the rain.

Sarah guessed it was late afternoon by the light, although she wasn't sure she hadn't been unconscious for part of the trip.

Involuntarily, she took in a hungry gasp of air, as if she'd only been breathing with a half a lung under the tarp. The face that glared at her from over the cart's side was the young redheaded man who had helped drag David to the fence. He hadn't pulled the trigger, but he had helped kill him.

His eyes looked at Angie, questioning, and his face seemed to soften.

"Oy," Angie said, her voice softer and pleading. "We need to use the facilities."

The man looked away and the leader joined him at the side of the cart. "Jesus!" he said. "Smells like you already did. What pigs! Come on, Aidan, get 'em out. Blimey, what else would you expect from the Irish?"

"Jeff!" the driver called. "Take over here and let me do that, eh? You've had all the fun today."

The young man called Aidan pulled the gate down in back and Sarah and Angie scooted toward the opening. They were stopped in the middle of the road, but Sarah hadn't seen another traveler. Angie scrambled out first and Sarah watched the two men's faces as she did. They must have been bored, she thought. They were enjoying the distraction. She looked into the face of the man called Jeff—the one who'd murdered David—and she carved his features into her brain.

One day. Some day. If not me, it'll be someone like me. I'll see you punished.

Before Angie was all the way out of the cart, Jeff reached forward and grabbed her breasts, pulling her all the way out. She squealed in pain as he wrenched her out of the cart and dropped her to the ground while the other men laughed.

Sarah's heart pounded as the third man came around the side of the cart. He was homely, his face pocked with old acne scars. It's true, she thought with her fear rising inside her. People born ugly will act ugly. She jumped down from the cart and went to stand next to Angie, who was glowering at Jeff as he climbed

37

back into the driver's seat of the cart and picked up the reins. Sarah looked around and then held up her hands.

"Can you untie us?" she said. "I can't get my...my..." It occurred to her that she didn't want to be anywhere near these animals when she had her pants down, but short of soiling herself, she had to try.

Aidan glanced at Angie again, then pulled out a knife and stuck it between the cords of Sarah's wrists. Her hands sprang free as soon as they were cut and she quickly massaged them, but forced the automatic *thank you* that was on her lips back into her throat.

"Try anything and I'll tie your hands to your feet for the rest of the trip," he said, as he cut through Angie's cords.

Angie and Sarah edged away from the road and into the ravine, where they lowered their pants and relieved themselves. She could hear the other two women whimpering and she guessed they were having their bonds cut, too. Before she was quite finished, the ugly one came and peered over the ravine at them. He laughed and then turned away.

Angie zipped up her jeans and rubbed the red marks on her wrists.

"They're fucking animals," she said, her face flushed with anger. "I'm not even Irish, nor you neither."

Before she could answer, Sarah heard a scream from the road. She fastened her jeans and bolted up the side of the ravine. She saw that the ugly one had one of the other women down on the ground. Her scream had been silenced by the large, filthy hand that gripped her face. She lay motionless as he ripped at her skirt with the other and positioned himself between her legs.

"Old enough to be your mother, ya randy git!"

"I think this *is* his mother!"

"Nah, I've had her. She ain't this fine."

The men's raucous laughter echoed down the empty road.

Without thinking, Sarah charged. She felt Angie's fingers gripping at her from behind, but she shook her off and sprinted across the road.

By the time she reached the two on the ground, the oaf had obviously removed all obstacles to his goal as his naked backside was pumping vigorously. Before Sarah could reach him, an arm whipped out and pulled her off her feet and swung her away from them. When Aidan set her on her feet, he backhanded her full force into the side of the cart. Sarah's head cracked against the wagon and all light and sound snapped out as she slumped to the ground.

When she awoke, her hands were bound again and the cart was once more moving. Either it was dark out or the tarp was covering them with no gap, and Sarah could barely make out the forms of the other three women with her. She ran her tongue over her teeth and found at least three loose ones. Her head ached badly and her arm felt on fire. That must have happened when they'd reloaded her unconscious body back into the cart, she thought.

"You awake, Sarah?"

Sarah turned to see Angie's anxious face next to her. "You scared the shit out of me,. Why did you do that? That was crazy."

Sarah's eyes tried to adjust to the dark and see the woman who'd been raped. She sat where she had before, holding the younger woman and staring where the opening in the tarp had been, as if hoping to catch a glimpse of the scenery.

Sarah looked back at Angie and closed her eyes. She was definitely seeing double, so she guessed she probably had a concussion.

"You gotta stop that shit, Sarah. They are gonna bloody do what they're gonna do. Just let 'em!"

Sarah opened her eyes and saw that Angie looked genuinely distressed.

"Trust me, they'll do all of us before we get where we're going. You want to live to escape, you gotta pick your battles."

Sarah knew she was right. She had been foolish this afternoon, with no plan or weapon beyond her horror and anger.

If I get killed, I'll never see John again.

As if reading her mind, Angie reached out to touch Sarah's hand and Sarah saw that she was tied again, too. "You really don't have any family?"

Sarah took a long withering breath and willed the emotion to stay in check. Her voice was a whisper. "A son."

"Is he young? Young enough to need his Mum?"

Sarah looked at Angie and forced the tears not to come. "He doesn't think so," she said, and tried to smile.

"So see? You gotta stay in one piece, however you need to do that, for his sake."

Sarah nodded and then shifted against the cart. Some of them must be asleep, she thought. Normally she could hear voices from the front. Two on the cart front and one—Gareth, she thought they'd called him—riding point on a green gelding.

"How about you?" Sarah asked.

Angie's face relaxed but she shook her head. "Not yet," she said. "But I aim to live long enough to do it some day." She shrugged. "I got a boyfriend."

Sarah looked away and felt the terrible agony of the day close around her like a vice she couldn't escape from. She wasn't even sure it was her voice that spoke, but it must have been. "I had a husband. A good man. A loving father. My dearest friend…" She put her hands to her face and a terrible keening wail came from deep inside her. She could hear one of the drivers, either Jeff or Aidan, knock hard against the side of the cart. "Shut up in there!"

Angie's hand squeezed Sarah's. "Shhh, Sarah," she said. "Keep it in, petal. Keep it all inside for now."

Sarah took a shuddering breath and nodded. Using every inch of strength she ever possessed, she shoved the desperate, bottomless, grief deep inside her.

Chapter Six

Denny Correy rolled off the young teenager, slapping her bare bum as he did. He wouldn't have her leaking all over the floor for him to step in. It was for precisely this reason he didn't allow the little piece in his bed. "Off you go now," he said, as he stood to pull his jeans back on. She scrambled to her feet and snatched up her clothes as she bolted for the door. It was annoying to see the look of fear on her face—and the rush she was always in to vacate his chambers.

It was pretty clear he'd have to up the ante with the girl soon. Tell her it wasn't enough just to open her legs to him. If she ever wanted to see her little brother again, she'd have to at least pretend to like it.

It would have been preferable if he didn't have to tell her how to act.

The last year had been a wild ride in more ways than one. In all his thirty years it never would have occurred to him that the same laws that had restricted and impinged on him for so long would actually be the making of him. After the bomb—or the Great Equalizer as Denny liked to call it—all the high and mighty had been dragged from their mansions, stripped of their high-tech toys and torched in their Daimlers and Jags.

That last one quite literally, he thought, smiling to himself as he dressed.

Yes, an England without electricity, without cars, without laws, however temporary it was—and make no mistake, there

were definite rumblings of the cranky old bitch righting herself—
was just the place for a sod like him to plant his flag. And thrive.

He glanced at the rumpled sheets on the floor and saw there
was blood again.

In fact, there was no reason to think he couldn't keep all
that he'd built after the lights went back on. The commodity
services he offered would always be needed.

"Yo, Denny! You decent yet?"

The voice came from the anteroom outside his bedroom.
He knew Meyers, the acting Chief Constable for these parts, was
waiting for him. He grinned at what he must have thought
watching the girl dash past him naked and trembling as a fawn,
his seed dribbling down her long legs.

"Enter," he bellowed, his good mood restored at the thought
of the fat bastard's randy envy of him.

He settled himself behind the large oaken desk in the corner
of the room. When he had first found the house—deserted just
days before by the looks of it—he had chosen the largest upstairs
room as his headquarters. Over his shoulder and through the
ceiling to floor window, he could see the long needle of smoke
from the chimney in the middle of the factory.

His factory. He smiled to think of it, flexing his hands in an
attempt to limber up the crippled fingers on his right hand—the
one smashed to a pulp two years earlier in a prison yard fight.

He looked up to acknowledge Meyers's entrance.

"Pfew!" the man said, arranging his bulk in a wooden chair
opposite the desk. "Smells like skank-sex in here."

"The very best kind," Denny said, grinning at the man.
"Almost as good as rape."

Meyers's eyebrows shot up. "That wasn't rape? Sure looked
like it to me the way the lass was making good her escape." He
laughed.

Denny fought for control of his instant rage, comforting
himself with thoughts of the girl's punishment for embarrassing
him like this. *She'll be lucky to have legs left to exit his bedroom at any
speed*, he thought, trying to calm himself.

"To what do I owe?" he drawled, forcing himself not to reveal to the fat fuck how he'd gotten to him. "I assume, Chief Constable, that you continue to enjoy the fruits of my labors?"

The corpulent slug was a frequent, and free, visitor to Denny's small prostitution ring. A small price to pay, he thought —especially since *he* wasn't paying it—to ensure that the grass-roots law and order group in the area that Meyers headed continued to leave him and his lot alone.

Meyers sighed heavily, as if it pained him to have to tell Denny his news. Denny developed an image in his head of the man swinging from a rope from the center beam of his chicken-processing plant in order to assuage his impatience.

"About that little matter we discussed last time…" he said.

"You'll have to remind me."

"You using kiddies in the factories has got a lot of the women in the area up in arms."

"Fuck 'em."

"Yeah, well, if it's all the same to you, I'll respectfully decline. But they're making enough noise and, well, like I said last time, the whores are another thing, and I really think the women can push this to a point where I don't think you want it pushed."

"What are you saying, Meyers?" It was all he could do not to pull out the SIG semi-automatic from his desk drawer and put them both out of their misery.

"Look, don't get me wrong," Meyers said. "I am a mere tool of the people." He held his hands out in a helpless gesture. "If the greater good decides to make a move against you…"

"Are you insane? I have an *army*. Anything you come at me with—"

"Don't misunderstand, Denny! We are *all* totally happy with our arrangement. But truth be told, why would *you* want to fight if you can avoid it? I grant you we wouldn't win against you, but we'd do some damage. Maybe even shut down the factory for a time. It's like I told you last time, the women of the district—our wives, mind!—are determined to rescue the poor bitches, who I happen to know for a personal fact give themselves freely to the paying men of the area—"

"In fact, give themselves to those women's own husbands and boyfriends."

"Of course! But saying the women have no power wouldn't be the truth. And this is what they want. If you make us fight you to appease them, well nobody wins that way."

"Just for the pleasure of watching you take a knife in the gut, I'm tempted to let your women wage their war against me. I'll have *them* working my chicken factory and filling my whore house when the smoke clears."

Meyers, wisely, said nothing.

"Let me ask you, Meyers, do you know where I recruit my whores?"

"My understanding is from your raids on the English villages along the river which were hit the worst by The Crisis, aye? The ones that didn't re-band or reorganize after it all went down?"

Denny nodded, narrowing his eyes at the constable. "That's right. And most of those villages are an easy day's ride from Correyville." Denny resisted the urge to feel the twinge of pride at the sound of the name of his town.

Meyers's eyes widened as the light behind them clicked on. "You're thinking of moving your recruitment efforts further afield."

"It's already in process."

"That's brilliant." Meyers rubbed his hands together at the apparent ease and happy resolution to the problem. "I feel confident the ladies of the district will be much mollified, as long as you leave the English rose alone."

"So glad I could help. Is that all?" Denny steepled his hands in front of him on his desk and regarded the Chief Constable. It had taken him all of one hour to come up with the idea after the last visit from the little fear-spewing worm and his veiled threats. Although Denny's first impulse was to kill the messenger, he knew there would just be another Chief Constable in his stead.

In a rare flash of maturity and conciliation, he had decided that the best route around this particular problem would be to appear to be accommodating to the present government. It could only aid him in his dealings in the new post-EMP world as the UK slowly got back to its feet.

Besides, Meyers was right. Using Irish whores was actually a bloody brilliant idea. There had already been at least one occasion where a newly recruited whore—who had been taken from her village not days before and insufficiently drugged for her first day on the job—had been put in a room with a john from her same village. It hadn't discomfited the john. In fact, the man had reportedly been delighted to tup—every way to Sunday —a woman he'd known and desired for years, but who had, in fact, been married to another. It had, however, caused a problem with the other whores when it became known.

Recruiting his whores—or factory workers if they were too old or too ugly—from outside the country would alleviate that problem very nicely indeed.

Susan Kiernan-Lewis

Chapter Seven

Donovan sat on his big bay at the river's edge and watched as the cart's wheel tracks disappeared into it from the bank. He had hoped to catch up to them before now, before they could pull some crap like this. He scanned the banks in either direction but saw nothing to draw his attention. They had gone in here. Likely they would've crossed, but they could just as easily have come back out on the same side. The point wasn't getting across the river necessarily.

The point was covering their tracks.

Although a fisherman by trade, Donovan had hunted enough to know a little something about tracking. But a river was the grand equalizer. They might as well have disappeared into thin air.

He dismounted and led his horse to the river, where he scooped up water in his hat and let him drink. It had been mildly unpleasant at midday with the rain starting in, and the day had gone from blustery to bracing. He glanced at the sun in the sky, slowly sinking against the horizon. Things were only going to get worse.

Even he had seen the folly in leaving after dark. He couldn't see their tracks, couldn't see the inevitable signs of a cart rolling through glen or across little-used country lanes. He only knew that a cart needed to stay on a road and this was the only road even barely passable. And he knew he couldn't just stay back at camp and do nothing. So he'd slept in his saddle and waited for first light to pick up the tracks before the early morning drizzle erased them and—thank God for the mud!—had followed them here. If it hadn't been for the deep crevices carved into the thick earth by the heavy cartwheels, the rain would have defeated him.

And now the river had done exactly that.

He looked upriver. If they were heading to Dublin, he should be able to pick up their tracks again somewhere along the bank when they reconnected with a road of some kind. On the other hand, if they weren't heading to any specific town, but rather a cave or hideout of some kind, they might come out of the river at any point and no one could say where.

And all the while he stood here and watered his horse and looked up and down the river, Sarah was perhaps being tortured or raped. Knowing that mouth on her, he thought grimly, she was at least as likely to get herself killed. He flapped his hat out, spilling the residue water against his leg, and then remounted.

He squinted up at the descending sun. It was months since anyone had a working wristwatch, the batteries long since having run down, and he sorely missed his own. He guessed it was after four o'clock. That meant she'd been taken roughly twenty-four hours ago. He had at least three hours before he lost the light. Might as well head toward Dublin as anywhere.

Why would they take her? What else was in the cart to make it so heavy? Donovan eased his mount into the shallow shoals of the river, keeping his eye on the bank to pick up the trails again. What if they hadn't gone to Dublin? *And if they did, how the fook am I gonna find her in friggin' Dublin?*

The snap of a breaking branch caused his horse to jerk its head up, and Donovan forced himself not to tense in the saddle. He scanned the scrubby woods that lined the riverbank. The noise had been close. Someone was close...and watching him.

Ah, bugger this, he thought, resting his hand on the stock of the shotgun tucked into its saddle sheathe. "I can hear you," he shouted. "So you might as well show yourself!"

He waited, scanning the bushes for any movement, his hand hovering on his gun when a small rustle of bushes just south of where he was standing in the river opened up. He watched in astonishment as a pony emerged, leaves sticking to his bridle and cavesson as if he were an Indian's war pony.

When he saw John Woodson ride forward, his face rigid with determination, Mike's shoulders relaxed. *I might've known,* he thought, shaking his head. But he realized with surprise that a part of him had been waiting for the boy all along.

"What took ya so long?" Mike called out to him. He saw the lad relax immediately and trot over to join him.

"You're not mad?"

"Actually, I was just thinking I could use a little help about now. Come on."

With the two of them scouring both sides of the river at once, they were able to determine that the cart had not come out on the other side anywhere close, but had probably walked in the shallows a mile or more.

"North or south, do you think?" John asked as he sat his pony and shaded his eyes as he stared in the direction of the plummeting sun.

"Neither," Mike said, unsaddling his horse and tossing the saddle on the ground. "If it was me and I didn't want people to know I was heading some place obvious I'd walk my horse in the river for a spell."

"So you think them going in the water means they're going to Dublin?"

"That would be my guess. Or any town between here and there."

"But taking a cart through the water…" John frowned as he watched the current in the river eddy around the grasses hugging the bank. "That's desperate. They could tip over so easy."

"I imagine they *are* desperate," Mike said, and then was sorry he had. The boy didn't need reminding of how bad the situation was for his mother. Mike couldn't help but notice how pale he looked. Earlier he'd chalked it up to the fact that John's life had just been devastated, but now he watched him waver in his saddle. It wasn't just mourning or fear. The boy looked ill.

"Climb on down here, John," Mike said. "We can't do anymore today."

"Every minute we stay here is a minute Mom is moving away from us."

"They have to rest, too."

"Maybe they don't. They've got a cart. Maybe they take turns driving and they just go all night."

"The horses'll need to rest. As do we. Untack your pony, son."

He watched John slowly give up the idea of pressing on. As much as he clearly wanted to, it was also just as clear the boy was spent. He slid silently from his saddle and snaked the reins over the animal's neck to lead him to the camp.

Mike hated to speak the words, especially as how the boy looked to be holding himself together with a wing and a prayer, but they needed saying and then they could move on. He took a long breath. "I'm so very sorry about your father, John. Truly sorry."

John nodded, his eyes collecting with the tears he'd worked hard not to shed. He turned away from Mike to loosen his pony's girth. "Thanks," he said so softly that Mike nearly didn't hear him. Mike gave him a moment and the two made camp wordlessly until Mike had a small fire going.

"There's only cold jerky and tack," Mike said. "But I thought the fire would be…good." He wanted to say comforting. He felt so helpless in the face of such world-shattering grief. He handed John a piece of the chewy goat jerky. The two sat facing the fire without speaking for several minutes.

"What did you do with the mines?" Mike finally asked.

John looked up, surprised. So caught up was he with his own thoughts, he appeared to have momentarily forgotten that Mike was there. "Dad left them at the goat pond between the pastures."

"He didn't throw 'em in?"

John shook his head. "At least not before I left." He looked up at Mike. "You think you can use them now?"

"Somehow. Yeah. We can use them."

"That's good," John said, staring into the fire. "It's nice to know he was right about them after all."

Except the reason he was right about them was the death of him, Mike thought darkly.

He noticed that John still held the jerky in his hand, untouched. By the fire's light, he could see a fine sheen of sweat on his face. "John? You feel alright, boy?"

John looked up at him dully and then turned his head to vomit in the dirt behind him. Mike caught him in his arms before he could fall over into a faint. He held the unconscious boy in stunned helplessness.

After a fitful sleep with Mike sponging his face every few minutes through the night with cool water, John had rallied enough by daybreak to be able to sit up on his own, though he was still weak. Mike had run through every possibility of what could be ailing the child but he didn't recognize the symptoms. He wondered at first if it could be something only American children got, but he quickly discarded the idea. The Woodsons had been in Ireland a full year now—ever since the lights went out all over the world trapping them here, far from their home in the States. Whatever had made him sick, at least he seemed to be getting a little stronger as the day wore on.

"We need to get going," John said weakly. "Every minute we stay here—"

"I know, son," Mike said. "I know. And we will. As soon as you're strong enough to sit a saddle."

"That may be too late, Mr. Donovan!"

"Shhh, boy. Preserve your strength." It couldn't be something he ate. He hadn't eaten anything. Mike packed up the camp and saddled both horses. The sun, what there was of it, was directly overhead. Barring any complications or unseen impediments, they should be able to make it back to the main camp by nightfall.

The anguish in Mike's chest at having to turn back was matched by the look in John's eyes. He went down to the river to fill a bag to douse the remnants of the fire ring with, and gave the lad the privacy he needed as the tears streaked down his face, and his young heart filled with the painful hopeless longing for the mother he would now not see today.

They had to stop twice. Both times Mike was forced to dismount and settle John on the ground. Both times he felt the fevered cheeks and uneven, rasping breathing and wondered in creeping unease if there would be anything for Sarah to return to.

Dear God, am I supposed to rescue her in order to bring her back to sit by two graves?

"I'm feeling better, Mr. Donovan," John said weakly.

"You look better," Mike lied, handing him a cup of water, heartened that the lad didn't seem to need any help drinking it.

"I guess thanks to me we're not going to make it home tonight, are we?"

Mike watched the boy's face as defeat and fear competed for dominance in his gaunt expression. "We'll get home when we're meant to," he said.

"Only, if I'd never followed you, you'd be half way to Dublin by now. If we never find her, it'll be my fault."

"Stop it now this instant! Stop that kind of talk, young John Woodson. Is that what you'd want your mother to be hearing you say?" The woman's voice jolted Mike to his feet.

He slapped his hat against his pant leg as Fiona entered the campfire leading a tall grey mare. "Holy shite, Fiona!" he exclaimed. "Where the hell did you come from?"

"You know, if *I'm* able to sneak up on you then you do know that just about anyone in the county could, too, don't you?" She knelt down next to John and Mike was gratified to see her quickly take charge. She smoothed the boy's hair across his forehead and pressed the back of her hand to his cheek. "Looks like the fever's just broken," she said. She patted him on the shoulder and smiled down at him. "I know you feel like hell, me darlin', but you're on the mend."

"Great," John said weakly and closed his eyes.

"What the hell, Fi," Mike said as he took her horse and pulled its saddle off. "What are you doing here?"

"It's glad you should be that I'm here, Michael Donovan!" she said, sitting down next to John and laying his head in her lap. "I have news, so I thought to take the chance I'd find you. Although I must say I was hoping to find you a bit further along than this. You're just four hours from camp, you know that?"

Mike sat down next to her and ran his hands through his hair in frustration. "I know. The lad's sick. I needed to get him back."

"Take a minute to hear what I've learned and then you can go on and make up the time. I'll bring young John home after he's had a wee nap."

The thought that he could resume the search for Sarah brought Mike to his feet. It wasn't until then that he realized he had deliberately and consciously tamped down his anxiety and frustration about having to turn back. He stood and grabbed his saddle, swinging it up on the bay's back in one fluid movement.

"Tell me as I saddle up."

Fiona glanced at John to make sure he was sleeping and joined Mike as he tightened the girth on his gelding.

"I've got three things to tell you. First is that Caitlin is causing problems again."

Mike frowned and pulled the stirrups down from the saddle. "What kind of problems?"

"Well, she's always been the one saying how this is all the Americans' fault and like, but now she's saying…" Fiona lowered her voice. "She's saying how David deserved what he got and that it was justice."

"She's fecking barking," Mike said with disgust.

"Sure, maybe, but there's them that's listening to her. Because she was Ellen's sister—*and is your sister-in-law*—she fancies she's got a certain status in the camp, you see. There's some told me she's set her cap for you, Mike."

"Don't be ridiculous."

"She's telling some that the two of you'll be married before Michaelmas."

Mike snorted. "Well, it's nonsense and gossip."

"Don't be brushing it off as just gossip, brother dear. You'll have to deal with it sooner or later, no mistake."

"Fine. Next?"

Fiona took a long breath and put her hand on Mike's arm to force him to stop packing his saddlebag. "You cannot be gone for long, Mike. We need you."

He turned to face her and he felt his impatience bristling off of him.

"Put a time limit on it," she said firmly. "Say, a week. If you don't find her in that time, she's lost to you. Accept it and come back to us."

"I won't promise that."

"Because you'll throw away the good of the community to run after another man's wife?"

Mike reacted as if she'd slapped him and Fiona knew she'd gone too far. "I'm sorry, Mike," she said. "I didn't mean that. But the fact is, it's not just Caitlin saying all this is the Americans' fault and yet you go running after one of them—"

"*One of them?* Fiona, this is *Sarah.*"

"I know."

"I don't know if you do, girl. *Sarah,* who's had her husband murdered and been dragged off, hurt and terrified, her son left behind—"

"Lower your voice," Fiona hissed. "You'll wake him. I love Sarah, you know I do. But there's anti-American feeling over all and you've got to put the needs of the community over—"

"I don't care if she's Osama bin feckin Laden," Mike said heatedly. "I'm going after her and I won't come back until I find her."

Fiona stared at him, but her hands dropped from her hips, defeated.

"So what's the third thing?" Mike asked as he turned to resume packing his saddlebag.

She took a step back from him. "The third thing is that three armed men took a couple of women from a village on the other side of Balinagh."

Mike stopped to turn and listen to her.

"They killed their men, too."

"Is that all?"

"Rumor is they're English and headed back there."

"Cor! That's two hundred miles away."

Fiona could see she'd stunned him with her news. His hands stopped working on the saddle and his eyes looked out into the night as if somehow he might catch a glimpse of the one he sought.

"It's worse than that, Mike. If this is the same group what took Sarah they're not on the Welsh coast but nearer to *London*. Forget making it to Wexford or Arklow on old Petey there." She nodded at Mike's horse. "We're talking *across* the Irish Sea and a trek of a thousand miles."

Susan Kiernan-Lewis

Chapter Eight

The question that haunted Sarah, even in her dreams, was: *should she fight them now and try to escape or, as Angie seemed to believe, should she endure and wait for her moment?*

When she thought of all that she had waiting for her—John, thoughts of her parents—it all seemed even further away than before. For the first time since coming to Ireland she allowed herself to think the unthinkable: she was never going to get back to the States and she would never see them again.

This was blasphemy and absolutely not allowed in the Woodson cabin. But as she sat in the back of the cart, pressed in tight with six terrified women and not knowing what her future could be, if she even had one, the idea that she would someday be pumping gas again on Beach Boulevard in Jacksonville, Florida was as ludicrous as thinking she could escape her current nightmare by making herself invisible.

She had spent a good deal of time blocking certain thoughts from her mind. Thoughts so debilitating and useless that they stripped her of every ounce of strength or power she ever had. She willed herself not to think of John being told that his father had been killed. She dug her fingernails into the palms of her hands to will herself not to envision his sweet face as he realized he might never see his mother again.

She willed herself not to think of David, not his laugh or his beautiful eyes or the way he held her and always made her feel safe and loved. And when she failed, as she so often did, she felt herself just a little bit weaker, a little bit more lost.

Should she try to escape? Or should she bide her time and just make sure she survived the journey? Should she fight? Or should she just endure? And with every minute she hesitated, she moved farther and farther from John.

Could she make them believe she was passive? After attacking the rapist in the road the day before, she thought it would be hard to rewrite their concept of her. Either way she chose would have unpleasant consequences, that much she knew.

Which one is the way back to John?

Her eyes settled on Angie, who was watching one of the new girls nervously. When Angie saw her looking, she edged over to her.

"I don't like the looks of this," she said, indicating the chubby blonde who sat bolt upright on the floor of the cart, knees pulled up to her chest, her eyes darting everywhere.

Sarah understood what she meant. The girl didn't look frightened. She looked pissed off. *That was dangerous.*

"Oy, what's your name?" Angie whispered loudly to the girl.

She flashed an annoyed look at Angie but answered. "Janice," she said sullenly. "Do you know who these tossers are? Do you know what's going on?"

"No," Angie said, "I just know not fightin' 'em is the way to stay alive."

The girl gave her an incredulous look. "*Stay alive?* You think they mean to murder us, then?" The three girls who had been dumped into the cart with her began to squawk and cry. An abrupt pounding on the side of the cart came from where the two men sat on the driver's seat. "Shut up in there, ya cows, or we'll shut ya up!"

"Feck you, ya fecking bastard!" shrieked Janice. She started to stand up in the cart. Sarah gasped at her foolishness and she and Angie both lunged to grab her and pull her back down, but it was too late. The cart came to an abrupt stop, throwing all the women against each other and the floor.

Sarah waited and held her breath as the tarp was wrenched off the cart and she could see that it was night. The man Aidan rode up on his horse and took his hat off, slapping it against his leg. "What's going on, Jeff? We'll never meet the boat at this rate."

Boat? Sarah would have tried to get Angie's eye if there wasn't so much going on.

"Which one of you bitches yelled?" Jeff, the man who had murdered David, stood at the foot of cart. Even in the semi-dark, Sarah could see the fury and the madness in his face. She felt herself involuntarily shrinking back into the farthest corner of the cart.

Janice still stood, but Sarah could see a little healthy fear had infused her. She wiped her hands on her slacks. "I just wanted to know where you was taking us, like," she said. When he didn't immediately respond, she added, "The men in my village will come after you. You can't steal us away like we was nothing."

Sarah stole a glance at Angie, but she was watching the exchange between Janice and Jeff with intense fascination. Sarah wasn't absolutely positive the woman wasn't smiling.

"Will they now, darlin'?" Jeff held out a hand to her and beckoned her to come closer to where he stood. "Then perhaps we should just let you go if you're going to be so much trouble to us."

The word *nooooooo* was trying to form in Sarah's throat and in her mouth, but nothing came out except the softest groan. She watched the drama before her like it was a bad movie, one with an inevitable and terrible ending. She watched Janice hesitate and then move boldly forward to grasp Jeff's hand and be helped out of the wagon to the ground. Jeff turned and raked the tarp back over the rest of the women.

The darkness covered the women and deadened the sounds of Janice and Jeff's voices until there was nothing but silence. After several minutes, the cart began to move again.

Janice never returned.

Sarah watched the faces of the other women, the two who had been taken before her, and the three who had been taken with Janice. Their eyes were wide, the whites of their eyes stark in the darkness. There was no scream, no cut-off shriek to herald whatever fate had befallen poor Janice. There didn't need to be. Every single desperately terrified woman sitting in that cart from hell knew exactly what had happened to the poor, brave, stupid girl.

They rode in gut-clenching silence, each of them processing the evil that held them, the monsters who had ultimate power over them, and the sickening fear of what tomorrow would bring. Sarah's attention was focused on tomorrow, too, but also on a niggling thought that had begun to bother her and just wouldn't go away.

She couldn't be sure, but just before Jeff threw the tarp to cover them she was almost positive that he looked at Angie.

Sometime the next morning, Sarah was awakened by a terrible odor. Pulling herself up to a sitting position, she realized that more women had been added to the cart. She now had a young woman nearly in her lap, and when she looked around she could see there were two additional people in the cart. She licked her lips and tried to assemble her thoughts coherently.

There was no way she would have naturally slept through the cart stopping and three more people joining them. Her mouth was dry and her head pounded. Up to now she had assumed they were the effects of her concussion, but now she believed it was much more likely they were all being drugged. How else would they easily and silently pass close by villages and townships with their cargo of stolen women? It was one thing to cow them all into an enforced silence, but even threats are powerless against hysteria. She looked over the somnolent heap of sleeping women and saw that Angie was awake.

"They didn't let her go," Angie said, her voice low but clear. "Janice? They didn't just let her go."

"You think?" Sarah's voice was raw and raspy. She tried to remember the last time the men had stopped and given them water.

"It's more important than ever that we not fight them. You see that, right? These bastards are insane."

"We got more sometime in the night."

Angie nodded. "I was awake when they came in. I heard 'em talking and we're nearly there now."

"Where's there?"

"I don't know but the trip's almost over."

Sarah looked away and saw a wedge of daylight from underneath the tarp. She was surprised to see the legs of a gray horse go by. That wasn't Aidan's horse. A stranger had just passed them on the road. She looked at Angie but she had her eyes closed.

They were on a road with other people. And for the first time, Sarah wasn't too drugged. She thought for a moment. *If I scream out and alert someone that we're back here and...and it doesn't work, they'll kill me. And John is an orphan. Or they'll kill me and they'll kill whatever innocent traveler happened to hear me.*

Her eyes filled with tears as she watched the legs of another horse and another mounted traveler pass the cart.

Sarah bent her head and prayed. She had prayed many times since this nightmare had begun. The difference was, this time she prayed a desperate plea that had been lodged in her heart since she had first awakened in the back of this filthy cart from hell.

She prayed God would help her believe Mike was coming for her.

At midday the following day, the cart stopped. After several minutes, one of the men reached in and pulled Angie out of the back. Moments later, Angie lifted the tarp and gestured for Sarah to come out, too. When Sarah stuck her head out of the back, she saw the cart was poised on a long pier leading to a steam-powered ferry. There were no other people or vehicles around them.

She jumped down on the pier to join Angie. Aidan, sitting on his horse behind them, never once took his eyes from the two of them. She could see the bulge of his handgun under his jacket. Just turning her face to the sharp and bracing air of the sea brought tears of relief to Sarah's eyes after the dank, claustrophobic world under the tarp. It took a moment for the realization to register that they were about to leave the country.

Angie smoked a cigarette and turned her face upward to catch what few rays of sunshine escaped from the bank of grey clouds overhead. Sarah couldn't help but wonder how in the world Angie had rated this honor. She hadn't been out of the cart long enough to have performed a sexual service for any of the men. *Maybe a promise of it had been enough?* That also didn't make sense given the number of rapes so far on the trip.

"If they intend to ransom us," Sarah said, keeping her voice low, "why are they taking us out of Ireland?"

Angie looked at the gaping sea as the waves lapped against the dock. "You're right. It doesn't make sense."

"What do they want with us? What possible benefit are we to them?"

Angie glanced at Sarah and her eyes dropped to Sarah's breasts.

Sarah spoke with frustration. "If *that's* all they wanted, they can do that right here in Ireland."

"It doesn't make sense," Angie repeated, looking back at the water. "They're definitely taking us to England."

"You're English."

Angie looked at her. "I was in Ireland on holiday when The Crisis hit."

"So why aren't you thrilled to be returning to England?"

Angie shrugged. "Like you, I don't really have family back there."

"You're lying." Sarah glanced at the men as they spoke to the ferry driver. "Are you with them?"

"Why would you say that? Are you barking? *Them?*"

"Then what is an English girl doing in Ireland—"

"I told you! I was on holiday!"

"Where is it you said they grabbed you?"

"Other side of Darnagh. I was camping with me boyfriend."

"Oy!" Aidan barked at them. "You two keep your voices down."

Sarah ignored him. "What happened to him?"

"They knocked him out and took me."

Sarah watched her closely. "That story sounds rehearsed. You're with them."

Angie's eyes hardened and her face took on a transformation. "Fuck," she said. "Well, it doesn't matter now." She threw her cigarette down and ground it out with the toe of her boot. A boot, Sarah now saw, that looked remarkably new and shiny. Angie turned and motioned to Aidan behind her. "Get her back inside and tell Jeff to move over. I'm done sitting in this shite."

As Aidan jumped down from his horse, Angie looked at Sarah. "Look, the one thing I told you that *is* the truth is that if you mind yourself nobody else gets hurt. Tell them inside, too. Everybody behaves, and we all arrive alive."

Aidan grabbed Angie's hands and cut the knot in one swift movement. Without another word, he pulled back the tarp and grabbed Sarah by her arm. She looked wildly around to see if there was anyone anywhere to see that she was being shoved into the back of a cart full of sobbing, doomed women.

There wasn't.

Back inside and under the tarp, Sarah leaned against the side of the cart and felt the first jolting pitch as the vehicle moved onto the small ferry. She looked at the lone woman across from her, staring blindly into space in numbed shock. From a gap in the tarp, Sarah could see the blue of the ocean of St. George's Channel behind the woman's head.

And beyond that, England.

Susan Kiernan-Lewis

Chapter Nine

The moment Caitlin saw the two of them ride back into camp without Mike was the moment she knew she had already won.

The boy sagged in his saddle she noticed with a smile, but the look on Fiona's face worried her. Fi was tough and she could smell bullshit a mile off. She could definitely be a problem if Caitlin was to successfully finish what she started.

She watched as several of the other community families rushed out to greet the two. *Like friggin' royalty. Like the little Yank was the feckin' crown prince returned to his kingdom. Now that the little shite's da was gone, there was nothing standing in the way of the Yank bitch crawling into Mike's bed, and all of 'em being the picture of the perfect little family.*

Nothing except her.

A smirk formed on Caitlin's face as she watched Fiona help the brat down from his horse. Two children around his age ran up to him, but he shook his head as if he barely had the strength to make it to his bed, let alone play a game of stickball. Too right, Caitlin thought as she watched him stumble after Fiona toward her cottage.

Looks like he'll be needing tending. Likely Fi has her hands full these days, what with big brother running after the new widow.

Likely she'll be glad of whatever help a loving sister-in-law could give.

***

Mike had never been to the east coast of Ireland. In his mind, he expected it to look much like the west coast, which he knew well. As he sat on his horse looking down onto the busy harbor, it occurred to him that the difference was that this coast, the one on the channel and facing Wales, looked a little more civilized than what he was used to. His coast was wild— uncontained by land or shuttle boats taking commuters to and fro. Although there was no denying the awe-inspiring beauty of the coast, he knew which part of Ireland *he* preferred.

It was midday and the scene below him was controlled chaos. An outdoor market stretched from the bulkhead where the ferry was tied all the way through town. Even from where he sat —easily a half a mile away—he could hear the noise and clamor of the market.

This is what we should still have in Balinagh, he thought. Except, without a natural conduit like the channel leading straight to the UK, there was no reason for people to come to it, let alone stay in the region. Most people around Balinagh had left months ago to be near family or better resources in the towns and along the coast.

Only a barking mad Irishman would stubbornly insist on creating a community out of the godless wilderness.

As he moved down the worn pasture path down the steep hill to the town, Mike kept his eyes on the ferryboat lashed to the long pier that jutted out into St. George's Channel. He wasn't positive this was where they would have come. Mike had lost whatever possible tracks might have been Sarah's. It was possible, if they had more raids, that they crossed the channel further north up the coast.

Now, as he descended to the town, he realized he was going strictly on hearsay from Fiona's sources, logic, and hope. If he was totally off the mark coming here instead of further up the coast, he'd likely never know. And since the alternative was to turn around and go back to camp without even a whiff of the trail of the bastards who took her, he pressed on.

He knew he should rest and water Petey—it'd been a long and tiring trip, with rain most of the way—but he was keenly aware of the time. The lights and electricity may be out, but one thing stayed the same: it wasn't going to get any easier the colder the trail got.

He saw the covered cart as soon as he was close enough to make out shapes on the ferry. It was easily large enough to carry several people in back and the tarp covering it was loosely tied. *In case people needed to breathe.* He stood in his stirrups the last few steps down into the town to get a better look. A young woman sat in front with two drivers, both of whom looked like rough trade. One of the men had his arm around the woman but she kept shrugging him off.

Sarah might be in there.

When he stepped from the pasture path to the cobblestones of the town's main drag, he worked to keep Petey at a walk although it was all he could do not to gallop him straight for the ferry landing.

Did I figure it right after all?

It made so much sense. This was the most direct route back to the UK, especially if you had cargo that wouldn't stand close inspection. The closer he got, the better he could see the young thugs with the cart. Even the woman looked rough, her face hard and ugly. Mike strained to see if the back of the cart moved at all—anything to indicate there might be human cargo hidden under that tarp.

"Whoa! Hold up, yer honor!"

Mike jerked his mount to avoid hitting a large bald man standing in his path.

"Watch where you're going, you idiot!" Mike blurted. He could see over the man's shoulder that the ferry was making last minute preparations for debarkation.

"Oh, idiot, is it?" the man said, reaching out to grab Petey's bridle.

"Get your hands off my horse."

"Jimmy! Liam! Give us a hand over here, will ya?"

Mike saw one of the men on the cart on the ferry jump down from his seat and go to the back, where he lifted up a corner of the tarp to peer inside.

Why would he do that unless there were people back there?'

Two men appeared on either side of Mike's horse. One of them grabbed at Petey's reins, trying to snatch them from Mike's grasp.

"What the feck?"

The other man deftly slipped Mike's rifle from his saddle scabbard.

"I'm afraid you'll be needing to come with us, squire," the bald man said as Mike twisted in his saddle to try to grab for his rifle. When he turned back to face the bald man in front of him, he saw the snout end of a Colt 45 pistol, which the man was aiming at his head.

Chapter Ten

Sarah was stunned to realize she slept even fifteen minutes during the wretched and lengthy channel crossing. Interspersed between the sounds and smells of the remaining women's vomiting and cries, she had turned off her brain and given herself up to oblivion. The agony of reawakening to her nightmare was softened by the renewed strength the rest had given her.

It was three days after the attack. When Angie had convinced Sarah to resign herself to enduring the trip without fighting, and when she believed that there might be an end to it, Sarah had devised a method to keep track of how long she was gone. Now, after Angie's treachery was revealed to be just a way to keep her and the rest of the women manageable, she tried not to think of all the opportunities to escape she had let go by.

Three days since the attack meant that Mike's camp had long since galvanized into action. While it was true she and David had taken a step away from the group, she knew they would try to find her.

Mike would try to find her.

Three days and nights. Mike and his posse would be on horseback and travelling faster than the loaded cart full of women.

Why hadn't he found them yet? Would he be able to track them to the coast? Would he know they'd left the country?

Three days and no hint that anyone was coming for her.

Her captors seemed, if anything, to be even more relaxed than when they started. They were drunk most of the time now that Angie was riding with them. They seemed to abdicate all control to her.

How had she believed even for a minute that Angie was a victim like herself? She never looked afraid. Unlike the rest of them, who all sported either bruises or busted lips from their handlers' impatience, she had never exhibited any signs of abuse. Looking back at the first two days of travel, it seemed preposterous to Sarah that anyone could have believed Angie was one of them.

The cart heaved dramatically to one side, triggering hysterical shrieks from the seven women huddled in the back. Sarah determined that the crossing was over. She listened to one of the men cursing as, from the sounds of it, he roughly attempted to re-harness the horses to the cart for the exit from the ferry.

The canvas flap hiding the women jerked open and Angie peered in. "Shirrup, back here," she said harshly.

Immediately, the women's cries reduced to moans and muffled sobs.

"You'll have a chance to use the facilities after we're off the boat. I'll need you to move quietly and quickly when I tell you to, is that clear?"

The women all nodded, clutching each other in fear as if Angie were the personification of the devil himself.

They weren't far wrong, Sarah thought, narrowing her eyes at the woman.

"Where are you taking us?" Sarah asked.

"Ah, now, I'm not at liberty to spoil that particular surprise. Just know that it won't disappoint and that it's better than lying dead in a ditch. Just ask poor Janice."

"Why are you doing this? For money?"

Sarah thought she saw a shadow pass over Angie's face but the woman quickly regained control.

"I'm doing it because it's my job, petal. That's all." Angie ended the conversation with an abrupt jerk of the canvas flap that closed the women back in and blotted out the slim wedge of light.

An hour later, the cart was parked under a large grove of ash and aspens. Sarah and the seven other women had been allowed to relieve themselves without interference in a long ditch that ran parallel to the road. It occurred to Sarah that now that Angie didn't have to play the part of one of the victims, there would likely be no more rapes or beatings. She was definitely the one in charge.

Angie stood at the top of the ditch watching the women while the men watered the horses and smoked across the paved highway. Like the roads in the area around Balinagh, the road had been unused for over a year now. Already the sun and the weather had buckled the asphalt. Bushes grew wild on the perimeter.

What little news she and the rest of them had received about conditions in England or the rest of the United Kingdom after The Crisis had indicated that England hadn't been as badly hit. From what she could see—miles and miles of unused highway—that did not bear out.

She climbed up the side of the incline toward Angie. "I can't imagine what would cause you to do this to other women," Sarah said when she reached her. "Are they holding your grandma hostage or something?"

Angie grinned at her. "You know what I see when I see you, Yank? What I saw the very first time they threw you in the back of the cart three days ago?"

Sarah wiped her hands on her jeans and looked away, forcing her face not to show her emotion. She didn't want to think three days back. *David had still been alive three days back.*

"I thought, blimey, we got us a cuckoo. You know that story? We went shopping for wrens and robins and we pulled us a big Yank cuckoo into the nest. Let's just say I expect a bonus for landing you."

"You got kids, Angie? Looks to me like you got childbearing hips. Maybe more than one?"

"Shut up, Yank, or I'll put the gag back on. Might wipe my arse with it first."

"Your kiddies know what Mummy is doing these days? I bet you got a refrigerator door full of their finger paintings back home. Maybe you got one showing Mummy putting a knife in someone's back. Maybe Daddy?"

"Shut up, I said! You don't know anything about me." Angie took a step toward her and Sarah forced herself not to move.

"I know you're a mother, same as me."

"Then you don't know shit. Get back in the cart." Angie shoved past Sarah and stood at the top of the ditch. "Let's go! Nose powdering after we get where we're going. Lunch is served once you ladies get your arses back in the cart."

Sarah looked down the long lonely highway. There were no hikers, no riders, no horses, no carts. She could still smell the sea and she knew it had been less than an hour since they'd made the crossing. But wherever they were off the coast of England, it was deserted and remote.

The rest of the women struggled up the side of the ditch and hurried to the cart. Sarah noticed that they all avoided eye contact with the men. There had been one more rape before Angie revealed herself but none since.

Once everyone was seated in the back again, Angie left the canvas off so they could get some air. The gesture depressed Sarah. It meant they were going nowhere near a town or any other place inhabited. The level of laughter and horseplay among the men increased too.

They aren't worried, Sarah thought. They know they're in the homestretch now.

5 Days after the attack.

Sarah and the seven women ate and slept in the back of the cart. They were allowed out twice a day for bathroom breaks but everyone stayed tied. Sarah's wrists had rubbed raw, bled, scabbed over, and rubbed raw again dozens of times over. Their captors were in a hurry. That was clear. They took turns sleeping in the front of the cart so that they didn't need to make camp at night.

In the two days as they trudged eastward across England—through rains and evil winds, drizzles and even a spitting snowfall—they never saw another living person.

The other women in the cart were as close to zombies as still-living people could be, Sarah thought. Like her, most if not all of them had seen loved ones murdered before they were abducted. Two of the women had been raped. All of them sat in the cart, compliant, and numb with fear. They didn't engage Sarah or each other. A couple, mother and daughter it looked like, clung to each other. The rest behaved according to what they all knew to be true without a doubt—they were on their own.

Midday on the sixth day, Sarah knew they were close to the end. Usually after lunch Angie stopped the cart and let the women out for a moment. Today, she jumped down from the driver's bench and, with Jeff's help, secured the tarp closed over the opening in the back, blotting out the light. Sarah tried to catch her eye to get some hint of what was happening but Angie was all business. The other women began to move restlessly in back. They, too, knew that something was coming. Whatever horrors they had been keeping back in the darkest recesses of their minds were about to come rushing and screaming to the foreground.

Sarah peeled a corner of the tarp away from the side of the cart and got down on her hands and knees to peer out. For an hour or more, all she saw was sky. Just about the time that the women were starting to relax again, the cart picked up speed and they began to talk in excited, panicked tones. Sarah could see buildings now, and other people on horseback moving alongside the cart. She could hear, too. It wasn't the sounds of normal traffic pre-Crisis, but it was the unmistakable hum of a town in full activity. She heard voices calling, laughing, a horse's scream and the constant clop-clop of more horse-drawn carts on the road with them.

"Be quiet!" she whispered to the women and they silenced immediately. It was dark under the canvas, and rank with the smell of unwashed bodies and stark fear. She could see the whites of the eyes of the woman who sat closest to her. They all stared at her as if waiting for her orders.

Well, I imagine you'll be told what to do soon enough, Sarah thought. *I guess we all will.*

When the cart stopped suddenly, Sarah was still bent over to look through her gap in the canvas and fell forward toward the opening. She scrambled back but the women had surged forward and filled her spot. She felt a knee in the small of her back and her breath pushed out of her. Suddenly, the canvas tarp whipped back and the sweet breath of afternoon air came rushing into the foul-smelling cart. Sarah stayed on her hands and knees, trying to steady herself while the women receded like a noxious tide of noise and odor.

"Shirrup!" Angie's voice was hard and shrill. As Sarah looked up and blinked into the light, she saw Angie and Jeff standing at the end of the cart. He unhooked the back panel and held out his arms to her. She hesitated.

"This is where you get off, petal," Angie said. "Hurry up, we have a few more stops today. Move your arse."

Sarah crawled to the edge of the wagon and felt Jeff's hands capture her under her arms and drag her off the end of the cart. She fell to the ground and the pavement slammed into her face, cutting her lip open on her tooth.

"Who else, Ange?" Jeff asked, nudging Sarah with his steel-toed boot to make her move out of his way.

"That one," Angie said. "The old one and the kid, too."

"Aw, Ange, you're no fun," Jeff said. "I was looking forward to having a go at the tyke."

"And that one there with the big nose."

"But she's got tits! No one cares about a big nose with those tits!"

"Let's go, ladies," Angie said. "You, you and you, out! Right now. I don't want to have to send my friend in to get you."

Sarah staggered to her feet and looked around as the two women and the teenager scrambled out of the back of the wagon. The cart had stopped in front of the entrance to a long dirt driveway. Behind her was the town they'd just ridden through. She craned her neck to see past Jeff. Down the driveway was a long series of shacks and huts strung together by ramshackle walkways. It looked like it had once been a factory of some kind. The windows were broken out, but Sarah could see smoke pouring out of the chimneys at each of the joined buildings.

A deserted workhouse in the middle of nowhere.

Only it wasn't deserted.

Jeff turned and grabbed Sarah's bound hands and looped a long rope through her bonds, attaching her to the two other women and the child. She could see the other women in the cart looking even more terrified than before they stopped. The end of the line for Sarah and the other two women seemed, clearly, to be some kind of factory. Even from this distance, Sarah could see women coming out of the door with buckets of water and going back in.

Whatever they were making in there, she thought, at least they didn't seem to be turning people into soap.

At least she didn't think they were.

Jeff brought her rudely back to the present with a rough jerk on the rope that ripped into her raw and bloodied wrists. She bit back a cry of pain. He saluted Angie from where she sat at the front of the cart and began to walk down the driveway, leading the women.

Sarah turned to see Angie watching her as she was led down the front drive. Their eyes met. Angie didn't smile. Her eyes looked hunted and sick.

The smell of the place was beyond what her senses had ever experienced before.

Sarah entered behind the other women through the large double doors. As soon as she stepped foot inside, the illusion of a factory vanished and was replaced by the image of a fifteen century insane asylum. With only what natural light there was from the overhead windows—a bank of ten windows, each easily twenty feet high—vision was handicapped to distinguishing human form from animal.

Sarah stopped abruptly as the young girl ahead of her bent over and threw up the meager lunch she'd had an hour earlier. Before Sarah could think to sidestep the puddle of sick, she was assailed with the most intensely evil odor she had ever endured. Her hands flew involuntarily to her mouth in attempt to physically stop entry of the terrible stench into her nose or mouth. It was the smell of hell itself. A simmering pestilence of sewage and excrement, festering sores and foul air that was thick against Sarah's lips and nose. She gagged and drew in a long, shallow breath through her mouth.

Her eyes watered in the fumes and she blinked to clear her vision. Jeff was still pulling them further into the interior of the hellhole. She could see now that he had a scarf wrapped around the lower part of his face. As she stumbled forward, the floor of the place slick underfoot, she saw the people. Hundreds of them lined the main corridor where Sarah and the other women were being led. On either side people were standing or kneeling, pleading with them, their arms upraised, their hands clasped in prayer. Many were naked, but those that weren't were dressed in filthy rags.

They looked like they were starving. They looked like photos Sarah remembered seeing of concentration camp victims before the Allies rescued them.

The noise of the place was unholy, matched only by the relentless stench. A roar of machinery laced the people's pleas like an undercurrent of percussion. Behind the line of begging wretches, Sarah could see bodies lying in various stages of decomposition. Beyond that were the long snaking lines of the factory workers standing at their stations, their backs to the door.

Up ahead, Jeff was talking with a stooped over, one-armed elderly man. The old man nodded continually as Jeff talked, never once looking him in the eye. Finally, Jeff thrust the end of the rope into the man's hand and walked back out the way he had come. As Sarah watched him, she found herself memorizing his walk, his eyes above the scarf.

If hope of seeing John again was what kept her alive, imagining this man's eventual just deserts was what kept her sane.

He passed her without a glance in his hurry to exit the reeking bedlam.

Sarah turned to look at the people who still stood in the aisle, entreating her with muted cries of anguish. A young man, totally nude, screamed in frustration and Sarah thought she saw that his tongue had been cut out. She looked away in horror and gripped the rope in front of her as if it were a lifeline and not the very thing pulling her deeper and deeper into the furor and chaos. She forced herself not to look at the tragic souls with their arms outstretched to her. *How can they possibly think I am in any position to help them?*

But she knew. They were once like her. Strong, well fed. Clothed. Alert. They had once walked through those double doors.

A sharp jerk on her hands jolted her attention to what was happening in front of her. The old man who had been given their rope was in the process of untying them. Up close, Sarah could see he wasn't really that old at all. But he was stooped and one-armed, and she bet he didn't come into this place that way.

When he roughly disengaged her bonds, Sarah cried out in pain. Her wrists were badly abraded. She felt she had left a thin layer of skin on the ropes he whipped from her hands. He dropped the rope on the ground and motioned for her and the other three to follow him. Sarah noticed the young girl had her arms wrapped around the waist of the woman who was probably her mother. Sarah didn't know whether to be glad or sorry for that.

The other woman, whose large nose had saved her from whatever had been behind Door Number Two, rubbed her wrists and kept her eyes on the back of their new jailor. She had been one of the new ones, Sarah thought. Her nightmare was only two days old.

They followed the man through the corridor of naked, weeping humanity into the very heart of the noise and confusion of the factory, for that was clearly what it was. The closer they came to the backs of the standing workers, Sarah could see bits of feathers floating in the air. As they came up to the workers, the feathers formed a virtual explosion of fleece and eiderdown that hung in the air like mushroom clouds of fluff.

As they hurried past the workers, Sarah could see that the women—there were very few men, and they all old—were killing, plucking and gutting chickens. The noise was at such a tumultuous peak that it was obvious the cacophony came from the terrified birds—most of them shitting themselves in their violent panic—and the sounds of the hand cranked machinery that smashed the carcasses to dust.

*If ever there was a hell on earth…*Sarah thought as she watched the glazed, robotic looks on the chicken workers.

The man stopped at one spot on the factory line and grabbed the girl from her mother. He shoved her into line and held up a finger to make her look at him. She tore her eyes from her mother and watched him as if hypnotized. He grabbed a live chicken from the crate to the left of the girl, wrung its neck and placed its still flopping body in her hands. He pointed to the basket of chicken feathers. In the clangor of the factory, it was impossible to hear conversation of any kind.

And then the girl, who up until a year ago probably had only used her hands to text her BFF or get a fill-in on her gel nail set, grabbed the spasmodic chicken and began frenetically yanking its feathers out. Sarah saw the man nod with satisfaction and then turn to look at the girl's mother. He indicated with a jerk of his head that she was to stay with the girl. Sarah watched the mother's face twist into tears of relief as she jumped up to the place to the left of her daughter and grabbed a live chicken.

The man continued walking until another gap in the line revealed itself and he repeated his tutelage with the big-nosed woman. A few steps later, he indicated a spot in the line and Sarah stepped up. He stood next to her and waited while a young girl handed the woman to her right a newly killed, largely plucked chicken.

Sarah watched the woman cut the chicken down its breast with a sharp knife and then pull the ribs apart before handing it to the man. He reached into the body cavity and pulled out a handful of warm, bloody offal. Sarah saw him quickly toss gizzards, heart and liver into a bucket in front of her, and the remaining viscera onto the floor. The woman directly to Sarah's right waited for the gutted chicken with a small hatchet in her hands. The man handed her the chicken and Sarah watched her detach the bird's feet and head in two whacks.

He stepped back and motioned for Sarah to take his place. The woman to her left handed her a newly cut chicken and the woman to her right tapped her hatchet with impatience.

Sarah stood and gutted chickens for the next five hours. At one point she tried to communicate with the women around her to ask where the facilities were that she might relieve herself. The man quickly appeared, but before she could speak he brandished a short stubbed whip and brought it whistling down across her shoulders. Stunned, Sarah whirled on him without thinking. He backed away from her, then grabbed the young girl in line and, in front of Sarah, beat her back and buttocks with his whip, his eyes on Sarah throughout.

She quickly took her place back in line and didn't look up again until a loud bell clanged and all the workers stepped down from their places in line. She followed the women she had worked next to all afternoon to her bed for the night.

Too exhausted to think of eating and too nauseated to keep it down anyway, Sarah fell on the thin covering on the floor that was her pallet. The women's dormitory was a smaller room off the main work floor, but the smell was no less foul. Sarah lay on the pallet, grateful to be off her feet. Her legs twitched and aching pain clawed up to her thighs.

How in the world would she last another day? Except for the high windows in the main killing floor, she had seen no other way out of the factory except the double front doors. A few women were allowed to go out to fetch the buckets of water they were constantly throwing down on the floor to wash away the blood and the sticky offal, but otherwise no one left or entered the building.

The light had plunged the factory into darkness except for one lantern in the dormitory. Sarah could smell food being cooked but she was too tired to lift her head to see who was doing it or if they were sharing. For the first time since she came to the factory, she heard voices and conversation around her. Soft, murmuring voices and even a chuckle filtered through her subconscious, although Sarah wasn't sure she hadn't fallen asleep and dreamed that.

Was it the middle of the night? Was she awake? Her fingers and feet vibrated with exhaustion and the exertion of being held taut all day. When she closed her eyes, she realized she had been breathing out of her nose for hours and hadn't realized it. The smell no longer seemed that bad.

She was so tired she didn't realize a hand was pressing on her shoulder until she felt it through her blouse and the thin rag that served as a blanket. She jerked around to face the woman who had stood next to her all day chopping off chicken heads and feet. For a moment, Sarah wasn't sure she wasn't dreaming her, too.

"You're thirsty, luv," the woman said, holding out a plastic cup to Sarah.

Sarah sat up and reached for the water, not caring if it were radioactive or laced with cyanide. She drank it down and groaned with the relief of quenching a thirst she hadn't even registered that she had. "Thank you," she whispered, the memory of the poor girl's beating coming quickly to mind.

"We can talk a bit in here," the woman said as she took the cup back. Sarah guessed her age to be close to her own. She had kind eyes, but her hair had been cropped short, as if she had been sick.

"How long have you been here?" Sarah was grateful for the kindness and she tried to smile, praying it didn't look like something manic and unnatural.

"Not long. Just long enough to know the ropes."

"How did you come to be here? Does your family know?"

"My family is gone." The woman looked away and then back at Sarah. "It's just me now."

"Did they come to your village and take you?"

"You sound different. Where are you from?"

"I'm American. My name's Sarah."

"I'm Desdemona. People call me Dez. Where did they find you?"

"I was living in Ireland. They...they killed my husband to take me." It didn't feel any more real to say the words, but the pain at hearing them was just as bad.

"I'm sorry about that. We'd heard a rumor that they was going further afield for the recruits. Ireland, huh?"

Sarah shook her head. "Recruits for their poultry processing factory? They've kidnapped me for this?"

"That's not how it works."

"How what works? And those people by the door...the ones that look like they're about to keel over? Who are they?"

"They were us, six months ago." Dez's mouth hardened when she spoke. "But it won't be me. It damn sure won't be me, I can tell you."

"Is there no escape? I thought there were laws in England even after the, you know, the bomb."

"We have laws," Dez said with disgust. "But the people in charge are paid to look the other way."

"Don't you have a village? People to look out for you?" Sarah thought of Mike's community. Everyone from very different walks of life had come together to forge a new kind of clan that watched everyone else's back. If it weren't for her and David's stubbornness, she would probably be safe within their compound right this minute.

"I was a paralegal in Kent. I had a boyfriend, who I haven't seen since The Crisis, may God rest his soul. He was a fool so I'm sure he's dead. I stayed in my apartment for a while until the looting and the gangs drove me out, then I was living in the street. It wasn't like that where you're from?"

Sarah shook her head. "No, we...there's a community run by this head guy and it's all good and we...they look out for each other."

"Well, that's nice, I'm sure. There wasn't anything like that where I was. When Correy's goons found me, I was ready to be found."

"Correy?"

Dez laughed. "Yeah, we're in Correyville. Didn't you know? I guess it's like that community you was talking about, only instead of some Irish guy running things it's the devil himself."

"Dez, there's got to be a way out of here. I've got a family to get back to. If you wanted, you could come with me."

Dez looked down at the empty plastic cup and then over her shoulder. The rest of the women were either sleeping or talking quietly in small groups. Whoever had cooked had passed the food among the group.

"You don't need to bother. You're not staying."

"What do you mean?"

"They brought you here so you'd be agreeable to where they *really* want you to be. I've seen 'em do it fifty times or more already."

"What do you mean, *where they really want me to be*? Why didn't they just take me there?"

"Coz most women don't take to whoring if they don't have something worse to compare it to. Me, I was pushed into a corner a few times early on after The Crisis—for food, mind you —and it didn't kill me." Dez shrugged. "But they ain't asking me."

"How do you know they'll give me a choice?"

"Because they have you pulling guts. It looks like nothing, but there's a skill to it, especially what I do. They got you pulling guts because they want you to go screaming for the door."

"And the door leads to their prostitution operation?"

"Yeah. Those girls eat good, and they have nice beds. They don't get walloped for nothing nor have to smell shite every minute of the day. You want to be there, Sarah. Trust me."

"And you think they put me *here* so I would then gratefully give my body to whomever paid me."

"Well, they're not paying *you*, but yeah. I sure as shit would." Dez looked around the room. "There's not many would turn down the offer if it was made to them."

"But some did."

"Yeah, well, some would rather die, wouldn't they?"

Sarah sighed and fell back onto her pallet. The stench seemed to be reviving as she looked around the darkened room. "I have a child," she said. "Dying's not an option."

"Well, then I guess you're going to the whorehouse."

Susan Kiernan-Lewis

Chapter Eleven

Two days sitting in the back of what used to be a dry cleaners. Two days of wondering where Sarah was and if that was really her on the ferry.

Two days.

Mike sat at the counter and looked out the window onto the street of Boreen, County Wexford.

Two days. Just long enough to cool her trail down to make it impossible to ever pick up again. *It had been her. He knew it.*

A light tap on the door prompted him to his feet and he stood watching the front door—still with its welcoming customer's chime intact—open on the form of a tall woman holding a covered tray. As usual, she was accompanied by a man —never the same one—with a gun.

"Aideen," Mike said, his eyes never leaving the man and his gun.

"Good morning, Mike," she said. She was a good-looking woman, Mike had to admit. Big where it counted, delicate everywhere else. "I'm afraid we'll be seeing the back of you today."

"Oh? Finally going to shoot me, are you?"

Her laugh was a rich, throaty one and nearly prompted a smile from him too. If circumstances had been different, he found himself thinking.

"Liam, you big mug, I told you not to bring that in here. It's not necessary."

Liam frowned and put his gun back in its holster. "We don't know that for sure," he said, eyeing Mike suspiciously.

"Now, Mike," Aideen said, spreading out the tray of food on the counter. "We've had this discussion before. You know that no town can function without rules, and I am sorry that you were caught in them. But tolls are important these days. Especially now. We couldn't run the town without them."

Mike sat back down and reached for the cup of tea on the tray. "I'll be getting me horse back today? And me rifle?"

"Of course. We're not uncivilized. Edgar doesn't enjoy incarcerating people."

Yeah, right.

"But we've had the use of your horse for two days and so your toll is paid, and also the fine, mind, for breaking the law in the first place."

"The law? Which would be entering the town without first asking permission?"

"Ah, now, Mike, don't be like that. I've told you before, the law pertains to anyone on horseback or horse-drawn vehicle and it's a good law and we'll stand by that. What with you coming into town without a punt in your pocket, what else could we do?"

"But I'm free to go now?" Mike stood up.

"Aye, but I thought I might make a suggestion?"

"I'm listening."

"You're keen to cross to Wales, am I right?"

Mike nodded.

"Well, that's expensive, ya see. And what with you as broke as—"

"What's your suggestion, Aideen?"

"Work on my father's farm for two weeks. He'll pay you enough for a round-trip passage to the UK."

Mike hesitated. "I'll need a fare for another on the way back."

Now Aideen hesitated and Mike thought her eyes grew a little brighter. "Oh, I see. A runaway wife?"

"No. Just a friend."

She extended her hand across the tray. "Two weeks and you'll be on your way again. You have my word."

He hesitated. In the two days he'd had to cool his heels, he realized he needed to be smarter about what he was doing. Partly the reason he'd been caught unawares by the toll—and Edgar— was that he was too focused on his goal and he missed all the important clues around him.

He shook her hand. "Two weeks."

An hour later, he had his horse and rifle back and was riding alongside Aideen's pony trap to her father's farm.

He glanced around the scenery in this part of Ireland. While the cliffs and crags still buckled beneath the green sod like the area he was from, there was something more tranquil or tame about this part of his country. His eyes lighted on Aideen as she held the reins on the trap. She couldn't be yet thirty, he thought as he watched her curly brown hair cascade down her back, her face freckled from the sun and lack of makeup.

She'd brought a food tray to him for two days in the back of the dry cleaners and spoke cheerfully to him each time. But she had a story. He could see it in her eyes, eyes that weren't as cheerful and ready as her easy smile.

He stretched his back and wondered how far away from the coast her father's farm was.

If his plan wasn't to turn right around and head back to Donovan's Lot, then he needed to use his head better about how he went about things.

He had to get to the UK because that's where Sarah was.

That meant he had to get on the ferry because that was the only way, short of swimming it, to get to the UK.

The ferry cost money.

He had no money.

He'd take the time to make the money.

He could run around like a goose trying to make everything happen fast and get nowhere. Or he could put his shoulder to the plow, probably literally, for two weeks and ensure he got to England.

Now if only Sarah could hold on that long.

Chapter Twelve

9 Days after the attack.

Sarah wondered if they would ever come for her. After three full days on the line, she was seriously balancing whether her odds were better breaking out of the factory at night or waiting until they took her to the whorehouse, where there were bound to be more opportunities.

If they were going to offer her the option at all.

Dez assured her they would ask her, they were just making sure she was amenable. Sarah picked chicken viscera out from under her nails and wondered if the smell would ever come out of her hair. The days were long and grueling. If she hadn't known that deliverance was coming, she had to admit it would have been much, much worse.

Where was Mike? Was anybody coming? Had they given up on her? She forced herself not to think what John must be going through—all alone. She knew Fiona would mother him, take care of him.

Still, she had to get back to him.

It was late on the third day, just before the clang of the day's bell was about to sound, that they came for her. She recognized the man called Aidan and someone else she had never seen before. Her hands still wringing with chicken entrails, she felt a strong hand clamp down on her elbow and pull her away from the line.

"Cor, she stinks! Can't we hose her off first?"

"Just bring her. Don't bother tying her, she won't try anything."

Sarah didn't even have a chance to get eye contact with Dez before she was dragged out of the factory. The light was fading when they opened the double factory doors and prodded her outdoors. She was grateful it wasn't earlier in the day. Likely, she would've collapsed like a squirming mole at first glance of the sun. As it was, for her purposes she knew the night was her ally.

"I was gonna have a go at her before we delivered her, but I'm not sure I've had my shots." The man that Sarah didn't know was a rough sort. He was big, easily six-three, with a thick skull and a slack, protruding bottom lip. Aidan referred to him as Gil.

"You don't want to touch anything in there you don't have to. Besides, Denny would have your balls on a platter you touch her before him."

In the three days since she had been bound, her wrists had scabbed over and she didn't relish the idea of having them broken open again. She went meekly to the back of the cart wondering how long the trip was and if she'd have a chance to slip off. She was stopped before she could climb in.

"Nah ya don't, little sister," Aidan said. "Hop up top between us." Aidan lifted the reins and patted the seat next to him. "And we're no happier about it than you are." With sinking heart, Sarah climbed onto the driver's bench and sat next to Aidan. Gil pulled himself up and wedged her in.

It was clear why they didn't feel a need to bind her hands, at any rate.

With the factory receding in the distance over her shoulder, Sarah felt a gnawing feeling of anxiety and trepidation working up from her gut to her shoulders.

Would they expect her to go to work *tonight*? Were they taking her straight to the whorehouse?

She looked frantically from side to side hoping to see someone who might recognize that she wasn't a willing rider with these two men. But there was no one else on the road this evening. Wedged in between them, Sarah had never felt more helpless or more like prey in her entire life. She could practically feel the hunger and urgency pinging off the man, Gil, as he sat next to her, his face twisted into a lethal contortion of anger and need.

Someone who hurt others for the pleasure of it, she found herself thinking, although why she thought she knew that she couldn't say.

Wherever they were taking her, she thought, could not be more uncomfortable or dangerous than where she sat right this minute.

She was, of course, absolutely wrong.

The ride wasn't long enough. Before it was totally dark, the horse cart turned a corner revealing a long curving driveway that led to a large three-story mansion. Before The Crisis, it must have belonged to someone rich and powerful Sarah thought as she regarded the house on their approach. Kerosene lamps hung in several of the windows illuminating the rooms even from the outside.

Whoever lived there now was powerful, that was for sure. Jags and Bentleys may not drive up and down this bricked entranceway any longer, but the man who lives here is a king in every other way that matters. Dez said his name was Correy. As they rode toward the mansion, Sarah knew the man they were taking her to hired cutthroats and murderers to abduct innocent women and children to work in his filthy, vermin-ridden factory and as sex slaves to whomever still had legal tender.

By the time they stopped the cart in front, Sarah wished she was back in the factory.

Gil jumped down and Sarah immediately joined him to avoid any chance he might try to assist her.

"I'll take her from here, gentlemen."

Sarah looked up the stairs at the verandah, where a stout woman stood, her arms crossed in front of her. If it weren't for the fact that she had screaming orange hair piled up into a beehive hairdo, Sarah would've thought she was the housekeeper.

91

She followed her up the stairs, aware that the men were coming, too.

Sarah followed the woman through the house and down the main hall. She could hear raised voices at one end of the house, but she couldn't hear what they said. She needed to hurry to keep up with the woman ahead of her. The men had fallen away at the foyer and Sarah was grateful for that. Finding the right moment to slip away from this woman would be easier if she didn't have to watch her back, too.

The woman opened a door off a back room and motioned Sarah inside. She took one step in and her resolve began to falter. The room was steamed with the fragrance of orange and rose petals that rose off the large claw-footed bathtub situated in the middle of the room. Sarah stared at it with wonder.

"Clothes." The woman said the word as if she was giving an order she expected to be obeyed without hesitation.

Sarah blinked at her and then the tub and unbuttoned her shirt. She dropped it, her bra, underwear and jeans to the floor.

"Kick them over here."

Sarah obeyed, then went to the tub without being told. She gripped the sides and eased herself into the hot pool of sudsy water, an involuntary groan escaping her as she did.

The woman watched her for a moment and then said, "Get clean everywhere. You've got ten minutes." And then she swept Sarah's clothes from the room with her foot and left, closing the door behind her.

It would never have occurred to Sarah that the one time she had had in nine days to escape would be the one time she was almost physically incapable of doing so. She needed the bath, the soak, the perfume, the heat, the water. She leaned her head back and dipped her head in the water, feeling the grime and the pain of the last week melt away. Like finding rest in unlikely conditions and food she wouldn't have fed to the dogs a week ago, she needed this restorative for whatever lay ahead of her. She held her breath and submerged totally. When she came up, she could see the filth coating the top of her sweet-smelling tub of water. She reached for the shampoo that had been left out for her.

She hadn't had shampoo in over eight months. She squeezed it out onto her head and massaged it into her scalp, feeling gently for the place where Aidan had slammed her head into the side of the cart. When she dipped her head back again to rinse the soap, she noticed that the bubbles were no longer grey. The shampoo had swung the tide. She stood up just as the woman reentered the room with a wide, fluffy towel in her arms, a change of clothes draped over a forearm.

"Figured I wouldn't have to tell a Yank how to get clean," she said in a clipped English accent. "One is never sure what to expect with the Irish, however." She handed the towel to Sarah, who quickly toweled off and wrapped it around her body.

"Put this on." The woman held up a negligee. It was black, short and totally see-through. She held out a pair of crotch-less panties in her hand.

So that's the way it's going to be. Sarah reminded herself that she was clean and that was a start. It wasn't a gun. But it was better than what she had an hour ago.

She reached for the outfit.

Thirty minutes later, Sarah stood in the middle of a man's bedroom. She knew it was Correy that she was waiting for, not a john. The head guy himself was going to interview her. The woman who had arranged her bath, clearly a madam of some kind, had made it clear that she was to sexually avail herself to Correy.

After dressing in the skimpy negligee, she was led to Correy's bedroom.

Where she waited.

The bedroom was masculine, almost painfully so. It looked as if someone was trying very hard to show that he was very male.

That almost never boded well.

Sarah's heart was pounding as she waited, seated on the man's bed, which was made of heavy brocades and velvets. She couldn't imagine how he kept them clean now that washing machines were no more. He probably had poor peasant women banging them out on stones in the river. She shivered. In all the times she had to think about this moment, one thing she never thought would happen…was this moment.

It had never occurred to her—even after all that Dez had said about it—that she might actually end up having to give her body to someone. And not just *any* someone, but someone vile and wretched and evil. She felt goose bumps creep down her arms and she rubbed them away.

Could this really be happening? Was this really going to happen? She glanced at the orange-headed madam, who sat in a chair by the window looking out. Sarah felt absolutely naked. The negligee easily revealed her breasts and she couldn't help hugging her body with her arms to cover them.

Once, the woman looked at her from the window and commented. "You'll need to drop your arms when he comes in. He won't be charmed by attempts to hide them."

Who was this monster?

As she waited, Sarah took a long breath and reminded herself that the road back to her son had to go down this path. It wasn't by way of the poultry factory—which was a dead end in every way—and it wasn't by way of someone coming to rescue her. Tonight may be a terrible night. It may in fact be the worst night of her life, but it was a necessary night in order to get to the other nights—nights where an opportunity would present itself and she would be able to run.

The door banged open, startling both women. Sarah's hand flew to her mouth, but she quickly dropped it as the madam had warned her. She sat on the bed, feeling like she was nothing but a pair of breasts and a few strips of lace and panties.

He walked in and straight over to her. If she hadn't known him to be the monster he was, she would have taken him for a friendly young man who was eager to make her acquaintance.

He smiled openly at her. He wasn't bad looking, with blue eyes and straight teeth, but he didn't look nice.

"Well, well, well, so this is the Yank. Very nice, I must say. Sarah, is it? I think Angie said?"

Sarah cleared her throat. "Yes, that's right."

"Jolly good. Love that American accent. Reminds me of *Friends*. You ever watch that show? Phoebe was my favorite. Good tits. How's your arse?"

Sarah stared at him. "Excuse me?"

The madam from the window walked over. "Turn around and let him see your arse, stupid."

Sarah slid off the bed and turned away.

"Bend over," he said.

Oh, dear God, he's not going to do anything right here, is he?

Sarah put her hands on the bed and leaned over.

"Oh, very nice, indeed," he said. For a moment, Sarah thought they were done. She was about to turn back around when she felt his hand slide up her bottom and yank her panties down and off. "How many times do I have to tell you, Maggie, I hate these things?"

"Sorry, Mr. Correy."

"Get out!" he screamed.

Sarah turned to go but he grabbed her by the arm and held her by the bed. "Not you."

When she tried to turn to face him, her heart pounding in her ears, her face red with fear and revulsion, he held her immobile between him and the bed. She felt him rub his pelvis against her naked bottom. She grimaced and bit her lip to endure it. He leaned over so his mouth was near her ear while both his hands held her hips in place in front of him.

"Now, here's what you need to ask yourself, luv," he whispered hoarsely into her ear. "Is fighting me, or anyone else I send to roger you—which will surely force me to slit your throat and throw you on the growing pile of useless bitches who crossed me—going to get you back to your boy? Angie said you had a son. If you're dead, you have zero chance of ever seeing him again. You see how this works?"

Sarah took in a breath and held it.

"I asked you a question."

"Yes, I understand."

"I love how quickly you Yanks see the writing. So, you'll be stripping down without my having to do it for you. You'll await me in my bed, no matter how long I take. And you'll do me just fine, no matter what I ask you to do. Do we understand each other?"

Sarah nodded, her hands gripping the bed in front of her. He gave her bare ass one last hard squeeze before he slapped it and pushed away from her. "Chin up, darlin', English women have taken it up the arse for Mother England for years. I don't recollect the exact phrase but it's something like that. I won't mind a bit if it helps to think of your boy while I roger you." He laughed roughly and moved to the door. "I'll be back."

Sarah nodded again and waited until the door closed behind him.

She was alone.

Jumping off the bed, Sarah ran across the room and jerked open the first drawer in his tallboy. T-shirts and underwear were neatly stacked. Rifling under the clothes, she found nothing she could use to protect herself. Hearing footsteps outside the door, she paused. When they passed, she pulled open the second drawer to find only jeans. Sarah touched the rough denim fabric and then, hearing a different set of footsteps, hurriedly pushed the drawer shut and ran back to the bed.

She could tell that whomever was about to enter the room wasn't Correy. Correy was slim and short. The footsteps were heavy, indicating a large man. She arranged herself on the bed and tried to calm her hurried breathing. Her eyes darted around the room, looking, searching for something, anything, she could use for protection. And then she saw the doorknob begin to turn and she found herself holding her breath.

He literally filled the doorway with his bulk. The man, Gil, stood at the entrance to the bedroom, a leer planted firmly across his face, his eyes never raising any higher than her nearly naked breasts. He took one step into the room and shut the door behind him.

Susan Kiernan-Lewis

Chapter Thirteen

He stood in front of her, his hands on his hips and grinned, his eyes never meeting hers.

He looks at me like I'm a thing to be devoured, Sarah thought, with rising panic. She slipped off the bed and stood in front of him, not sure why she moved, but not able to help herself. She wasn't trying to escape, exactly, but it didn't matter. The grin disappeared from the man's face and his lips curled back to reveal yellow and chipped teeth. He slapped Sarah hard, knocking her down against the bed.

"Bitch! Who told ya you could move?"

Sarah's mouth filled with the taste of her own blood. She scrambled across the bed and turned to watch him as he moved around the foot of the bed to cut off her escape. She had meant to give in. She'd told herself she would do what she had to do to survive. She didn't know why she couldn't stop herself from moving away from him.

He cracked his knuckles and advanced on her, his eyes again on her breasts. "Denny said you're too old for him so you're all mine, sis. I wouldn't think of yelling or anything coz I pretty much got the green light to do whatever I want, and it's up to you whether there's anything left of ya afterwards to go on to Maggie's or I haul your arse back to the factory. Ya understand me, bitch?"

Sarah stared at him and felt the helplessness sift through her. She couldn't do it. She could not allow him to climb on top of her. Her mind was a whirl of motion and a thousand different thoughts and images. Would she ever be the same again if she let him touch her? Would she be anything worth having back as a mother?

Her eyes narrowed as she watched Gil undo his belt and drop his pants on the floor. He still had his socks and boots on and Sarah thought she saw something flash from the top of his sock. He was wearing a shoulder holster but she couldn't see if there was anything in it. Whatever she did, she needed to do it now. She looked frantically at the nightstand by the bed but there was nothing there, not even a book or a paperweight.

"Denny said we can't use the bed so move over here by the couch. If I have to come get you, I'll make sure it hurts bad."

She watched him waiting for her, his stiff member holding his shirtfront up like a sagging tent pole. She nodded and moved toward the couch. She had only one trick in her bag and if she screwed it up he'd kill her. But if she didn't at least try, she would surely die a slower, different way.

As she passed him, she turned to him and said, "I was hoping it would be you ever since we first met this morning."

He grunted in surprise. She saw his eyes were not on her face. She counted on it. She pushed her chest out higher and placed her hands on his arms. "I want you to do me," she said plainly. He hesitated just long enough, his eyes mesmerized by the swaying of her full naked breasts so close they were nearly touching his arm.

She brought her knee up sharp and hard between his legs.

He emitted a strangled breath and she pushed him off balance. He fell onto his back against the wall and folded up with a long, wailing groan. She didn't waste the moment. Using her fear and revulsion to push her to take the next step, she knelt over him and grabbed the blade she'd seen in his boot.

Don't think! Just do it!

"I'll kill you for this you bitch…" he groaned.

Sarah drew the blade across his throat and watched his eyes spring open wide as she did. A gasp of air hit her knuckles from his exposed windpipe. She knew it was enough and she couldn't wait any longer. Before she was even standing, she shed the negligee on the floor. She grabbed the gun from his harness, then ran to the dresser and jerked open the second drawer for the jeans.

She turned and listened to sounds from the hallway. She heard laughing and women's voices. Over her shoulder, she could hear that the wheezing had stopped. She pulled on a pair of jeans and grabbed a t-shirt from the top drawer.

She checked that the gun was loaded then tucked it into the back waist of her jeans. The knife was sticky with blood but she held it in her hand in case she met anyone on her way out. She glanced out the window and sent a silent prayer of thanks that it was already dark. She would have to leave through the window, across the roof. She was barefoot but it couldn't be helped. She didn't know how long she had before Correy reclaimed his bedroom, but she knew she needed to be long gone by then.

With the knife still in her hand, she pulled the window open and crawled out onto the sill. Correy's bedroom faced the back garden, not the front, and she counted that as a major stroke of luck. As she negotiated a five-foot drop from the window ledge, she glanced back in the bedroom to confirm what she already knew. Her would-be rapist lay propped up against the wall, his hands still cupping his naked crotch, eyes staring unseeing at the ceiling. She could see the line of red across his throat even from eight feet away.

She dropped onto the second roof below the bedroom window and crouched on all fours to inch her way to the roof edge. There was a first story roof eave over the back door entrance. Once she made it that far, she could drop the rest of the way into the bushes. She might come away with some bad scratches, but at least she wouldn't break anything. She could see the dark lawn stretching all the way to fence perimeter about one hundred meters away. Once she was down, she should be able to make it to the back fence at a dead run in seconds. The woods on the other side looked dense and thick, but that was to her benefit.

While she didn't worry about the fence being electrified, as she released her hold on the roof edge and dropped into a hedge of hazel shrubs by the back door it did occur to her that Correy might have security or dogs. She landed painfully in the center of the bush with branches lashing her face and neck and immediately fought to free herself. She took a quick inventory as she ran for the back fence. Her feet had taken the worst of it, but still only stings at this point. Figuring she'd stand a greater chance of running into sentries at the fence, she ran straight across the lawn. If a dog caught her, she'd kill it with her knife.

If she ran into a man, same thing.

The grass was cold and smooth under her feet. She felt the gun pinching into her back as she ran, but also felt an exhilaration as the evening air pushed against her and she saw the fence come nearer and nearer.

Nine days of abuse and imprisonment, threats and beatings. Nine days of crying silently for her losses, of praying and hoping for rescue, of waiting for something to happen.

And now she was running free. Running directly back to her boy.

And she'd be damned if anyone would stop her.

Chapter Fourteen

The work was hard and Mike was glad of it.

Ten-hour days of plowing fields, feeding livestock, cleaning out stalls and pigsties, and mending fences left him falling asleep over his dinner and nights of dreamless, uninterrupted sleep. He slept in the barn near Petey, which suited him fine, and counted the days until he'd earned enough to ride back to Boreen.

Meanwhile, he stepped into the routine of hard physical labor and forced himself to put his worries away until the job was done. Aideen lived in town with her young daughter, but came each Sunday and Wednesday to cook enough to tide Mike and her father over for the days in between.

Her father was a right bastard.

Small and wiry, with a ferret face that seemed to push in on itself when he grimaced, Fionn Malone worked alongside Mike as if they were inmates on a chain gang. His dour and humorless manner infected the atmosphere of every room he entered. Mike was glad to retreat to the barn each night.

The second Sunday that Aideen came to cook and clean, she asked Mike if he would ride back to Boreen with her.

"Only, there are some *gougers* on the loose lately," she said. "And I've left it too late today. You can ride back in the morning."

Mike knew it was easily a two-hour ride each way and there was no way Fionn would pay him for the excursion. His shoulders sagged at the thought of delaying his trip across the channel by even one more day. But he couldn't let Aideen ride back in the dark either.

"I promise you'll be paid for your time," she said. "I've got one or two things needing mending at my place, too."

"Not married, Aideen?"

"I *was* married, Mike Donovan. But me Darryl was killed soon after the *Yank's Gift*." When he frowned, she said, "Surely they call it that where you're from? It's because it's thanks to the Americans we're all living like savages, you see?"

"It's an American I'm looking for."

"You and everyone else around these parts. But seriously, I wouldn't advertise the fact. People aren't too pleased with the Yanks these days. Just last week, a woman was tarred and feathered for saying she thought the Americans make good movies."

"A bit drastic, surely?"

Aideen shrugged. "People are frustrated. The worst of it are the rumors that say the US was totally unaffected."

"I'm sure that's wrong."

"Are you? Seems to me it's exactly what you'd expect from 'em. They start all this bother and we end up paying the price for it."

That evening, Mike tied Petey to the back of Aideen's pony trap and drove her back to Boreen.

Before they left, Fionn had him clear out of the house for an hour while he and Aideen talked of family matters that didn't concern him. When he and Aideen rode back to town, Mike couldn't help but notice she'd been crying. He hoped she and her father weren't dealing with some kind of health crisis.

What else could it be? The old bastard was hardly in danger of losing his job.

The trip took longer by pony trap, and Mike swore he could feel every bump in the road. Plus, it wasn't an activity that overwhelmed him like the farm work did. His mind, especially with the quiet mood Aideen was in, was free to roam and think the worst. When he wasn't worrying about where Sarah was or what she must be going through, his thoughts inevitably turned to Gavin and wondering about how his community fared.

While he tried to believe they could survive without him, he had to admit the people living there—twelve families, sixty individuals all total—were remarkably capable of making some seriously stupid mistakes.

Fiona's pessimism aside, he couldn't help but think this break from his directorship would give Gavin the opportunity he needed to grow up a little.

He sighed as he watched the dark shapes along the side of the road morph and dissolve into bushes and leafless trees.

Who was he kidding? What with Caitlin's mischief and Gavin's immaturity, the community was, without doubt, in total chaos right now. And here he was pitching hay and driving the farmer's daughter down country lanes.

The world really had gone mad.

While the night was quite dark, the hour probably was only a little past nine when they stopped at a house to pick up Aideen's eight-year-old daughter, Taffy. She was half asleep, stumbling to the pony trap for the short ride back to Aideen's apartment in Boreen. The girl was pretty, with large dark eyes. Her skin was dark, too, attesting to the fact that her father had been of a different race from her mother.

That night, Mike slept on an old mattress in the hallway of Aideen's apartment. He couldn't help but notice she behaved as if this was the first safe and secure night's sleep she'd had in months.

If she was so afraid, why she didn't just move back in with her father? Then he remembered Fionn's glowering face as they loaded up the pony trap and figured he probably had his answer.

The next morning, he nailed a window sill back together for Aideen and cleaned out the worst of a neighboring apartment that people were clearly using as their own private dumping ground. The little girl, Taffy, was quiet and hung close to her mother, but Mike had been able to coax a small smile from her before he got ready to leave.

"I can't thank you enough, Mike," Aideen said, handing him a sandwich of fresh bread and cheese.

"No problem." He looked toward the channel, beyond which he knew Sarah must be battling to stay alive.

"It was a lot to ask," Aideen said solemnly and put her hand on his wrist. "I want you to know that I'm aware of that. If you're ever…" she looked over her shoulder to see that Taffy was out of earshot, "needing a friend…a close friend, well, I'm here."

Mike was surprised. Aideen was a handsome woman and no mistake. Her figure was slim, with large breasts, and he'd be lying if he hadn't imagined at least once or twice in a fevered moment the feel of her round bottom in his hands. But there was something off about the invitation that he couldn't place his finger on. Maybe because, as friendly as Aideen had always been, even as rotten as their acquaintance had started out, there had never really been any heat or chemistry between them.

Probably just another sign of the times, he thought wearily. When a woman finds she needs something that only the stronger sex can provide, like protection or rebuilding windowsills, she thinks of her own innate skillset first.

"I'll keep it in mind, Aideen," he said, smiling warmly at her. "And I thank you for the kind offer."

"Sure, it's nothing. Now you'd better get going. There's a gathering slated for later this morning and I'll feel better if you're well out of town before it gets going."

"Is it some kind of anti-Irish parade, because I thought we were all Irish here."

"No, it's just that, Irish or not, you're not from around these parts and this is a gathering about what to do with outsiders."

"The Americans? Because I can almost guarantee you won't see too many of 'em around here. They're rare."

Aideen laughed. "People just need to vent, Mike. And if burning an American flag is going to make them feel better about the fact that they don't have milk for their tea, well, then they just need to do it."

The section of town where Aideen's block of flats was located was nearer the waterfront than the road leading out of town. Mike realized when he finally had to dismount to lead Petey out of the narrow and crowded market streets that Aideen hadn't exaggerated the congestion. As he pushed through the crowd of gathered townspeople, he saw homemade American flags draped across rails and barrels, ready for the first match.

It felt like such a waste of time and energy to pour hatred into being mad at a concept rather than buckling down to the immense amount of work there always was to do these days. He couldn't imagine how many hours it must have taken the women in town to create those flags—some looked like works of art in their craftsmanship—only to destroy them at a party that wasn't going to make anyone feel better after it was over.

When he saw a young man lounging by one of the ale barrels waiting for the festivities to start, Mike had the nagging feeling that he'd seen him somewhere before. As he made his way through the crowd, he examined the boy's clothing and his hair, trying to place where in the world he had seen him. Suddenly, a snapshot formed in his head of a man jumping down from the horse-drawn cart on the ferry to look inside the back of the cart.

Was it the same guy?

Mike squinted and pulled hard on Petey's reins as he approached him. It could be him. But did it make sense that a week later he'd be back on this side of the channel?

"Hey!" he said, getting the lad's attention. "A word?"

The young man looked at Mike with the same expression Mike was used to seeing on Gavin's face when he knew he needed to be respectful but there were things he'd rather not be called on.

Guilt, I think they call it.

The boy instantly stopped leaning on the barrel and straightened up to take stock in whatever kind of threat Mike might be to him. "Whatdya want?" he asked, a vein of insolence in his voice.

"You seen an American woman?" Mike asked. "About this high, dark hair? Came through here a week ago in the back of covered cart?"

The boy looked at him in confusion, and the honesty of his look made Mike realize that he didn't know him after all, had never seen him before.

But by then it was too late.

"Oy! This bugger's asking about 'is American girlfriend!"

Before Mike even had the chance to open his mouth to refute it, they were on him.

Chapter Fifteen

Angie had never seen Denny so unglued.

And she had once watched him attempt to draw and quarter a man with his bare hands.

"I want the bitch dead," he said. He sat in his study, fists gripping a heavy paperweight that Angie had reason to believe would be lobbed at her before she would be allowed to leave. While technically not Angie's fault that the Yank bitch had murdered Gil, stolen a gun and escaped from Denny's bedroom, the fact that she had brought her in—what was supposed to be her great achievement—perversely made her the one responsible.

Angie only hoped Denny wouldn't try to use her as a temporary substitute for whatever he was thinking of for the Yank.

Goddam her! If I catch her first, Denny better hope there's something left for him to murder.

"Angie? May I hear your plan, please, of how you intend to correct this cock-up?"

Angie knew the reasonable tone hid a malicious intent. She had heard him speak in that same voice on occasions when a knife to the kidney was his next move.

"She'll try to head back to Ireland," Angie said, hoping her voice didn't shake. "We'll have the main roads covered. I am confident we'll pick her up by lunchtime."

"Really? Lunchtime? So should I save my appetite for dessert? Is that what you're saying?"

"Yes, Denny."

"Because I have to tell you, Angie, that regardless of how I may look to you, I am really, very upset."

Don't speak. He wants you to respond. Don't do it.

Four men stood with her in the library. She tried to imagine the kind of person who had lived in this house before Denny took it over. There were so many books lining the shelves, it seemed incredible to believe one person, or even one family, could read them all. Likely they were just for show. She wondered how Denny had taken possession of the place. Did the original owners leave of their own accord, or had Denny helped them along?

She turned to the men, two of who, Jeff and Aidan, had been with her on the trip to Ireland. "We'll need five horses. Make sure you've got enough rounds for your weapons."

"I don't want her dead."

Angie nodded and then dismissed the men with a hand gesture. When the door closed behind them, she braced herself. She knew she couldn't go until he released her. She'd learned that the hard way. Today, that release could be anything from demanding she get on her knees in front of him to a beating that would prohibit her from getting out of bed for a week.

Or anything in between.

On impulse, she cleared her throat. She knew she was taking a chance, but what did she have to lose? As soon as the thought came to her head, she banished it.

Dana.

She had everything to lose.

"Got something to say, Angie?"

"The bitch has a kid."

"So you've said."

"At the compound near where she was taken. After we get her, I was thinking we might go and get him." She lifted her eyes from the carpet to see the effect of her words and was rewarded by what looked to be a genuine smile.

"Angie, my girl," Denny said, standing up and tossing the paperweight onto the floor, where it hit with a thud and rolled impotently across the room to thump against the couch leg. "You are a feckin' genius." He turned from her and went to look out the window.

It was a cold day, but sunny. Not bad for a picnic by the river or a walk in the park, Angie thought. But not good at all for running barefoot and practically bare-assed though the woods and the highways.

"Now go get her."

Susan Kiernan-Lewis

Chapter Sixteen

11 Days after the attack.

Barefoot, hungry, and afraid of just about every person she glimpsed from the safety of her ditch, Sarah had spent the last two days travelling exclusively at night and hiding by day. She knew Correy wouldn't just let her go. At least she had to assume he wouldn't. Making it clear of his property without raising the alarm had given her the hope and the energy to walk the entire first night without stopping to rest.

She knew she had to get as much distance between her and Correyville as possible. The problem was she had no idea which direction she should be traveling.

Hoping for the best and accepting that she might have to backtrack, she moved quickly in the steep ditches that lined the now rarely used highways. More than once, she stumbled over corpses in the dark. Her determination not to be one of them forced her from reacting as she normally would. She told herself that decomposing bodies were just one more hurdle in a nightmare of obstacles that stood between her and being with John again.

The first body she fell over nearly unglued her. As she lay in the mud and stared at the rotting head, seeing the lips that once sang or kissed or laughed, she forced herself to shake the thoughts from her mind. And when she did, she leaned over and peeled off the dead woman's shoes.

In the morning of that first day, she found a large elm tree and climbed it, praying that Correy didn't have whatever the English equivalent to a bloodhound might be. She wedged herself in the highest forking branches and slept on and off until it was time to slip back into the darkness and walk on.

Somewhere in the wee hours of that second night, her thighs aching and her lips cracked and scabbed over, she met the gypsies. She heard them a good mile before she spotted them. They were nearly a dozen ragtag homeless crouching around a fire that had been built at the base of an overpass. She knew she could avoid them by skirting wide around. But in addition to the singing and laughing, she smelled meat cooking and the aroma drew her to the group as decisively as a collar and leash.

She was starving.

She watched them for a while from the shadows. There were six men, four women and two children. She watched them huddle together for warmth and affection and hand feed each other like they were on a picnic. The men looked harsh to her, with chiseled features and jagged hair. The women all looked old and the children cross-eyed and silly.

Her intention was to beg for food, but if she had to she would take it by force. She knew they could overpower her if it came to that and she prayed it wouldn't. She didn't want to kill anyone else. She hoped nobody would make her do that.

She stepped out of the dark and stood waiting for them to see her.

The music stopped and she watched as all twelve heads swiveled to look at her.

"Hello," she said. "May I join you tonight?"

She wasn't at all sure what she must look like to them. Her clothes were ill fitting but she looked obviously female even so. She remained where she was standing.

Finally, one of the men stood up and held a hand out to her beckoning her toward the circle of warmth. "You'll be welcome."

The leader of the gypsy band was called Declan. Sarah realized it must be a sign of the new times that few people offered a surname any more. Declan's family had been living under the overpass for nearly three months. They'd been chased out of most communities pretty steadily ever since The Crisis.

Sarah's intention after sharing their food with them was to leave immediately. She didn't know how far she'd already come or how far she needed to go. But now, if anyone were to speak to this group, they would know how close Sarah was. Even so, it was very hard to leave.

"If you've come from Correyville as you say, you're only about ten kilometers outside. But kilometers only matter if you're measuring a distance to something, don't you think?"

Declan was intelligent but simple. Sarah couldn't help but think that he and Mike would get on very well. Plus, incredibly, Declan seemed happy with what he was doing. Sarah liked him immediately. The food they offered her was some kind of woodland creature, either possum or rabbit. She didn't know, she couldn't tell, and she didn't ask. It was hot and delicious and she ripped the meat from its bones like she were a wild animal herself.

"How far is it to the coast, do you known?"

Declan accepted a cup of something hot from his wife and passed it to Sarah. She smelled the aromatic vapors of alcohol coming from over the lip of the cup. She drank deeply.

"In miles or time is it you want to know?"

"Miles, I guess."

"I don't know."

Sarah grinned. "Okay, then time."

"Well, that depends. Can you do twenty-five miles in a day?"

"I'm traveling at night so it's a lot slower. I don't think so."

"Traveling at night because you're fearful of strangers?"

"That," Sarah said evasively.

"Or people who are not strangers to you?"

Sarah sipped from the warm wine again and handed it back to Declan. "I don't want to cause trouble for your family. The people who are after me are evil."

"You'll never get where you're going traveling by night," Declan said as he leaned back against a tree and lit up a pipe. He grimaced. "Ran out of tobacco almost a year ago now. Ragwort doesn't draw well and it tastes like shite, but it's still a comforting habit." He pushed a stick into the fire and one of the children came and curled up in his lap. Sarah thought the child looked to be about five.

"So how far do you think the coast is from here?"

Declan shrugged. "Two hundred miles, at least."

Sarah tried to remember the cart ride after they left the boat. She had slept through some of it but it had easily taken the bulk of three days. How was she ever going to make two hundred miles on foot traveling in ditches by night? It would take her months and Correy would surely find her. She closed her eyes, as if the news was too much to take in.

"But that's the long way, mind."

She opened her eyes. "The long way?"

"Aye. Nobody takes the shortcut, you see. That'd be daft. But you, Sarah, you might just be crazy enough."

"Why does nobody take the short way?"

"Because it's straight through the Brecon Beacons which is five hundred miles of wilderness, wild animals and bandits."

She stared at him.

"But it cuts off nearly a hundred miles of going by highway and nobody—not whoever is after you nor anybody else—is going in there if they don't have to."

"I have to," Sarah said with determination.

Declan put down the wine cup and leaned over to hand Sarah another piece of meat from the spit in the fire. "I believe you do. You can travel by day without worry, at least until you come out t'other side."

"And then?"

"Then it's another sixty miles of watching your back to the coast. But you should be safe 'til then."

Sarah finished chewing and stuck the animal bone in her jeans pocket. She didn't know when she'd eat again and she could at least suck on it if things got bad.

And things were almost certainly going to get bad.

She stood up. "How far did you say I'm from this Beacons place?"

"Around thirty miles. If you continue on as you're going, you'll see a sign for it. It's a national park. Or at least it was. The people coming after you won't expect you to go in there."

"Because I'd have to be crazy."

"Aye, that's right. You'll be safe from them. But there are other things to worry about in there. Mind, keep your eyes open." Declan stood up and set the child down next to the fire. He took a few steps over to the where a pile of knapsacks were and dug around and returned with one. He handed it to Sarah.

"There's some jerky in there, and some hardtack. It's not wonderful but it'll keep you from starving. Once you're inside the Beacons, you'll need to catch some food for yourself. I wouldn't count on the kindness of strangers. I tucked a slingshot inside. Do you have a knife?" Sarah nodded and took the bag from him.

"That's good. You know how to skin and gut what you kill? Only I notice you don't sound like someone from round these parts and most people have had to get their hands dirty since the bomb went off."

"I know how," Sarah said. "I can't believe how generous you've been to me. I wish I could do something for you."

"We have everything we need."

Amazingly, Sarah thought he really believed that. "You sound Irish," she said. "Is that where you're originally from?"

"Aye, it is."

"Well, Ireland is where I'm going. If you ever find your way back there, I come from a community of people who would love to meet you." She waved a hand to the rest of the group, who were huddled sleeping around the campfire. "All of you. And you would be very welcome were you to come. Ask for Mike Donovan's place."

"Thank you, Sarah. Now you'll need to be going if you want to make any time at all. You won't manage it to the Beacons by day's light, so you'll have to decide whether to risk it or stop."

"May I hug you?"

Declan laughed and held out his arms. "Cor, I don't know where you're from," he said, "but it most certainly is not from around here."

She hugged him tightly and felt his goodness and his generosity help to wash away the horrors of the people she had met in the last two weeks. She released him, hoisted the bag onto her back and, after a brief nod of thanks, slipped back into the shadows.

If she had to guess, Sarah would say it took sixteen hours from the gypsies' campfire to the sign that said "Brecon Beacons National Park 5 kilometers." Six hours walking in the dark and praying she hadn't gotten turned around, and ten hours waiting for the shroud of darkness to cloak her entrance into the park. In the end, she was too afraid to risk walking by day. It was painful to be so close, but Correy's people had to figure she would go back the way she came and she was still too near the main highway, the A7. If there was ever a perfect time to find her, this would be it.

She found a good elm tree across from the park sign. Just looking at it gave her optimism that sanctuary was close. She hid herself among the branches and found a secure perch where she could doze off without falling. Her stomach growled and she ate the small bits of jerky that Declan had put in the pack for her. He had also included the dented wine cup and a thin, patched blanket, and Sarah blessed him with real tears when she huddled shivering under it against the night's cold.

The days were the worst because, with no activity, it was hard to turn off her brain. And her brain was full of fears and what-ifs and terrible memories. She tried to will herself to sleep, but the occasional movements below of travelers kept her alert and fretful. She just had to survive undetected until nightfall, then she'd find a cave or a campsite and really sleep.

For now, she just had to not be seen and not fall out of the tree.

When evening fell, it was hard not to climb down before it was really dark. The longer she sat in the tree, the more keenly she felt John's pain and imagined his tears. And the more frantic she became to get back on the road toward him.

Finally she slipped to the ground. She hadn't seen or heard anyone in over an hour. These days, most people made sure they were some place safe before night fell. As usual, Sarah stood absolutely still for a moment and listened. When she was sure she was alone, she walked over to the ravine that ran parallel with the highway and looked in. On more than one occasion, she had found people sleeping in the ditch.

She preferred the corpses.

There was no moon and she was tempted to jog along the highway instead of getting back in the ditch. Five kilometers were at least a solid two hours at the rate she had to move in the ravine. On foot on the highway, even in the ill-fitting dead woman's shoes, she could make the distance in less than an hour. The urge to get somewhere she could feel safe and not have to constantly look over her shoulder was paramount.

She decided to risk it.

Turning away from the ditch, she hoisted her pack on her shoulder and began to jog in the direction of the park.

In twenty minutes, I'll be a third of the way there, she told herself. *If it gets dark at nine, then I can be in the park and bedded down by ten.*

She checked that her gun was still snugly fitted in the small of her back and held the slim blade in her hand and picked up her pace.

With no moon to go by, she tried to count the minutes but decided that was too distracting when she needed to be on the lookout for people. Her experience with Correy's group had told her that when they came, they would come noisily. She assumed they wouldn't bother with carts for this errand, nor would they come on foot. She was banking on the fact that she would hear—she would literally *feel*—mounted riders coming down the road toward her well before she could see them.

The gun she took off Gil was a semi-automatic pistol. It had a full clip of 15 rounds. As far as Sarah was concerned, if she had to she could take out at least a dozen before going down herself, especially if she was in a good strategic position when they found her, like in a tree. Problem was, they knew she was armed. *They would probably dress accordingly.* Nonetheless, the gun gave her strength. *No matter how my story wraps up*, she found herself thinking, *I'm not quitting without taking a good many of them with me.*

Winded and distracted by thoughts of which direction they might come from, the sound of a branch snapping jolted her out of her near complacency. Silently, she slid into the ditch on her stomach and pulled out the gun. She tried to soften her panicked breathing—the only sound in the night for miles. Her eyes darted down the highway and into the brush across the road. It sounded like a branch, so that meant the woods. Was someone in there? Someone watching her? Following her?

She lay without moving, her fingers growing slick with sweat around the handle of the gun, but she was too afraid to risk wiping her hands on the ground or her jeans. Had she imagined the sound? If it didn't come again, did that mean whoever it was had seen her jump in the ditch and was now waiting for her? She blinked and tried to see in the gloom of the darkest part of the night, but the trees and bushes across the road remained impermeable and solid.

She knew she had all night to make a distance of what now was probably only a little more than a mile. All night to wait this guy out, whoever he was, and not do something crazy impatient like jump up and try to run the rest of the way to the park entrance.

All night.

She took a steadying breath and was about to stand up and chance that it was her imagination after all when she saw him. He materialized out of the shadows from deep within the woods. At first she thought she might be hallucinating. He stepped quietly, almost gently, onto the vacant highway and lifted his nose high up to catch the scent.

Catch her scent.

Sarah's heart pounded in her chest at the sight of the sheer size of the black bear. How could something so big creep so silently? She aimed the gun at the animal's head. She'd read that some bears have skulls so hard that bullets fired from terrified hikers just ricochet off them, serving only to enrage the beast and prompt it to charge.

Could it smell her? Could it smell her fear?

Frozen and determined not to move unless she had to empty the entire clip into the animal, which she was fully prepared to do, Sarah fought not to allow the whimpers of terror escape her trembling lips. The bear rose up on his back legs and staggered to the middle of the road. The odor from his foul-smelling pelt reached Sarah like a slap. When it hit her she jerked and the gun, slick with her perspiration, slid out of her grasp. She gasped and lunged for the falling gun just as the beast snapped its head in her direction, its eyes roaming, flashing and scanning the ditch until it found her.

Groping desperately for the gun that had skidded to the bottom of the ditch, Sarah scrambled further into the ravine. She looked back over her shoulder just in time to see the monster standing at its full height, roaring in fury. And then he charged her.

Susan Kiernan-Lewis

Chapter Seventeen

Angie saw the bear first. Because she was on foot and because the bear was clearly distracted by something else, it hadn't noticed her. And that would have been fine. She could have just waited and let the animal go on its way.

Obviously, Jeff and his lot had other ideas.

"Cor, blimey, it's a fucking bear!"

The first shot whistled by Angie's ear and she dove into the dirt along the side of the road to avoid being what she was sure would laughingly be referred to as collateral damage by those assholes should she get accidentally shot in the back. She stayed down while the air blistered with what sounded like a fusillade of bullets tearing into the bear, the bushes, the ground and, as they would later discover, even one of their own horses.

Angie waited patiently for the slaughter to stop. It had been her idea to look for the Yank at night. After three full days of no trace of her, Denny was murderous in his intention to kill *someone* if she wasn't recaptured soon. It seemed an obvious solution to look for her by night. That's when the stupid bitch was sleeping, right? That's when they'd catch her napping.

Unfortunately, it also meant going out with these idiots in conditions even less manageable than when she was faking being a kidnapped victim in the wilds of Ireland. And because she insisted on walking point, the clods seemed to be having trouble remembering that she was in charge.

She stood up now. "You bloody idiots!" she yelled to them. "Do ya think you've told everyone within a fifty kilometer radius that we're here? So much for sneaking up on her!"

The men laughed. "Don't get your knickers in a wad, Ange," Jeff said. "Or if you do, I'll be happy to help you unwad them."

The other men laughed again.

"Was that my horse you daft feckers killed?" Angie said, walking toward the bear carcass. She looked at the mountain of steaming, brown, bloody fur. She put her hand to her nose. "God, he stinks." She turned on the others as they rode up to where she stood. "Where did he come from? I thought we killed 'em all off back in the Middle Ages. *And* you nearly killed me in the process."

"We had to kill 'im, Ange," one of the men said as he dismounted. "He coulda gone for us or killed the horses."

"So by all means, let's *us* kill the horses before he can," she muttered. She snatched the reins out of his hands. "No sense in trying to tip-toe around now. You lot have made it clear we're here."

"Hey! That's my ride!" The man pulled the reins out of Angie's hands and raised a hand to her, but before he could take a step, a stunned look came into his eyes and he dropped to his knees. The reins fell from his fingers as he smacked face-first into the asphalt of the highway. Angie looked over his body at Jeff, who sat on his horse directly behind the man on the ground.

"What did you…?" Angie looked at Jeff and then the body on the road in front of her. "Shit, Jeff. Did you just knife him?"

"It's called maintaining order, Ange, and I'm surprised I have to tell you about that. What kind of respect you think you'll have with the men if you don't enforce it? You can thank me later. Bill, grab the reins and hand 'im to Angie. Good lad."

The young man named Bill, his face white at the sudden murder of one their number, literally jumped to grab the horse's reins, causing the already agitated animal to shy violently and bolt away from the group.

"Go get 'im, ya daft bugger!" Jeff yelled at him as the boy turned and raced after the panicked horse. Angie shook her head and walked over to the ditch by the bear's carcass. She pulled out a flashlight and directed the beam into the ravine.

"Find something?" Jeff walked his horse over to her.

"I don't know, but the bastard was looking at something before you guys came roaring up. Something in the ditch."

Jeff swung down from the saddle and the two of them peered into the ravine. "Nothing but a couple of corpses down there," he said.

"Go down and check it out."

"Aw, shit, Angie. We can't check every dead body we find in every ditch from Hereford to the coast."

"You want to tell that to Denny if we have to explain why we didn't find her? You want to explain how there was one ditch you were too much of a pussy to go down into and maybe that was the one ditch she was in?"

"Those bodies are fucking dead down there, Angie. Jesus, you can smell how dead they are from here."

Angie looked at him and he sighed and handed her the reins. "Speaking of pussy," he muttered. "I must be barking to think this'll lead anywhere but me picking maggots outta my hair."

Angie directed the flashlight onto the pile of bodies. It looked like two but might be more. It was hard to tell where one set of arms and legs ended and more began.

"Aw, Christ, it's revolting! This one's fecking head isn't even attached. Are you happy? Both are dead in the most disgusting, rotting, possible way that any poor bastards can be dead. Or would you like me to bring some bits up to you to prove it?"

Angie glanced back at the dead man in the road. If Jeff still had his knife on him she'd have him make sure both bodies were dead. As it was...she was tired and the night was a complete balls up. One lost horse. One dead horse. One dead man. And another night where the bitch was still free.

"Never mind," she said to Jeff as he climbed out of the ditch. "The night's a disaster. We'll start again in the morning."

*****

Sarah waited until she could only hear the mourning doves herald the new dawn, and still she waited. Finally, she pushed the decaying corpse off her from where she'd pulled him so many hours before and scrambled up the side of the ditch, snatching up the gun from where she'd dropped it. In the half light of the new day, she could see that the corpse she'd slept with last night —and she had actually fallen asleep at one point—was a decayed and rotting lump of flesh that could be either male or female. She said a silent prayer of thanks to whoever it was and climbed up to the highway.

It was not yet quite light, but nowhere near as dark as she needed it to be. She ran, slapping at the things that still crawled in her hair and down her shirt, trying to remind herself as she had for the hours she'd endured their tickling last night that their very revolting nature had saved her life.

She ran as if she were outrunning wild horses on her trail. She ran as if John were at the end of the road. She ran knowing she was racing the light to stay alive. When she saw the exit ramp to the park she didn't hesitate, but veered down it and never stopped until she saw the park entrance, a large sign that spanned the four-lane that led into it, weeds and bushes flourishing from the cracks in the pavement.

As soon as she entered the park, a feeling of peace descended on her. She slowed her run to a jog and tried to remember what Declan had told her about finding her way inside the Beacons. It was five hundred miles of rough terrain and it wouldn't do for her to wander all five hundred of it and not come out the other side any closer to her destination.

She found a wide elm tree and pulled herself into the first layer of steady branches. She was still close enough to the entrance that she didn't trust Angie and her gang wouldn't follow her in, but she wanted to rest and she needed to think. From where she sat she was surprised to see a considerable amount of animal activity. *This place must be deserted if the rabbits and hedgehogs were roaming about without fear*, she thought. She felt in her bag for the slingshot but decided she needed to get further into the park before trying her hand at it.

From what Declan told her, she needed to travel due west as much as she could for as long as she could. If she found a cliff or some other natural impasse, she'd take the time to find her way around it. Until then...she looked up in the sky to see the sun was nearly at its apex. She climbed down and moved deeper into the park. There was a walking path but it had been overgrown since The Crisis, as clearly nobody was keeping up the maintenance on it. That suited Sarah just fine. The fewer people, the better.

When she came to a little creek, she prayed it wasn't polluted and dropped to her stomach to drink and wash her face. The sun was directly overhead, but in just a t-shirt it was still too cool. Shivering, she searched the area for sticks and kindling. She thought she was probably a good three hours inside the park and she hoped that was enough. When she piled the sticks on the ground, she took the longest one and dug the end of it into the ground. John had showed her how to find true north back in Jacksonville when he was working on a badge for his Scout troop. She saw the shadow it made was on a level spot and she brushed it free of debris. She placed a tiny pebble at the tip of the shadow it cast.

She had water at this spot and she thought she was far enough in. There didn't appear to be any trees wide or tall enough to sleep in though, and that worried her. It felt good to be walking around in the daylight after two days of hiding by day.

Did she really feel safe enough to build a fire?

Her stomach growled and she pulled the slingshot out of her bag. She'd seen evidence that there was plenty of small game in the area. Just the thought of cooked meat made her mouth water. She hid her bag under a bush and walked down the overgrown path a bit until she found a large rock she could climb on to hunt from.

Thirty minutes later, she came back to her campsite empty-handed. She examined the pebble on the ground to see that it was now several inches away from the tip of the shadow. She put another pebble down on the new tip of the shadow and drew a line in the dirt with a stick between the two pebbles. If she had done it right, and that might be a pretty big if she realized, and she stood in front and between the two pebbles, the first on her left, then she should be facing true north. That meant that due west was to her left in a straight line. That also meant that she had travelled the last three hours going north instead of west. But it couldn't be helped and at least now she knew.

Hopefully.

Gauging by the sun that it was about two or so in the afternoon, Sarah decided to dedicate the whole rest of the day to finding food. If she could get at least one meal under her belt, she'd travel a lot farther the next day.

She shivered again and considered running in place to try to warm up, but decided it wasn't wise to deliberately wear herself out. She took the slingshot and gathered up the sharpest stones that would fit in the pocket and practiced hitting a tree near her camp. She was a terrible shot, throwing the sling down in frustration at one point.

Maybe she should try to find fish in the creek instead? But she had no line or hook or bait. She sat and stared at the slingshot and felt the possum bone from last night's meal with the gypsies poking her through her jeans. With more hunger and weariness than she ever remembered feeling, she got up and filled her pockets with stones and retrieved the slingshot.

It was nearly nightfall before she returned to her campsite, but she came back with two decent sized rabbits. It was all she could do not to gut them with her bare hands and eat them raw. She was hungry enough she thought she could do it without gagging. The long afternoon of hunting had been punctuated with many hours of worry and fear and thoughts of John and

David and Mike. It had been thirteen days, nearly two weeks, since David's murder. Two weeks of mindless terror for Sarah and relentless worry and sadness for her boy.

13 Days after the attack, she thought, wishing she had a journal to write it down in. As long as she used her brain to remember where she came from and how long it had been, she felt there was hope and she could stay sane, or at least grounded. She knew that didn't make sense but somehow it helped.

And now the fire. She had never made one herself from just flint and sticks, and tonight she didn't even have the flint, just rocks. She put a slim stick against a rock in a nest of dry leaves and rocked it back and forth in her hands, alternating the tempo in hopes of creating the necessary friction to make the spark she needed.

An hour later, her back aching and damp with sweat in spite of the dropping temperature, she still hadn't succeeded in catching the leaves on fire. She tried to remember how John did it for the Scouts or how David did it on at least a half dozen occasions at the cottage during their first year after the lights went out. She remembered seeing him use a stick as a spindle and rubbing it between his hands—his large, capable hands. She tried to emulate how she remembered him doing it. And as she worked, the bodies of the two rabbits seemed to mock her.

Dear God, would she really have to eat them raw?

She kicked herself for not figuring out the fire question earlier, because now it was too dark to go looking for berries, and unless she was going to eat the meat uncooked she had another hungry night ahead of her.

And a cold one.

Night fell quickly once the light started to go. She dropped the sticks and the spindle and the rock and went to wrap up in the thin blanket from her pack. She hated to sleep out in the open but there was no other option. There were no trees big enough to hold her in this section of the park. Declan had said there were caves, but after her run-in with the bear, Sarah felt better about her odds sleeping out in the open.

She pulled the gun out and dropped it in her lap and wrapped the blanket tightly around her shoulders and leaned up against a large rock. It still held a tiny bit of warmth from the day's sun. It was hard to believe she had spent all day hunting for food that she now couldn't eat. She was angry and frustrated with herself but she knew it couldn't be helped. She had made it this far and she was alive.

Tomorrow would bring another day of opportunities. Tomorrow she would eat. One way or the other.

She slept badly, awakening at every creak in the earth, every hoot or peep from any of the forest's birds and creatures. Every time she awoke, she gripped the gun in her lap as if she might need to defend herself against monsters in the dark, and every time she was soothed back to sleep by the calm, normal sounds of a forest just going about its business.

In the morning, she was ready to move on. She steadied herself against a tree after jumping up too quickly and feeling the leafy canopy overhead swirl and rock around her as a result. She would need to eat today somehow or she would be crawling to the coast. She went back to the creek and drank her fill, wishing she had something to carry water in. She packed up the rabbits in her pack and headed into the woods, going due west.

Even hungry, Sarah immediately noticed the difference in her affect. Declan was right. There was still plenty to be afraid of and she kept her eyes and ears alert for animals, or people, who might be lurking in the brush. But the constant fear she had lived with ever since she killed Gil and fled Correy's house, that was gone. Just looking around this wilderness it was clear nobody would be here if they didn't have to be. Surely not the likes of Angie and her riffraff gang.

No, she didn't need to worry about Correy here. And the peacefulness of that gave her a strength and an optimism that helped buoy her in the absence of the food she so desperately craved.

She decided to keep it simple. If she came across water, she stopped and drank as much as she could. When she needed to rest, she set up a stick to measure the sun and confirm that she was traveling west. If she found berries she recognized, she would eat them on the spot and strip the bush by filling her pack. Unfortunately, she didn't expect to find many berry bushes at this time of year. She would stop two hours before nightfall to make the fire. If she failed tonight, she would eat the rabbits raw.

It rained a cold, nasty rain midmorning that got stronger and more fierce as the day went on. Drenched and miserable, she realized that the matter of the fire had been taken out of her hands. She might as well eat lunch as opposed to waiting, because there would be nothing dry enough for her to make a fire with. In a way, it was a relief not to have to fight the battle.

Around noon, she found a stone overhang that gave protection from the worst of the storm, and, using the knife she had taken off Gil, she cleaned and skinned the rabbits. She cut off a small strip of meat and swallowed it without chewing. She caught water in the cup Declan had given her in the pack and chased the meat down with a cupful. Nothing came back up and so she did it again and again until she felt the agony of her stomach relent and although hardly sated, she was no longer starving.

14 days after the attack, she thought. *I'm alive and I'm fed and I'm moving ever closer back home.* She gave the first honest smile she'd felt since the attack as she drank from the gypsy cup and stared out at the forest through the curtain of rain.

By God, she was going to do this.

Two hours later, the trail was a flood of debris crashing down a flume of muddy water. Sarah sat on the rock and shivered in her wet blanket. The sun had never made another appearance after the rain started in earnest. A lost day. There was no way she could walk in this mess. A flash of lightning slashed at a tree a hundred yards away from her, accompanied by a crash of thunder. Sarah jumped. She pressed her body farther under the stone overhang,

There was nothing she could do but wait. Even once the rain stopped, if it ever did, the flooding could go on for days. The creek had probably overflowed its banks and now whatever had been dry land was underwater. She pulled the blanket tighter around her.

Forty miles in ideal conditions, she thought. *Forty miles of overland trekking where I might average fifteen miles a day if I find food enough to fuel me and nothing else slows me down.* That's three days if nothing goes wrong. That's three days on the *other* side of however long the storm would slow her down.

She glanced at the raw rabbit and realized she might as well eat again. She wasn't going anywhere at least until tomorrow. She said a prayer of protection for her parents in Florida in the hopes that they still lived, and for her boy and everyone at Mike's camp, and for herself and for poor Dez, and for Declan's family. She ate and drank, then curled up and slept soundly the rest of the afternoon and through most of the night. The last thing she needed to worry about was attack by man or beast. Not in weather that wasn't fit for either.

When she moved her cramped legs and awoke the next morning, the sun was peeking through the canopy of tree leaves and the birds were singing. She felt strong and although she was hungry, it didn't weaken her, just motivated her to get going. Careful not to try to make up for lost time and end up with a sprained ankle slipping in the muddy trails or over fallen tree limbs, Sarah moved steadily west. Her thighs chaffed badly from the wet jeans. She draped her blanket on her backpack in hopes it might dry from the autumn sun shining down.

For the first time since she'd begun her journey home, Sarah almost felt like singing. She walked and scanned the bushes around her for berries. It wasn't until late afternoon—about the time she was thinking of finding a place for the night—that she broke through a line of young pines to see she was at the precipice of a gentle cliff, at the bottom of which was a settlement of several dozen homes.

Sarah stood on the ridge in shock, her mouth open, as she looked down on the small village, each domicile with a smoking chimney of warmth and the unavoidable aroma of cooking suppers.

Susan Kiernan-Lewis

Chapter Eighteen

Sarah didn't hesitate. She needed warmth and a safe place to rest or she didn't stand a chance of surviving her attempt through the wilderness. She touched the Glock snug in the small of her back and descended the wooded hill to the encampment below. She didn't want to approach quietly. In her experience, people reacted poorly to be taken by surprise.

She prayed for the best and called out as she walked toward the settlement. "Hello, is anybody here? I am a friend. Hellooooooo."

The children saw her first and Sarah thought that was a good sign. It was much the same at Mike's camp. The kids were usually not focused on their work and were more easily distracted by something new. Three boys and four girls, all around nine years of age, ran toward her and then stopped. One of the girls called out behind her, "Mummy! A stranger's come!"

Sarah stopped and held out her empty hands. She smiled at the children and was relieved to see most of them smiled back. A woman wearing jeans and athletic shoes appeared from behind the line of children. She was wiping her hands on a small towel she had tucked into the waist of her jeans. She didn't look unfriendly, but she wasn't smiling either.

"May I help you, Miss?" she said, eyeing Sarah's clothing and looking behind her to see if she were alone.

"I'm traveling through the Beacons," Sarah said, smiling but feeling a rush of dizziness at the lack of food. "I was hoping I might stay with you for a night or two. I have food." She twisted her pack around and pulled out the two rabbits.

The woman smiled. "Well, you're welcome, of course. Are you alone?"

"I am."

She turned to address the children, "You lot go on and find Sandra's dad and tell 'im we have a traveler what's come visiting. Go on now."

The children disappeared in a rush back toward the interior of the makeshift village.

"My name's Sarah. I've become separated from my family and am trying to find my way back. I won't stay long, but a day or two would help me. I'm happy to work while I'm here."

The woman took a few steps toward her, her hand out for the rabbits. "I'm Lexi," she said. "Food is always welcome, but news even more so. You're welcome to what we have."

The group had banded together, not unlike Mike's community—family and friends of family and neighbors. Quickly realizing that the new times would require a different kind of friendship and harmony to survive, they elected a leader and struck out deep into the national forest to create their community.

"We knew there were few enough what would choose to live in here," Lexi said as she ladled up a large bowl of rabbit stew for Sarah. "But we have plenty of everything we need."

"Because we *made* it happen," her husband said pointedly. Adwen was a rough man, with arms coated in tattoos and a shaved head. Lexi told Sarah that he had been in construction before The Crisis, so he was good with his hands and knew how to give orders. In the changed world after The Crisis, that put him high up the ladder in the new society. "We learned how to hunt and we don't waste what we have. We plant what we need and guard the crops from the wild animals."

Sarah gratefully accepted her second bowl of stew. "I was attacked by a bear up on the highway about a mile from the entrance to the park. I thought bears were extinct in the UK."

Adwen nodded. "From the zoo. There's one not far from the park. The animals were starving after The Crisis. Not being used to hunting for themselves, most died pretty quick. But some adapted."

"No bears in here?"

"So far, just the normal stuff."

"How about wolves?"

"They were one of the ones that adapted. We haven't seen many, but they're in here with us."

"And foxes," a little girl said meekly.

Adwen grinned. "Yes, little one, and foxes."

Lexi and Adwen's home looked not unlike Sarah and David's own cottage back in Ireland. It was primitive but had been made comfortable. It had a dirt floor but Adwen was working to make a wooden floor for them. The couple had two small children, a boy and a girl.

"I worked as a secretary for one of the big Honda dealerships in Hereford," Lexi said. "When it all came down, me and my Adwen knew we had to leave the city. It weren't safe."

"All kinds of *human* animals were adapting to the situation, too," Adwen said, pulling a sleepy child into his arms at the dinner table.

"So we left," Lexi said. "We gathered together them what was interested in coming with us and we set out. We've been here a full year. We've never been threatened and we've never gone hungry. Not a single day." Sarah saw Lexi look at her husband with love shining in her eyes.

Adwen nodded. "The Beacons can be a fierce place," he said. "Not many would choose to live here. Do ya ken how it got its name?"

Sarah shook her head.

Adwen arranged the sleepy child in his arms and smiled at his son, who sat listening by his knee. "The Brecon Beacons are said to have been named after the practice of our ancestors of lighting signal fires on mountain tops to warn of invaders."

"They continued the practice," Lexi said, "even in modern times, but more like to commemorate or celebrate a special event."

"Like when Prince William married the Duchess of Cambridge."

"Only she wasn't a Duchess then, idiot," the little girl said to her brother from her father's arms.

"Now, now," Adwen said, patting the girl's leg. "Hugh's right. They lit the torches when the royal couple married."

"I'll bet it's a sight to see," Sarah said.

"Oh, aye," Adwen said, staring dreamingly into space as if seeing it in his mind's eye. "That it is. That it is."

That night, Sarah slept with a full stomach in a warm bed. In the morning, she met Lexi at the kitchen table with a large wooden bowl of green beans in her lap.

"What can I do to help?"

"You've done enough just bringing food to the table."

"Alright, well, what can I do to buy a flint from you?"

Sarah noticed how Adwen lit the cook stove the night before within seconds of their entering the cottage. The little house had been warm and snug all night long.

"A flint?" Lexi nodded. "You'll be needing one for your trip. I think we can help you with that."

The rest of the day—day 16 after the attack—Sarah pitched mulch onto dormant vegetable beds, dragged buckets of water from the creek to the lean-to where the settlement donkeys and goats were kept, and mended tent tarp with a needle nearly as thick as her finger and about as sharp. She would have left on the third day, but the cold November skies opened up again and for three straight days drenched the little settlement, forcing everyone indoors for the duration.

No longer troubled by hunger, Sarah spent the long hours worrying about John and the trip ahead of her. In an attempt to give Adwen and Lexi a break from her constant presence, she began to spend part of her days in the communal lodge, a large hut at the end of the main byway off which the other huts and cabins sprouted. There, the women in the settlement gathered to swap advice and support one another. If there were babies, they were there in the arms of their mothers. It was where the elderly congregated too.

Sarah had been surprised to see them—it was the older population that had suffered the most from The Crisis. With no medicines and no accommodations made for their special needs, old people had been the first to succumb. This group sat closest to the cook fire in the communal lodge. There were only three old women, but they sewed and minded the children and dispensed what wisdom they could, given the situation.

Evvie was the first to greet Sarah when she peeked into the hut. Her hair was white, not grey, and Evvie kept it twisted into a bun at the nape of her neck. Her eyes were very blue and twinkled, even when she wasn't smiling.

"Hello, there," she said to Sarah. "I heard we had us a Yankee Doodle in our midst." Her smile dimpled at her own joke. "I'm Evvie, Lexi's mother."

"Oh, I'm so pleased to meet you," Sarah said, holding out her hand. She wondered why Evvie didn't live in Adwen and Lexi's cottage but thought it was possible she and her son-in-law weren't a match made in heaven.

She sat down next to Evvie and saw that the old woman was making lace. "That is so pretty," she said, indicating the strip of worn lace.

"A bit silly under the circumstances," Evvie said, sighing. "Lexi has mentioned on more than one occasion that I'm a bit useless."

That totally did not sound like Lexi to Sarah. "Y'all seem to have settled in here pretty well," she said.

"Oh, my goodness. Are you Scarlett O'Hara? Because I loved that movie as a girl."

Sarah laughed. "Well, I guess it's true you can take the girl out of the South but not the South out of the girl. Where are you from?"

Evvie smoothed out the lace and picked up her tatting needles again. "I was born in London," she said. "Lived there all through the war, met my first husband..." She looked up at Sarah. "Not Lexi's dad, mind. I had a career on the stage."

"You were an actress?"

"I was. After my husband died, I met Alvin and he wanted babies so I quit."

"Wow. Where's Alvin now?"

"Oh, dead. I'm tough on husbands. That's what my third husband, Mark, says." Evvie laughed and shook her head and then she sobered. "I do wonder what must have become of him. We heard such terrible things of what was happening in London."

"Why weren't you in London with him?"

"I wanted to see my grandbabies. The Crisis happened during my visit last year."

"I'm so sorry, Evvie. I'm sure you must miss him very much."

"I do," Evvie said quietly. "Still, my Mark is very resourceful. I do believe he will try to find a way to me, you see. In spite of what my daughter and her husband think."

"Love will find a way."

"Exactly."

Fearing that the conversation might veer toward Sarah's own husband and not feeling at all ready to deal with it, Sarah steered the topic away.

"I'm from Ireland, and over there we all thought that The Crisis hasn't been so bad for the British people."

Evvie snorted.

"I know," Sarah said. "It's just that we were hoping England was getting itself sorted out and then y'all could come help us."

"I don't imagine my country will be sorted out in my lifetime."

Sarah noticed that Evvie spoke very matter-of-factly. She looked around the lodge and realized that the other women were sitting and listening to their conversation. She smiled at them and they smiled back.

"Is it bad out there?" one woman asked as she nursed her baby. Sarah realized that the child must have been born out here in the wilderness.

"It is," Sarah said. "I, myself, was kidnapped and only managed to escape by...by sheer luck."

"Kidnapped?" another woman said with a gasp. "Whatever for?"

"Oh, what do you *think*, Maizy?" the nursing woman said. "Use your imagination."

Maizy turned her horrified eyes on Sarah.

"You're lucky to be here," Sarah said to her. She glanced at Evvie, then back to the listening women. "I don't know how long it will take for proper law and order to kick in again, but right now hiding out sounds like a pretty good plan to me."

"So you'll be staying with us?" Evvie asked without taking her eyes off her needlework.

"No. I have a child in Ireland. I have to get back to him."

"They stole you away from *Ireland*?" Maizy said.

"They did. And that's where I'm headed."

"I went to Dublin once," Maizy said. "It took a long time to get there. And I wasn't walking neither."

Sarah stood up to leave. "It will take as long as it takes."

"When will you go?" Evvie asked.

"Tomorrow. The rains have finally let up. I've got a brand new flint to make my evening fires with and a pack full of vegetables and smoked meat. My blistered feet have healed and I've slept five full nights without once being afraid someone wanted to slit my throat or eat me."

The women laughed nervously, but Sarah noticed Evvie did not.

That night after dinner as Sarah was sitting in front of the cook stove with Lexi's two children and trying to remember a Harry Potter storyline to tell them, Lexi responded to a knock at the door. In the five days that Sarah had lived with the little family, this was not an unusual occurrence. Most of the families in the settlement had visited her to hear for themselves what news she had to tell about the outside world.

Tonight, Lexi interrupted Sarah's storytelling to ask her if she would step outside to speak with her visitor. Perplexed, Sarah set the little girl, Tabitha, down and went to the door. Adwen was out with the men tonight. He had a still that they were working on, and now that the long days of planting and tending the gardens were over for the season he spent much of his day there.

Sarah went to the door and was surprised to see Evvie.

"Evvie? You don't have to stand out here. Why don't you——" As Sarah turned to usher Evvie into the cabin, it occurred to her that it was strange that Lexi hadn't insisted her mother come in.

"No, dear, thank you," Evvie said. "I need to speak with you privately, if that's all the same with you."

Frowning, Sarah stepped out on the doorstep and closed the cottage door behind her.

"Is everything alright?" she asked.

Evvie shook her head, her eyes bright with unshed tears. "Of course, as you well know, everything is not alright and I'm sure they never will be."

Sarah put a tentative hand out to pat the old woman's shoulder. "Oh, Evvie," she said. "Things'll get better. And you're safe here in the meantime——"

"That's just it, Sarah," Evvie said. "I am very much *not* safe here. I have come to ask you if I might accompany you on your journey to Ireland."

Chapter Nineteen

Thank God for Aideen.

Mike propped himself up in the bed and watched her as she sat by the window sewing. In the four days that he'd been forced to stay with her after the mob beating he'd learned that bringing tea to prisoners was only one of the many jobs the woman did to cobble together a living for her and her Taffy.

She sewed, she manned market booths for owners with reason to be away, she tutored children, she ran errands, polished shoes, sold homemade muffins along with the wild berries she and Taffy picked in the summer time.

She was a hardworking, down to earth kind of girl. The sort of woman Fiona would bond with immediately. He grinned ruefully. Put a gun in her hand and give her a cheeky attitude and she'd look a whole lot like Sarah, too.

The crowd had been grateful for the pre-rally entertainment. They'd broken his nose, three ribs and loosened a few teeth. Not too bad, considering.

They could've taken his horse and his gun.

They could've killed him and thrown his body in the channel.

Aideen had heard the roar of the crowd and followed it to its source. While she had to wait until the mob had largely finished with him, Mike had no doubt it was her insistence that he was *not* pro-American and that he did not, in fact, even *know* any Americans that accounted for the fact that they allowed him to leave with her. Everyone knew Aideen. There was no way she would be harboring a Yank-lover.

As he watched her now, he realized that she never smiled or sang or hummed unless someone was watching—including little Taffy. He'd not realized that until he'd had occasion to watch her for nearly four straight days from his cot.

Aideen wasn't just unhappy like many people were since The Crisis.

Aideen was miserable.

Mike shifted his position and let a groan escape at the effort. She was on her feet, tossing down her sewing and approaching his bed.

"Can I help you?"

He waved her away. He'd already had the distinct displeasure several times before of having her help him to a spot in the alley where he could relieve himself. If he could manage anything going forward that had to do with his person or his pain, by God he would.

"Where's Taffy?" he said, gasping, trying to distract her from his struggles.

She frowned and watched him until he settled into a position, then went back to her chair and picked up the pants she was mending for someone in town. "She's napping. I'll be getting her up in a bit."

Mike knew that Taffy never went out to the farm with Aideen. In fact, Aideen paid hard-earned money to have a woman watch her while she went. He thought that was odd. As hard as Aideen worked for her money?

Damned odd.

"You tell your da I'll be back tomorrow?"

She nodded. "He wasn't well pleased that you've been gone so long. But it couldn't be helped." She got up and went across the room for a leather pouch. She drew out a bag of small gold coins, the new tender in post-Crisis Ireland. She walked over to Mike and set it next to him on the bed. "You'll have enough by next week," she said.

Mike thanked her but didn't touch the money. When he thought how hard she had to work—and the dump she and Taffy lived in—it almost felt wrong to be taking gold from her hands so that he could move on. He shook himself out of the thought. He'd already pushed back his time line by another five days. And when every day counted for so much, he wasn't even sure there was any point now.

"She must mean a lot to you," Aideen said. "Your American."

"She's a good friend. And she has a son who needs her."

"Oh, that's good then. No husband to worry about her except for you?"

Mike glanced in her direction but she was looking at the stitches she was making in the seam. "Her husband was killed two weeks ago."

Aideen looked up. "So now you're taking care of her."

"Someone has to."

"I didn't know it worked like that," Aideen said. Mike detected the slightest trace of bitterness in her voice. "It's good though if it does…in your world."

Mike wasn't sure what to say or if he should ask her about her husband. From the looks of Taffy, it was a mixed-race marriage and likely there had been some grief over that. Especially in this town. He found himself wondering exactly *how* her husband had died.

The next day, he rode back to her father's farm with her in the pony trap. With his ribs still mending, it would have been too painful to have attempted the trip on Petey's back. Another week or so—about what he had left to work in his agreement with Fionn—and he should be okay for riding.

When he got back to the farm, he spent some time settling Petey back in the stalls with the other animals. Aideen, usually so welcoming, had behaved almost standoffish when they got back to the farm and Mike, taking the hint, stayed in the barn and out of the way until she was ready to leave. He wasn't surprised if she was sick of him. It had been quite an imposition nursing him for the last several days. When he finally came into the house for his supper, he was surprised to see that she'd already left without saying goodbye.

Old Fionn wasn't much of a talker, which suited Mike. He ladled up the goat stew that Aideen had made and settled in front of the fireplace with the old man. To his left, the door to the single bedroom in the farmhouse was open and Mike noticed the bedclothes were rumpled, as if the old tosser had been napping all day instead of working. Mike shrugged and dug into his meal.

It wasn't his business what the old bastard did when Mike wasn't around.

Like his first week on the farm, Mike's schedule began to take on almost a comforting routine of early morning rising and hard work that left him tired in a good way. The sun was rarely out these fall days, but when it was it was hard not to feel the glory of being alive. Mike surprised himself at how much he enjoyed the work on the farm.

So different in many ways from fishing, but still outdoors for all that. He worked the land at Donovan's Lot just as hard and just as relentlessly as he did here on Fionn's farm. But the stress and worry of providing for so many weighed on him and sapped the joy that a simple day's labor gave him here.

Sunday came and Aideen didn't show.

The old guy opened cans of beans for their supper and said nothing of it.

Should he worry? Was Aideen just held up? He looked at Fionn spooning out his dinner straight from the can. He didn't seem at all phased by her nonappearance. *So was this typical?*

Mildly concerned but not ready to go riding into town to find her, Mike focused on finishing his week's work. His ribs were still sore but didn't inhibit his getting the chores done that Fionn was paying him for. The closer Mike got to payday, the more anxious he became about leaving and what he would do once he was on the other side.

When Wednesday came and still Aideen didn't come, he confronted Fionn.

"Do you think she's in trouble?"

Fionn frowned over his meal of cold beans. "In trouble how?"

"Because she hasn't shown up twice in a row now."

"Oh, she'll be here tomorrow."

Mike frowned. "How do you know that?"

"It's your last day, innit? She'll come to make sure you get your pay." He looked up all of a sudden with a fierce look on his face. "You're not tupping her, are ya?"

"Settle down, granddad," Mike said, trying to keep his voice light. "I'm not doing anything to her. Except being very grateful to have met her."

Fionn grunted and directed his attention back to his beans.

Mike went to bed early that night. One more day and he'd be on his way. One more day and he'd be on the ferry and then in Wales. He looked out the window of the barn at the moon waxing big and pale over the barnyard and wondered where Sarah was tonight.

Hang on, girl, he thought. *I'm coming.*

Fionn was right; Aideen did come the next day. Mike was so happy to see her, after worrying about her for nearly a week, that he didn't even mind that she seemed a little more businesslike with him than usual. The day had been a long one, with Fionn pushing him to do more than he normally did, trying to get a little extra out of him for his last day, Mike knew.

When Aideen drove into the frontcourt in front of the farmhouse in her pony trap, Mike called to her. "We missed you, lass. I'll be riding back with you if you'll give me a tick to wash up?"

She nodded without smiling. He could see her father waiting for her on the porch. Fionn went into the house without waiting for her.

Strange family, Mike thought as he went back to the barn for the bucket of clear spring water he'd brought up to wash with.

The water was cold and he was anxious to be gone. Both of those were responsible for the fact that Mike was at Aideen's pony trap and ready to go long before anyone would logically expect him to be. And both of those facts were the reason that Aideen, not expecting Mike to be ready yet, came down the steps of the porch thinking she was alone, her face mottled by tears and pulling down the hem of her skirt.

Fionn came out and stood on the porch. He wasn't smiling, but he was rearranging the front of his trousers.

At first Mike just stared at the scene and refused to believe what he was thinking. But when he caught Aideen's eye and she looked away in guilt and shame, he knew.

That sorry feckin' bastard…

"Mike, no!" Aideen grabbed his arm. Mike hadn't even realized he was climbing the porch stairs. He watched Fionn back away and slam the door. He heard the bolt fall.

"Son of a bitch!" He turned to Aideen.

"Let's just go, please," she begged him. "I've got the rest of the money and you never have to see him again."

"Whereas you do?"

"Mike, just get in the cart and let's go. Please."

Fighting every instinct that told him to go in that house and beat the ever loving shite out of that toad of a man who cowered behind the door, Mike turned away and lashed Petey's reins to the back of the cart. He got in next to Aideen and took the reins from her and urged the little pony onward.

He waited until they were a good mile away from the cottage, waited until she had stopped crying and her tears were dry.

"Why, Aideen?"

She took a long withering breath and let it out slowly. "Unlike the lucky women in your world, Mike Donovan, I have no knight in shining armor to swoop in and take me away from all this. I have a daughter. She has to eat."

"He pays for your apartment?"

Aideen nodded and looked as if she would start crying again. "It was all I could do to get him to allow me to leave at all. You think mending and picking blueberries is a living?" She turned on Mike. "You think I can feed my child on that? I'm doing everything I can to ensure I don't end up going back there to live."

"You can't do that."

"Well, thank you, but pep talks don't pay the bills. I'll do what I have to."

"Is there someplace else you could live?"

She hesitated. "Not really. I...I have an auntie in Wales. A cousin came through last month to say they were doing well and that I was welcome to come but..."

"You don't have the ferry fare."

Aideen laughed with mirth. "Absurd, isn't it? I sit at my window and stare out to sea and think, 'Right over there is a sane life, a happier life. Right over there and right out of reach.'"

"That's why you never bring Taffy to your father's."

Aideen put her hand to her mouth and closed her eyes but Mike could hear her words. "He started in on me when I was her age."

"Son of bitch."

"He's already starting to demand I bring her with me."

"Alright, I get the picture."

"I'm sorry, Mike."

"What in the world for? For having a shite for a father? For loving your daughter and wantin' to protect her?"

She broke down again and sobbed, and except for the sounds of her heartbreak only the wind through the early evening air flitting through the trees could be heard.

When Mike pulled up to the house of the woman minding Taffy, he put a hand out to stop Aideen from jumping out of the cart.

"How much did I earn for my passage?"

Aideen frowned as if she didn't understand the question. "Enough for you and your horse."

149

"And if I were a woman and a wee child instead?"

"Mike, no."

"It's either that or you let me go back and shoot the blackguard."

Aideen's eyes filled with tears and he could see vibrant hope fill her face for the first time since he'd met her. "But what about the woman you're looking for? How will you get to Wales?"

"I'll get there, Aideen," Mike said, putting a reassuring hand on her shoulder. "Or I won't. Go get your bairn. First things first."

Aideen threw her arms around him and held him like he was her lifeline. "God bless you, Mike Donovan, for coming into my life. I prayed for deliverance and he answered by sending you to me."

As her shoulders began to shake, Mike could feel her tears begin again.

Chapter Twenty

20 Days after the attack.

Evvie had no possessions except for the clothes on her back. When they left the village early the next morning, Sarah quickly fashioned a walking stick for the old woman and positioned her ahead of her on the path at least until they were well clear of the village.

It had taken all the willpower Sarah possessed not to tell Lexi what she thought of her. But even with the Glock backing her up, it occurred to her that people so coldblooded that they would routinely kill their elders to save on food would probably have no trouble killing a lone traveler intent on notifying the authorities or threatening to reveal their whereabouts to any bandits she encountered.

She had seen Adwen on more than one occasion eyeing her backpack with what looked distinctly like covetous longing.

Evvie's revelation had stunned Sarah. While it was true she noticed there weren't many old people in the community, she had assumed it was because it was a hard life. When Evvie told her it was because the elderly were taken out and slain on the eve of their seventieth birthday in order to preserve the community's resources for the younger and hardier members, Sarah was sorry to discover that she had no hesitation in believing it.

Evvie was much older than seventy. She said that had been a special allowance as a result of her relationship to Adwen.

The community had no issues with Sarah taking the old woman with her.

Just as long as she never come back.

"We're not monsters," Lexi said as Sarah stood in the doorway of her cabin before leaving. "We are doing what's necessary to survive."

"Thank you for all that you have done for me," Sarah said. The words tasted sour in her mouth but she felt them necessary to say. People who would kill their own mothers could kill a stranger for a shiny new backpack.

"Good luck in finding your way home to your boy," Lexi said, scooping up her own boy in her arms. She never addressed or looked in the direction of Evvie as she walked toward them from the lodge where she had spent the night. Sarah smiled at the little boy in Lexi's arms and turned to hand Evvie the walking stick.

The sooner they were out of this evil place, the better.

"I met some Yanks during the War," Evvie said when they stopped to rest on a mossy boulder overlooking a breathtaking valley of firs and oak trees. "I was only a child but they were all so handsome. They gave me gum."

She looked at Sarah, who was taking an inventory of their food. They had walked five miles before Evvie started to give out. "Can you imagine? Gum! We didn't have jam or eggs or decent bread at home, but I had Juicy Fruit chewing gum. I can still taste it. Like an explosion of all good things ready to happen."

Sarah looked over at her. "How old were you?"

"Eight. I'll never forget it. After that, we used to chase after them whenever we saw them and yell out, *got any gum, chum*? The Yanks loved it."

"You know you coming with me might make it a little trickier for Mark to find you."

"It'll be even trickier if I'm dead."

Good point.

"I don't even know what to say about all that back there."

Evvie shrugged. "Lexi insisted it wasn't personal. Two men and three women were murdered this spring." She paused. "Friends of mine."

"Dear God. Your own daughter!"

"Well, one of the men killed this spring was Adwen's father," Evvie said. "Although I'm told they never got along."

"I'm looking forward to you meeting Mike's group. And John. You'll live with us, of course. I mean, if you want to."

"I would love that. I don't suppose your group has any kind of medical supplies, do they?"

Sarah frowned. "I don't really know. Do you need medicine?"

"Oh, it's nothing. I was on blood pressure medication a few months back."

"You ran out, I guess."

"Other people have it much worse, I'm sure. How much longer, do you think?"

Sarah looked out over the valley and shrugged helplessly. "I think we have to get to the edge of that."

"Oh, my."

"Yeah, at this rate…I don't know."

"I'm slowing you down terribly, aren't I, dear?"

"Not really."

"I know I am."

"It can't be helped, Evvie. It is what it is, you know?"

"It will take as long as it takes."

Sarah smiled at her. "Yeah, something like that." She packed up the backpack and handed Evvie a thermos she'd stolen from Adwen's bed after she found out he was killing all the old people in the village. A part of her was hoping very much he came after to her to try to reclaim it. "I'll give you a toot of this if you think you'll still be able to walk a few more miles today. Once it's gone, I'll fill it with water."

Evvie took the thermos and the smallest of ladylike sips from it. She handed it back. "Good to go, Miz Scarlett," she said.

They managed another two miles that day before stopping for the night. Sarah had to consciously fight down her frustration. *It is what it is,* she told herself.

She found an old campground near a creek still swollen from the recent rains. There was a wooden lean-to damaged by the elements and lack of maintenance in the last year, but very serviceable. Sarah pulled out the two wool blankets that Lexi had allowed her mother to take and spread them on the ground.

"There's plenty of leaves around here," she said to Evvie, who instantly began gathering them in the long apron she still wore around her waist.

"It's the most useful I've felt in a year," Evvie said stooping to pick up the leaves.

"They'll help cushion our beds tonight and maybe we can get some to burn."

"You have a flint?"

"I do, but I've never used one."

"Oh dear."

Sarah looked at Evvie and smiled encouragingly. It had been a cold day that was only made bearable by their constant motion. With the fading light, the dropping temperature crept into their bones. A fire would be necessary tonight if they were to get any rest at all.

"Well, peckers up, dearie," Evvie said. "I'm sure we'll manage. Is there any food left?"

Sarah spread out their provisions. Several sticks of goat jerky, some cooked rabbit, and a few apples. Although hardly a feast, Sarah knew they wouldn't go to bed hungry. Tomorrow she would need to hunt something.

Before the sun left the sky completely, Sarah set to work to build a fire. She created a small pile of dried leaves on top of kindling that Evvie had collected. She took out her knife and began slashing it against the flint to get a spark. After a few moments, Evvie settled herself down next to her and spread out her skirts around her.

"May I make a suggestion, dear?"

Sarah turned to her and saw in her face the expression of someone who was used to having her advice ignored, her suggestions mocked.

"Please," Sarah said. She had never really watched David make a fire the few times they had needed to. She had no idea of what she was doing.

"I think you need to create a little house for the spark to jump into, you see?"

"Not really." Sarah tried to hand the flint to Evvie, but the older woman gathered up the dry leaves in her hands and began kneading them to form a small mass the size and shape of a sparrow's nest.

"You jab two sticks in the ground so that they arc into each other like a pergola."

Sarah watched with amazement and growing optimism as Evvie began to build her little structure of twigs and sticks. When she was done, it resembled an Indian teepee.

"Does the bird nest thing go inside?"

"All in due time."

Sarah felt an evil, icy wind slice through the little campsite and she braced her back against it. She still only had a t-shirt, but today she also wore the blanket that Declan had given her wrapped around like a poncho. She blew warm breath on her fingers and realized that this fire wasn't just a means of comfort for her. As cold as it would get tonight, they might need it to ward off any aggressive wildlife in the area.

"Now, take your knife...my goodness that is a wicked looking thing. Wherever did you get it?"

"You don't want to know."

"Anyway, in the middle of our bird's nest, put the flint flat side up and start scraping off bits of magnesium into the nest."

"I would never have known to do this," Sarah said as she began rubbing her knife edge against the flint.

"That's probably enough. Now turn the flint around to the round side and strike a spark into the nest."

Sarah slashed the knife against the flint and sparks flew everywhere. "It works!"

"Yes, but it's even better if the sparks go in the nest where the magnesium is."

"Yeah, good point." Sarah bent over the little bundle of tinder and zeroed in on the black flakes of magnesium at the bottom. This time when she struck the flint, one of the sparks caught and lit up the nest with a small flame.

"We did it! Oh my God, Evvie, you're a genius!"

"Now pick up the nest and tuck it into our teepee, Sarah."

Sarah could hear the excitement in Evvie's voice and wondered for a moment if Evvie was as surprised as she was they had made fire. She slid the burning nest into the bottom of the teepee and watched as the flames eagerly crept up the structure. She added more kindling and then a few larger sticks until there was clearly no danger the fire would go out.

"You totally just paid for your passage, Evvie," Sarah said, holding her hands out to the campfire. "I swear I think I can do anything if I'm not starving or freezing my ass off."

Evvie laughed and moved toward the fire, too. "Words to live by, petal," she said. "Words to live by."

That night they slept warm and with full stomachs. As usual when she wasn't concerned with immediate threats to her survival, Sarah fell asleep with thoughts of John and David…and Mike.

She couldn't blame Mike for not coming. As far as he could tell she must have disappeared from the face of the Earth. Even if he made it as far as Correy's place—and she prayed he hadn't—there would be no way for him to pick up her trail from there.

No, with twenty-one days between now and the day she was taken, there was no way her trail wasn't too cold to follow.

As much as he might want to, she knew Mike would never find her now. It was up to Sarah to find her own way home.

22 Days after the attack.

The next morning she and Evvie woke to frost on the ground and a fire that had gone out sometime during the night. Shivering, Sarah went immediately to Evvie bundled up in the corner of the lean to where she must have crawled in the middle of the night when the fire went out. She touched the old woman's shoulder and was relieved when Evvie turned to face her.

"Sorry I don't have a latté to offer you," Sarah said. "But if you want to wash your face before we head out, I'll go with you to the creek."

Evvie nodded and struggled to a sitting position. "Will you start the fire again?"

Sarah looked at the campfire and saw that the wood had all burned. If she stopped to relight the fire, she would have to gather wood first. "Do you mind if we don't? I'm really hoping to make better time today."

"Of course, dear," Evvie said. "I'll look forward to it all the more this evening."

"Did you sleep okay?" Sarah wasn't sure why she asked since they'd both obviously been pretty miserable the last part of the night. It just felt like the civilized thing to say.

"Very nicely, dear, until the fire went out."

"What can we do to make it last longer?"

Evvie stood up and shook out her blanket as she peered in the direction of the creek. "Let me think on that," she said, her eyes sparkling with life and mirth for the first time since Sarah had known her.

They walked nearly the whole rest of the day without stopping. Sarah knew that Evvie was pushing herself in order not to hold them up. They were so close now!

By Sarah's estimate, they were halfway through the Beacons. They had seen no other humans and, except for a few wild pigs that Sarah had half entertained the idea of going after with her sling shot, no animals either. The terrain was rough but not impassably so. A year earlier, day-trippers had walked these paths and picnicked along these streams and marveled at the many waterfalls.

But perhaps not in early November, Sarah reminded herself.

When it was time to stop, she could see that Evvie was totally done in. She took Evvie by the hand and led her to a clearing overlooking a small valley. They weren't near a stream, but Sarah had finally dumped out Adwen's hooch and filled the thermos with water so they didn't need to be. She spread out a blanket and insisted Evvie sit.

"But we've got hours yet of daylight," Evvie said, her voice broken with short breaths.

"We've done enough for one day," Sarah said firmly. She placed the knife and the flint in Evvie's lap. "When you feel up to it, put a fire together for us. I'll be back with dinner in an hour."

"You're leaving?" The ragged fear in Evvie's voice snagged Sarah and she turned to the woman.

"Evvie, we're in this together, okay? I mean, would I leave my knife and flint after I just figured out how to make fire?"

Evvie looked at the tools in her lap and Sarah could see some of the anxiety ease from her face. "I…I guess not."

Sarah came back and knelt by her. She put a hand on her shoulder. "You have every right not to trust people after what your dipshit daughter did to you, but that's not me. I will not leave you. Okay?"

Evvie looked into Sarah's face and her eyes were full to tears. "Okay," she whispered through a tremulous smile.

"Make us a fire." Sarah stood and pulled out her slingshot. "I'm going to go bring home the bacon." As she turned away, she stopped and then returned to Evvie and pulled out the handgun.

"Have you ever used a gun?"

Evvie eyed the pistol with what looked like growing horror. "Of course not."

"Well, it's not complicated." Sarah placed the gun next to her. "Not that I'm expecting you to need it, but if someone or something comes sniffing around before I get back…"

Evvie touched the gun with a tentative finger. "I will," she said.

That night, they ate what Evvie said was a badger but neither of them much cared. It was fresh meat. Sarah ate hungrily, only mildly concerned of what the smell of roasting meat might lure to the campsite. After they ate, they faced the fire and let the warmth and light renew and restore them from the long day of walking.

"How much longer do you think?" Evvie asked as she wiped her fingers on the tail of the tattered blanket draped over her shoulders.

"I don't know. I don't have a good method for estimating miles. I was pretty much just going to walk until we reached the highway."

"And then what?"

"Well, and then we walk to the coast and get on a boat to Ireland."

"How old is your boy? John, right?"

Sarah nodded. It didn't help to think of John. Up to now, she'd discovered that thinking of him weakened her and made her want to curl up into a ball and weep. "Twelve."

"That's young. Where's his father?"

Sarah cleared her throat. "Killed when they took me."

"Oh, dear Lord, Sarah, I'm so sorry. Just a few weeks ago?"

"Three weeks ago."

"You lost your husband just three weeks ago." Evvie shook her head as if unable to understand the horror of it.

"Well, it's not like I *lost* him, you know? I mean, I didn't *misplace* him and neither did he die of natural causes. He was murdered."

"I'm so sorry, Sarah."

"No, *I'm* sorry. I don't mean to go off on you. It's just...I can't believe it, you know? Oh, what am I saying? You of all people know what I'm saying. People are no damn good. That's all. And it comes out in the worst of times."

"Not true, Sarah," Evvie said, tossing a piece of kindling into the roaring fire. "People haven't changed because of the circumstances. The rotters are still finding a way to take advantage. But the good people are still good."

Sarah had an image of Declan and his family feeding and outfitting her when they had so little themselves. She knew Evvie was right. She just wasn't in the mood to agree at the moment.

"Whatever," she said.

"And your parents?" Evvie asked gently. "Are they back in the States?"

Sarah nodded. "No word from them or about them."

"You poor, poor girl," Evvie said. When Sarah looked up she could see the sadness and the pain wreathed in Evvie's face. She held her arms out and Sarah surprised herself by coming into them. Evvie was stout, whereas her own mother was slim from years of tennis playing and careful calorie counting. But everything else was the same. The love, the comfort.

And as Sarah began to cry, hopelessly, tirelessly, for her own mother, for her boy and her lost husband, she felt somehow renewed and stronger cradled in the old woman's arms.

25 days after the attack.

The day they emerged from the Brecon Beacons National Park, the sun shone bright against a relentlessly blue sky. It had taken a full five days to cover the distance of thirty hard miles. Sarah's jeans were loose and she'd taken to carrying the gun in her front jeans pocket. Evvie, too, had lost weight.

"Why are we not leaving the park?" Evvie asked when they stopped for lunch but didn't move on.

"I'm just making sure it's safe."

"Are you expecting your friends to be waiting outside? How in the world would they know at which point you might exit?"

Sarah knew Evvie was right, but still she hesitated. The memory of Angie goading her thug to search the corpses in the ditch was fresh and vivid in her mind. She didn't know if it was personal or if Angie was just psychotic—maybe a bit of both—

but that was nearly a week ago. By now she would be more determined than ever to find Sarah.

Sarah realized that a part of her was shocked that she had passed through the Beacons without mishap. She had fed herself —*and* an elderly woman—and kept them warm and safe through terrain that was rough and inhospitable and emerged unharmed on the other side.

Now if they could just stay that way.

"Sarah? Dear?"

Sarah looked at Evvie.

"It's not like you haven't had time to think of what you'll do when we got here."

"I know."

"And a journey of a thousand miles begins with a single foot forward."

"Not really helping, Evvie."

Evvie laughed and stood up. "I'm ready when you are, dear."

"It'll be harder to find food out there," Sarah said.

"You're stalling." Evvie picked up her slim knapsack and turned toward the park exit. "Personally, I have high hopes of finding a proper bed for tonight."

Sarah checked her gun and hoisted her pack onto her shoulder. Whatever was waiting for her, it was time to meet it head on.

"How far to the coast?" Evvie asked over her shoulder.

Sarah scanned the bushes beside them and ahead. The feeling of anxiety ratcheted up with every step she took now that she knew she was back on Angie's playing field. "Sixty miles."

"My, that's far. How long do you think it will take us?"

Me, three days, Sarah thought. *Us, more like six. If we're lucky.*

"I'm not sure. Maybe a week."

The highway at the edge of the park looked empty.

But that's what it would look like if they were lying in ambush.

She wanted to slink out around the perimeter, hiding in the bushes, gun in her hand. But Evvie was in a hurry to get back to civilization and trotted out of the park and up the long sloping drive that led to the highway.

Sarah pulled the gun out and held in in front of her with both hands. Her head swiveled from side to side trying to take in the full perimeter as they walked. By the time they reached the top of the slope—uneventfully—that led to the highway entrance ramp, Sarah was already tired and her neck hurt.

"Can we hitch a ride, do you think?" Evvie asked peering down the road, one hand on a bony hip as if about to thrust out a leg to entice the next would-be motorist.

"I thought we'd stay away from the highways," Sarah said dubiously.

"Oh dear, do you mind if we at least give it a try? I'm really hoping to find a hotel room for the night. Just the thought of a hot bath and a toilet where I don't have to use a handful of cold leaves to wipe me bum has given me the will to live for the last day or more."

"I know it's been tough," Sarah said, watching Evvie. Could they afford to go into town? Would they be less likely to attract attention because she was no longer a woman traveling alone?

"Here comes something."

As soon as she spoke, Sarah heard the comfortable clip-clopping sound of a horse drawn cart. The memory of the terrible four days she had spent in the back of a cart much like this one came roaring back to her and it was all she could do not to grab Evvie's arm and dive for the ditch along the side of the road. Seeing Evvie's excitement and hope as she watched the cart approached made her hesitate.

"What if they mean us harm?" Sarah asked, trying to calm her racing heart as she stood with Evvie and watched the cart come closer.

"Then you can shoot them, dear," Evvie said, smoothing back her hair into some semblance of order.

Sarah hid the gun back in her front pocket. "There's always that, I guess."

The cart stopped several yards ahead of them. A man in the driver's seat stood up. "May I help you, missus?" he shouted.

"We need a ride to town, if you'd be so kind," Evvie answered. "Can you give us a lift?"

"Aye, there's room if you'd like to come on," he said, motioning to the back of the cart.

"I don't like it," Sarah whispered hoarsely to Evvie.

"Think how much time we'll save," Evvie whispered back. She trotted to the cart. Sarah kept her hand on the gun in her pocket. The man was probably in his fifties, she thought, although Sarah knew the year since The Crisis had aged everyone prematurely. While his voice was rough and harsh, she could see when she got closer that his eyes were kind, if tired.

He had seen bad things.

And yet still he stopped to give two strangers a ride. In the back of his cart were two large bushels of root vegetables, mostly potatoes.

"If you don't mind sitting in back with the spuds," he said, gesturing to the flatbed of his cart.

"Not at all," Evvie said. "What town are you going to, may I ask?" She gave Sarah a quick look to ascertain that she felt it was safe and then walked to the end of the cart. With Sarah's help, she placed her feet in toeholds on the cartwheel spokes and pulled herself into the back. Sarah let go of the gun in her pocket and did the same.

"I'm heading to Carmarthen," he said. "And yourselves?"

Evvie looked at Sarah, who almost imperceptibly shook her head and gave her a warning look.

"Just a place for the night," Evvie said, her eyes still on Sarah. "Carmarthen will suit us fine. You're Welsh, then?"

"Aye," the man said turning around, touching his patched cheese cutter cap. "Davey Smail. I bought yon spuds in Llangadog two days ago. Carmarthen's been hit hard since the Yank's Gift."

Now it was Evvie's turn to warn Sarah not to speak with a severe look in her eye. "I don't believe I know that term, Davey. Whatever do you mean by the *Yank's Gift?*"

"Oh, it's just what some around here call the Black Out, ya ken? We don't know much about *why* it happened, but it's certain as the freckles on your face that it's the goddamn Americans what's brought it to our shores."

"Well, I'd say that's a safe guess," Evvie said and winced apologetically to Sarah, who shrugged. She closed her eyes and tried to appreciate the break from walking for what it was—a chance to rest up and still make some distance. But Davey's words reverberated in sinister tones in her head as she rode, leaning against one of the potato baskets.

Chapter Twenty-one

Day 28 after the attack.

The first night in a bed in nearly a month. The first bath that she wasn't terrorized in the middle of taking. The first time she was alone in a room without a dead body staring at her from the floorboards.

Sarah couldn't wait to leave…and Evvie wasn't budging.

"You said yourself the coast is almost five days distance," Evvie said. "Just thinking about walking for five days makes me want to sit down and never get up again. You do know I'm old, right?"

Sarah sighed. "I can't leave you here."

"Too right you can't!"

"But I need to go, Evvie. My son—"

"We've only been here one night!"

"One night is all we have money for—"

"You could work. The woman who runs this boarding house said she would be happy to let you work for our room and board."

Sarah watched Evvie cross her arms on her chest, her mouth pulled down into a pout.

"I can't stay, Evvie."

"And I'm too old to go!"

Sarah moved to where the older woman sat and picked up her hand. "The longer I stay, the more dangerous it is for both of us."

"You don't know that."

"I do. The people following me are desperate. If it was up to me we'd be sleeping in ditches and avoiding the highways altogether."

"I can't do that," Evvie said, her bottom lip trembling. "Just the thought of it…"

"I know." Sarah patted her hand. "So here's what we're going to do." She took a deep breath. "I'm going to work for the woman, Alice, just long enough to buy you a week's worth of lodging. That'll give me enough time to get home, get Mike, and come back for you."

"You're crazy, Sarah."

"It's the best plan I've got."

Evvie looked out the cracked and dirty window in the upstairs bedroom that she and Sarah shared. The town of Carmarthen had obviously once been a thriving tourist's mecca before The Crisis—or the Yank's Gift as almost everyone they met called it. But now it was a dingy, ramshackle collection of huts and poorly constructed houses and buildings. There was a large tent city along its perimeter, but from the looks of it, Sarah thought, that was where most of the crime, prostitution and violence were centered.

"One week?" Evvie looked out the window as if expecting to see demons or bandits lining up to break into the boarding house as soon as Sarah left.

"One week. And I'll be back."

That evening at dinner, Sarah made arrangements with Alice, the house's proprietor. She was a suspicious, tight-faced woman with bad teeth, but Sarah thought she could trust her. She wasn't sure she had much choice.

"So, you work for me for two days and I let the old one sit tight for a week."

"Board too, mind."

"Sure, sure. And when you come back, I get an extra twenty quid."

"That's right."

Alice shrugged as if to say it was all the same to her, but Sarah knew the house was only half filled with boarders who could pay Alice in any way at all.

"Where did you say you were from? I can't place your accent."

"Donegal." Sarah figured mimicking the way Fiona spoke would be an easier way out of the American accent problem than trying to sound English in England.

"Be faster if you turned a few tricks, you know," Alice said, peering at Sarah as if wondering if there was something physically deformed about her that prevented this.

"No, thanks. I'm a hard worker. Just tell me what you need doing."

"Oh, you can be sure of that. Starting tonight, unless you've got any more coin like last night? I didn't think so. The kitchen, if you please. Pedro will show you what needs doing. I hope you weren't planning on sleeping tonight."

Sarah worked five straight hours that night rinsing dishes after she'd first dragged in buckets of water from the only working well in the town, nearly a quarter of a mile away. The water was brackish and smelled bad.

She stripped all the beds in the house and dragged the heavy sheets and blankets to the basement where large vats and washtubs were filled with ice water. She sudsed and scrubbed the bed linens with coarse brushes. The temperatures dropped significantly outside and Sarah found her hard labor her only defense against the cold.

Just before dawn, dripping with sweat, she collapsed onto the wooden back steps of the house, so tired she didn't even feel the chill, her fingers blue and blistered, her legs aching as if she'd run a marathon. She looked due west—the direction where John was—and closed her eyes in prayer.

"Oy, want a bite?"

She turned her head to find a young girl bundled in a thick wool rug sitting on the top step of the stairs to the boarding house. She looked like a blonde Indian. Her eyes were large and almond-shaped, but her skin was light. She was holding out a meat pasty. Sarah took the pastry. She and Evvie had seen the stands set up on the main drag of Carmarthen, but the meat pies were expensive. It took all of Evvie's money for one night and board for two.

The fragrance of the pies had tortured Sarah long into the night as she tried to fall asleep. She sank her teeth into the pie and immediately groaned with pleasure.

"Good, eh?" the girl said. "You keep it. I've already had two."

Sarah forced herself to wrap the meat pie in a napkin and put it in her pocket. *Evvie will think she's died and gone to heaven,* she thought.

"Thank you so much," Sarah said, refocusing on the girl. "I'll save it for me mum."

The girl's eyes were bright and seemed to dance as she regarded Sarah. For a town full of so much desperation and pain, she looked remarkably well fed and cheerful.

"No worries. I seen you and the oldie-but-goodie come in yesterday. Where you from, then?"

Sarah recited the lie she and Evvie had concocted. "We're from Gloucester, heading for Narberth. I've a brother there working the fields."

"Sure you do."

Sarah blinked at the retort. Did the girl not believe her? In the dim light, it was difficult to see her expression. Come to think of it, what was this girl doing at the boarding house?

"And yourself?" Sarah asked. "Do you live in Carmarthen?"

"I'm from the Kale. Ever heard of 'em?"

Sarah shook her head.

"They call us Welsh Romanies, but basically we're gypsies. I'm Papin."

"Sarah."

"You've got a secret, Sarah." Papin smiled and Sarah was struck by the young girl's self-possession.

"I guess we all do," Sarah said, wondering if she was being missed in the kitchen and should be getting back. She stood up.

"A man asked me tonight about someone who sounded a whole lot like you, except for you not being American."

Sarah stopped in mid turn, her hand frozen on the wooden railing. She turned and took a step toward the young gypsy girl and squatted down on the step to look into her face. When she did, she realized the girl couldn't be more than thirteen years old.

"What man?"

"An Englishman with a lying face and hurting hands."

"He…he hurt you?"

"He took what I was offering, but wouldn't pay me afterwards."

The bite of meat pie threatened to come back up Sarah's throat. That explained how the girl had money. "When?"

"Tonight." The girl nodded in the direction of the street. "There's a pub before the tents. Him and his mates are staying there."

"What did you tell him?" Sarah's palms were damp and the cold night air lifted her long hair from her collar.

"Told him I didn't know no Yank. Which I don't, do I? What with you being from Gloucester and all. Or is it Ireland?"

Sarah's mind was a jumble of panic and questions. Had the girl revealed there was a strange woman just come to town and staying at the boarding house? How did the little gypsy guess it was Sarah the men were looking for? Were they asking everyone?

She and Evvie would have to go tonight. She couldn't leave her now. The men would question Alice, and likely Papin again, and end up with Evvie. She rubbed a hand across her face trying to imagine how she was going to do this with an eighty-year-old woman in the middle of the night with no food and no way to travel but on foot.

"What is it you want?"

The girl didn't answer immediately. She stretched out her legs and when she did, Sarah noticed that her thighs were bruised and her skirt was ripped. Sarah looked in the direction the girl had indicated.

"I want to go with you. Which ain't Narberth."

Sarah was astonished. "*Go with me*? Whatever for?" Was someone chasing the little gypsy girl, too?

Papin shook her head as if shaking off Sarah's question like an annoying fly. "Doesn't matter. Besides, I can help you."

Sarah watched her for a moment before speaking. "*How* can you help me?"

The girl brought her knees up on the wooden step and leaned forward eagerly. "I can move in with your mum while you get away. If she's with me, they won't think she's got anything to do with you." The girl's eyes were bright with excitement and her words gave Sarah a surge of excitement. *I can leave,* she thought.

But something wasn't right.

"How can you come with me and also stay here with...with my mum?"

"I'll stay just long enough so there's no suspicion on her, like. Then, when I can, I'll follow you. Tell me where you're going next."

"Alice knows I'm with the old woman."

"Alice doesn't care who's with who."

"But if they question Alice, she'll tell them."

"They won't question her. They don't even know yet about the old lady."

Yet.

"Oy," Papin said, "weren't you planning on taking a hike anyway?"

How did she know that? "Yes, but I'm coming back for her."

"Then it all works out. Besides, what option do you have? The bloke who asked me about you was a real wanker. I wouldn't want him after *me*."

Sarah sat down heavily next to the girl. "How long could you stay with her?"

"Until the men leave. Then I'll join you. Where is it you're going?"

Sarah paused. "The coast. To catch a ferry to Ireland."

Papin's eyes widened. "That's a long way."

"Especially on foot." Sarah glanced at Papin's ballet-slippered feet. "You still haven't said why you're so keen to come with me."

Papin stood up and brushed off the skirt of her dress. She looked to Sarah like a little girl playing dress-up in her mother's clothes. "Does it matter?" She looked at Sarah and smiled before turning and walking to the top of the stairs. It occurred to Sarah that the look she gave her was one she might expect to see from a much older, much more jaded woman.

Sarah turned to head back to her room to awaken Evvie and tell her the change of plans. The piece of meat pie still felt warm and moist in her pocket.

Susan Kiernan-Lewis

Chapter Twenty-two

Mike had been gone just shy of a month—one wasted month—and now it was done. The rescue mission was over. And wherever Sarah was, she was on her own, as in so many ways she'd always been. The weight of abandoning the search, even temporarily, was wedged tight into the base of Mike's throat, where he knew it would always be.

Was God punishing him for loving her when she belonged to another? He never thought the Almighty operated along those lines, but this failure felt very like a lesson being crammed down his gob.

It helped watching Aideen and Taffy step aboard the ferry, their bags packed, Aideen smiling more broadly than he could ever remember her doing. He watched the sharp and bracing salt air rake the two travelers. Aideen turned her face into it, as if she welcomed the assault, the clean slate, the new life that awaited her.

Donovan's Sacrifice, he thought bitterly as he sat on Petey at the top of the pasture and looked down onto the harbor, the ferry gone hours earlier. His failure spelled a new life for Aideen, but it was at the cost of being able to help the one woman who mattered most to him.

He turned his horse's head west toward home and Donovan's Lot. Whatever waited for him back home would be there still when he arrived. Whatever bollocks Gavin had made of things would be sorted out in time. He likely couldn't have destroyed a whole community in a month's time.

No, there was only one piece of wreckage that wouldn't soon be recovered from or easily survived by his failure.

John.

What the hell was he going to say to John?

***

The lad seemed a little better, a little stronger. Whether it was the endless cups of tea, the lack of chores, Fi's constant attention, or just the resilience of a young body overcoming the mysterious ailment Fiona would never know, but he was slowly coming back to them.

There was a day or two when she wasn't sure he would.

Fiona hefted the plastic laundry basket full of wet clothing onto her hip and squinted at the sky. There wouldn't be loads of sun, but neither did it look like it was about to rain any time soon. She smiled to herself as she stepped off her porch. She was fairly sure that her real job at Donovan's Lot was as Chief Worrier. She knew her brother felt *he* held that title, but he wasn't a woman. He wasn't even close. Nor until he grew ovaries could he ever be.

She lugged the basket to Mike's hut and set it down heavily on the first step of his decking. *Typical Mike*, she thought. He's worked to make everybody else's cottage as tight and windproof as they could be and left his own place to grow moss and catch leaks. Not for the first time, she caught herself, thinking, *If only Ellen had lived…*

A high-pitched squeal of a laugh caught on the breeze shuffled through camp and snagged Fiona's attention. *Speaking of Ellen…*She caught a glimpse of the dead woman's younger sister as Caitlin ran behind the tents that lined the main campfire.

What was the girl up to now?

True, the lass had come to her offering to sit with young John while he was the sickest, but then had been conveniently unavailable when Fiona suggested any real work for her to do. And as for sitting with the lad—Fiona pulled out a pair of cotton pants from the pile of wet laundry and draped it over Mike's porch railing—that had lasted all of one day after Fi caught Caitlin feeding the boy poteen. Remembering the incident, Fi colored with annoyance all over again.

"Are you trying to kill the lad?" She had grabbed the bottle from Caitlin's hands. "He's *twelve*, you eejit!"

Fi had seen an unpleasant side of Caitlin during that exchange, which ended with Caitlin flouncing out of the cottage and slamming the door behind her.

When Fi saw that John was fine—if a little woozy for the experience—she regretted her harsh words. *Still, it's hard enough to live during these times without having to live through someone else's foolishness on top of it.*

As she flapped out a wet t-shirt and positioned it next to the pants on the railing, she craned her neck to see what Caitlin was up to that involved scampering and squealing. She was *supposed* to be gathering kindling for the widow McGinty's cook stove. When no other sounds came from behind the tents, Fi shrugged and went back to her own chores.

After the poteen incident, Caitlin had opted to keep her distance from Fiona—and so, John—and Fiona had to admit she found it better for everyone all around. The following day when Fiona had gone to pour the poteen into a smaller bottle so that she could use the bigger one to store cooking oil, nearly a half a dozen undissolved aspirin tablets were glommed at the bottom of the bottle.

An innocent mistake, surely, on Caitlin's part, obviously trying to make the boy more comfortable.

But one that could easily have been fatal for him.

Susan Kiernan-Lewis

Chapter Twenty-three

The village of Bancyfelin was only five miles due west from Carmarthen, but it took Sarah all night to reach it. She hated to walk so close to the A40—surely the main conduit for Angie and her group—but she was afraid of getting lost. Besides, she had told Papin she would meet her in Merlins Bridge outside of Haverfordwest in two days' time. They had met again a few minutes before Sarah slipped away into the night—her promise of work to Alice unfulfilled and so her dependence on Papin all the greater.

It was Papin who told her Merlins Bridge would be a good halfway point at which to meet. Unfortunately, it was a direct route from Carmarthen on the worst possible road for hiding. Sarah cursed herself for not confirming with the girl that they were headed toward the point on the coast *that had ferry crossings*. In the end, she knew it didn't matter. If she had to backtrack, she would.

After the fifth group of noisy travelers forced her into the trees for another wasted hour of waiting and watching, Sarah finally decided to leave the highway for the pastures and woodland boundaries. Papin said that Merlins Bridge was only two days distance by foot, and what that translated into miles Sarah had no idea. Once again she realized she had placed her life in the hands of someone she had no reason to trust.

With the morning bearing down on her and what cover she had had up to then about to vanish, Sarah took off at a slow jog across the field. She knew she was off course. She knew she would probably not make the rendezvous at this rate. She also knew that traveling so close to the A40 was a death sentence. If she lost Papin, well, then she did. Mid-morning, grateful for not having seen another living soul, Sarah dropped over a broken fieldstone wall and rested, her back up against the wall. Evvie had insisted Sarah take the half-pie and she dug it out of her pack now and devoured it in two bites.

Her heart ached to think of Evvie, her eyes big and trusting but scared, too, beseeching Sarah to return for her. It had been a painful parting.

And then there was Papin. What was her story? If she needed to leave town, why did she need Sarah for that? And why volunteer to babysit Evvie in the meantime?

None of it made sense. Sarah closed her eyes and enjoyed the brief showing of the autumn sun on her face as it peeked through the clouds. If the girl showed up at Merlins Bridge then Sarah would honor her promise to bring her along. But if she wasn't there, Sarah wouldn't wait. Watching the sun retreat back into the clouds and the resulting icy gust of wind ruffling her hair, Sarah picked up her knapsack. Setting up sticks to ascertain her position wasn't helpful at this point. She needed to get away from the main road more than she needed to be heading due west.

She got to her feet and began walking.

In a way, the next two days were almost peaceful. With nobody's safety but her own to worry about, Sarah simply walked and slept, her mind locked in neutral. She killed a small rabbit in the afternoon of her second day, made a fire and cooked it before nightfall, then packed up her food and kept moving until late that night when she climbed a crabapple tree.

Walking across fields and pastures made her feel vulnerable, and although the area looked as desolate as farmland that's been abandoned could look, Sarah couldn't take any chances. Twice she had had to throw rocks at wild and ravenously hungry dogs—probably tame and beloved family pets up until last year—in order to continue, and with the smell of cooked meat on her, she couldn't risk sleeping on the ground, especially without a fire. Moving again made her feel like every step was taking her closer to John and not the fatigue nor the hunger could diminish the spring in her step that that thought brought.

While she felt relatively safe, she had to admit she had no idea where she was in relation to Merlins Bridge or the coast. She awoke in her tree on the morning of her third day since she left Carmarthen. It was thirty-one days since the attack. And it was raining. She pulled her wet blanket around her shoulders and squinted up at the billowing gray clouds overhead. Today was the day she was to meet Papin at Merlins Bridge. At least she wasn't hungry. She'd eaten the whole rabbit last night before falling asleep in the branches of her tree.

Without the sun, however, how was she going to be able to tell which direction she was walking? The last time she checked was yesterday morning, but she'd logged in many miles since then and with the meandering nature of her path—over stonewalls and around woods or any sign of human habitation of which there had been few but enough—she was sure she was no longer going due west.

Sitting in the tree, she tried to decide if she should continue in the same direction she had been going before she stopped. Ultimately, she didn't see another option. The sun didn't appear to be coming out any time soon and she had a strong urge to be moving.

She dropped to the ground, checked her provisions, ensured that her gun and knife were secure in her pack—she had stopped carrying the gun in her pocket, as it had begun to chafe badly on the top of her thigh—and headed out.

She walked in the rain until she saw the skies clearing ahead, which prompted her to move quicker. The sooner she got out of the weather, the sooner she could determine how badly off track she was and correct it.

As she moved toward the blue skies ahead, she noted that at some point in the trip she had mentally let go of the necessity of meeting up with Papin and was now focused strictly on just finding the coast. That thought surprised her and triggered her to say a prayer for Evvie's safety. Would Papin betray Evvie for whatever money Angie's thugs might give her? A chill ran down Sarah's spine as she remembered Jeff when he jumped into the ditch with her just a few days earlier.

If he only knew how close he had been to touching her warm, still living flesh under the two corpses lying with her in the ditch. She shivered, not in memory of her grisly ditch companions, but at the thought of what would have happened to her if the real monster in that ditch had discovered her alive.

Suddenly, she saw a man and a woman walking toward her across the pasture. Because she had just been thinking of Angie and Jeff, she instantly dropped to her stomach in a panic and watched the two approach. As soon as she hit the ground, she could see it wasn't them, but still she didn't move.

She watched them stumble along in the uneven footing of the pasture. Twice, the man reached out to grab the woman's elbow to steady her. Sarah turned on her back and pulled out the Glock. The rain, lighter now, still splashed into her face and she wiped it with the back of her sleeve, knowing she was about to give the two travelers a terrible fright. But there was nothing for it.

She stood up. She held the gun once more in her front pocket and she kept her hand in that pocket.

"Hello," she said in her best English accent. "Hello, there."

The couple stopped, the woman clapping a terrified hand to her mouth to stifle the shriek that Sarah nonetheless clearly heard.

"Don't be frightened. I want nothing from you except directions."

The man's hand went to his woman's arm and Sarah hated that she was causing them such discomfort. Lord knows she was well acquainted with what it was like to live with fear hunched around every dark corner.

"We have nothing to give you," the man said. He was about forty, Sarah guessed, and thin, although whether that was by nature or the last terrible year was unknowable. The fact that he refused to hear Sarah say she wanted nothing from them made her realize they had likely been badly treated.

"Where are we?" she asked, using her other hand to indicate the pasture. "I'm lost." Hoping that describing herself in a vulnerable position might make them relax, Sarah smiled. On the other hand, she reminded herself, she *did* have her hand on a gun and it probably looked very odd to the couple that she kept one hand in her pocket.

"You're in Wales," the man said.

Sarah nodded and tried to keep smiling. *This was obviously going to take awhile,* she thought with impatience. "How close are we to the coast?"

The man glanced at his companion and Sarah was gratified to realize it was the kind of look husbands give when they're about to provide directions but expect to be second-guessed by their wives.

"Thirty kilometers?"

His wife nodded.

Sarah's shoulders sagged dejectedly under her wet blanket. Thirty kilometers was around twenty miles. It was not welcome news. "Am I going the right way toward the coast?"

This seemed to surprise the man but he nodded. "Perhaps a little bit more that way," he said, indicating a slight course correction to the left.

"Thank you." Sarah smiled to indicate that the two could continue on their way when, on impulse, she asked, "Am I anywhere near Merlins Bridge, do you know?"

The woman spoke for the first time. "You've past it by about two miles," she said, not smiling. "Back the way you come and off that aways is Clarbeston Road."

"What *used* to be Clarbeston Road," her husband said.

"There's no markings on it," she said, "but you can't miss it."

"We're going that way," the man said and Sarah saw the woman snap her head to look at him. She was either surprised he'd suggest they travel together…or he was lying.

"Thank you," Sarah said. "I'll be along directly."

The man nodded and the couple continued walking. Sarah watched them go. It went against everything in her to retrace her steps when there was so much distance still between her and the coast. Backtracking two miles across the fields to meet up with Papin would cost her the rest of the morning. And how likely was it she was even there? Could she travel any faster than Sarah had?

Then when Sarah confirmed that the girl *wasn't* there, she would have to spend another couple of hours to return to where she was right now. And why? So she could assuage her guilt about not keeping her word to the little gypsy? Who would know? Sarah shifted her pack and turned in the direction that the couple had gone.

She would know.

She walked steadily until her longer stride couldn't help but catch up with the couple and then she walked with them, none of them speaking, which suited Sarah since her fake English accent was poor. When they reached the place that Sarah spent the night, the couple turned northwest and motioned for Sarah to follow them. She could tell when they shifted direction that the land was becoming more cultivated and that they were leaving the desolate fields behind. Tightening her hands into fists, Sarah took a long breath to calm herself.

She tried to remind herself that Angie would stick to the A40 as much as she could and that only people on foot or horseback would be able to comfortably travel these back roads. While Angie's lot was on horseback, there would be nothing in the way of alcohol or food or women to amuse them here. As she and the couple walked past crofts and what looked like abandoned holiday cottages, she prayed she was right and that Angie's men would stick to the larger towns.

"That there's Clarbeston Road," the man said to Sarah, pointing at a two-lane road that twisted and wound below them. Sarah would have to slide down a steep embankment to walk along the road.

"Which way is Merlins Bridge?" she asked.

The man pointed in the direction. "Though there's nothing much there now," he said, looking at Sarah closely.

Afraid she had forgotten to use her English accent, Sarah just nodded her thanks and turned from them to negotiate the drop down to the road. She forced herself not to look back up at them. She knew they were watching her. She wondered where they were headed.

Once on the road and feeling remarkably relieved to feel solid asphalt under her feet for a change, Sarah began to jog in the direction that the man had pointed to. The sooner she touched base at Merlins Bridge the sooner she could either retrace her steps—and that meant somehow getting back up that steep hill to the fields. The sun had come out now, which further buoyed Sarah's mood. With a re-emergent sun, she would be able to determine her direction again. Maybe she wouldn't have to backtrack at all to resume her trek to the coast.

She heard them before she saw them. Unfortunately, this time there was no handy ditch lining the road for her to hide herself. Sarah looked in panic at the tall hill to her left—the one she'd just descended—but realized that even if she could scale it in time it would only serve to make her more visible to whomever was approaching from around the corner on the road.

From the sounds of it, she could tell there were at least two, and possibly more, coming her way on horseback. She slipped her hand into her pocket to touch the reassuringly cold hard shape of the Glock and turned the corner to face what was coming.

Susan Kiernan-Lewis

Chapter Twenty-four

The shock at seeing the two of them was so great that, at first, Sarah could only stand her ground in the middle of the road, her hand on her gun and stare. It wasn't until Papin called out to her that Sarah realized what she was seeing was real. Papin, dressed in a long flowing gypsy skirt and a woolen jumper, was astride a bone-white Welsh pony, leading two other saddled horses behind her.

One of which carried Evvie.

"Oy! Don't shoot, ya daft bitch!" Papin called laughingly to Sarah. "I told you we'd find her!" she said over her shoulder as she trotted her pony down to meet Sarah where she stood.

"I don't believe this," Sarah said in wonder. "This is either a miracle or I got some seriously bad mushrooms last night out in the field."

"Oh, we're real enough, dear," Evvie said, her cheeks brightly pink against the cold day. Sarah could see she was gripping the saddle pommel instead of the reins.

"I know it's a change of plan," Papin said, jerking a thumb to indicate Evvie. "But the crazy old cow wouldn't stay by herself. What else could I do?"

Sarah touched the nose of Evvie's horse. He was a mixed breed but sturdy for it. "Where in the world did you get them?" It hadn't occurred to her until that second that right behind seeing John again—or Mike—would have been the unimaginably wonderful possibility of riding the rest of the way home.

"Oh, that's a trade secret, but we might not want to travel the main highways. I figured you didn't want to anyway. Besides, there was no way the old lady was going to be able to make it on foot."

"I'd greatly appreciate it, dear, if you'd stop referring to me as the old lady and such." Sarah could see that Evvie spoke to Papin fondly, with a twinkle in her eye.

"How did you even know I was here?" Sarah asked, moving to the riderless horse and tightening the girth on the saddle.

"Well, we didn't, did we? We got tired of waiting at the bridge and then some rough types came around and we thought we'd try waiting a little further on."

"I just can't believe y'all are here with horses," Sarah said as she secured her backpack onto the back of the saddle. "We'll save the hugs for later, okay?" She put her foot in the stirrup and swung easily up into the saddle.

The minute was she was astride again, after so many months of not riding, Sarah felt strong and in control again. Even a horse she'd never ridden before felt more naturally an extension of her body than walking.

"You don't ride, Evvie?" she asked, nodding at the double set of reins in Papin's hands.

"Never once," Evvie said ruefully. "But it beats walking."

"That it does," Sarah said, giving Papin a grin. The girl beamed with pleasure. Sarah touched her horse's sides with her legs and felt him wake up and move forward.

When she thought of how close she came to skipping Merlins Bridge and missing Papin and Evvie—*and horses!*—she quickly shooed the thought from her head. They were mounted, well fed, together again and only twenty miles from the Welsh coast.

Things were definitely looking up.

They rode for another two hours before making camp for the night. Riding or not, the trip was strenuous for Evvie, and upon being helped to dismount by Papin she sank to her knees.

"Whoa, Granny, you are seriously out of shape," Papin said, helping Evvie to a sitting position at the base of a broken stonewall while Sarah hobbled the horses nearby.

"I'm eighty-years-old, you impertinent brat," Evvie said good-naturedly. "I'm actually in amazing condition for my age. Can we risk a campfire tonight, Sarah dear?"

"I think so." Sarah handed her the flint and the knife. "I'll go get the bits for the bird nest thingy. Did you guys bring any food by any chance?"

While Papin pulled out the stolen provisions from her saddle roll and Sarah gathered kindling and leaves for the fire, Evvie laid out blankets against the saddles, one for each of them. When she got the fire going, the three sat for long moments just warming their hands and staring into the flames without speaking.

Even little Papin looked all-in, Sarah couldn't help but notice. She'd held up her end of the bargain in spades. She'd taken care of Evvie and gone several steps further by procuring horses and food. Sarah was having trouble imagining what she would have done without the little gypsy's help.

Papin used Sarah's knife to slice the long tube of salami and bread that she'd brought. She also had a large chunk of cheddar cheese—unimaginably rare in these days after The Crisis—that the three shared in celebration of how far they had all come.

"I've never toasted with cheese before," Evvie said, holding up her piece and smiling.

"It's the perfect thing to toast with," Papin said. "It's delicious, it fills you up and it's dead expensive."

"Maybe more than a toast, I want to give a prayer of thanksgiving," Sarah said. "Because until the moment that I saw you two again, I'd forgotten what it felt like to be grateful for my good fortune." She held up her cheese chunk and said, "To the three of us meeting safely again and to the journey ahead." She popped the cheese in her mouth.

"Hear, hear!" Papin and Evvie both said, eating their cheese.

"Although, I must say, a hot bath would be good about now, too," Evvie said with a sigh, prompting Papin and Sarah to burst out laughing.

"You old hag! You're never satisfied!" Papin said, reaching out and shaking Evvie's knee.

"You two obviously connected, I see," Sarah said.

"Well, she's a cheeky piece, it's true," Evvie said, smiling fondly at Papin. "But she's also a treasure and, trust me, I've cause to know." Sarah saw Evvie's eyes fill with pain and she knew she was thinking of her daughter, Lexi.

Well, that's fitting, Sarah thought. *Take away a crap daughter and replace her with...*she looked at Papin and smiled as the girl knelt behind Evvie and started to braid the older woman's long hair.

...with whom?

Sarah turned back to the fire and stared into its depths again. The horses gave them the added benefit of serving as an early warning device in case anybody approached in the night. She could sleep soundly in front of the fire knowing, short of someone slitting the throats of the horses where they stood, that no one could surprise them.

She turned back to see that Papin had tucked Evvie into her blanket and pulled her own cover around her shoulders. She nestled close to Evvie and closed her eyes briefly, as if relishing the sheer closeness of the other woman. It drove a needle of sadness into Sarah's heart to see it. *Poor little motherless Papin.*

Before Sarah took her place against her own saddle for the night, she did a slow and thorough perimeter check to make sure the horses were fine and that no sound or light was evident on the horizon. It was as quiet a night as one could experience, she thought. So still and dark, it truly felt like the end of the world.

Back at the campsite, she could see that Papin, like the child she was, had lost the fight to stay awake. She was curled up to Evvie, who had one arm around the girl.

"She's knackered," Evvie said in a whisper.

"I thought you were, too."

"Oh, I am. We left Carmarthen before dawn this morning."

"You made it here in one day? Well, I guess you would, on horseback."

"There'll be room for the girl at the place we're going?"

"Of course."

"And she'll live with us? And your boy?"

Sarah tossed another big piece of wood on the campfire. "That's the plan."

"It's almost like the new family unit after The Crisis is a bunch of patched-together misfits and orphans who need each other."

"Maybe that's the best kind of family."

"Maybe." Evvie used her free hand to smooth the loose hair from Papin's untroubled face as she slept.

"You going to be okay, Evvie?"

Evvie looked at her with a questioning look on her face. "Why do you ask, dear?"

"Well, I know riding beats walking but it's still stressful."

"I'll be fine, Sarah. I've got my girls with me, don't I?"

Sarah met Evvie's smile with one of her own. "You definitely do."

****

Mike sat on his horse at the fork in the path next to the stone cairn that marked the entrance to Donovan's Lot. He had hand-stacked this cairn with Gavin the summer they'd celebrated a record harvest—their first after The Crisis. He'd meant to put a sign of some kind on it but everything he thought of sounded too poncey. They weren't a country club for crissake.

At least from this vantage, it looked like the community was still standing. When the breeze turned, he could hear the light notes of children laughing. Always a good sign.

The trip to the coast had taken him two days. He'd allowed three for the ride back. The closer he got, the sicker he felt. He tried to remind himself that he'd only stay long enough to scrape together enough to afford a ferry fare and then he'd go back.

As cold as her trail would be by then, he knew exactly how futile the exercise was.

But it was all he had.

As he sat at the crossroads, bracing for his reentry into camp, he knew John would only have to see him ride in alone to know he hadn't found her.

He sat a moment longer, straining to hear the sounds of camp from this distance, trying to feel the moment of relief he always felt at coming home again.

Instead, with deepening dread, he nudged his horse past the cairn stone stack and down the dirt road that led to Donovan's Lot and his people.

****

The next morning, Sarah was sorry she hadn't taken the time to try to hunt a rabbit or hedgehog or something the night before. As a result, they had to start their journey with empty stomachs, and while the rain looked to be holding off, Evvie was already uncomfortable.

"It's just my arthritis," she said. "It comes on with weather."

"But it ain't raining, Granny," Papin said, looking up at the grey skies.

"No, dear, it's the *threat* of rain that brings on the misery in my joints."

When they were all three mounted, Sarah took Evvie's reins and led the way out of the pasture and across the field. She knew she wanted to stay away from any roads, but sooner or later they would come to a stonewall they would need to get across and she wasn't at all sure how they would manage that.

She and Papin could probably jump the walls but it was taking a chance. If the horses weren't jumpers, they risked broken bones, or worse. Sarah had to admit it would be pretty terrible to come all this way only to end up with a broken leg because she'd been too impatient to walk around a fence.

Tempted to trot, Sarah forced all of them to stay at a steady walk. The last thing they needed was an unexpected pothole to either lame one of the horses or unseat one of them. She sat straight in her saddle and massaged a kink out of the small of her back. The Glock had turned into the heaviest possible encumbrance to traveling, but the security it brought was worth it. She had now lost enough weight that she was able to fold down the waistband of Denny's jeans, allowing her to once more tuck the gun against the small of her back.

Just before lunch—which was the last of the now stale bread and remnant salami—Sarah made the painful but necessary decision to add extra miles to their trip when she realized that the thirty kilometers were measured by travel along the Clarbeston Road. Skirting the road by staying out in the open in the fields made her feel safer against the threat of Angie finding her, but it was at the cost of at least two more days traveling.

The three rode in silence until nearly dark. Twice Sarah had to dismount to try to reorient herself as to their location. Once, she sent Papin off to find anyone who might be able to give directions. It served the added benefit of allowing Evvie to rest. She looked to Sarah as if she were barely managing to stay upright in her saddle.

Papin came back from her expedition with the report that there was nobody on the road to ask. By Sarah's calculations, they were, more or less, on track to hit the coast by late the next day.

As the late afternoon gave way to early evening, it began to rain. By the time they set up camp—one that clearly wasn't going to have the benefit of a campfire—the lightning began to light up the sky with regular intervals. It had been awhile since Sarah had had to endure a full-on storm of any strength. And always then, she had been sheltered in a cottage. She could see that Evvie looked worried.

Did the Welsh get tornadoes? she wondered. *Or hurricanes?* Back in Florida, where she was from, it would be nearing the end of hurricane season.

"We gonna be okay, Sarah?" Papin asked as she and Evvie huddled under a stand of trees, the water pouring off the leaves and branches and affording little protection from the rain.

"We'll be wet," Sarah said. "And hungry. But we'll be fine." She hated to reward them all after such a long day of riding with a cold, wet night and no dinner, especially Evvie, who looked like she was having trouble breathing. But what else could she do?

"One more night and then we're at the coast and on the boat," she said. "We're nearly there."

Evvie nodded miserably and Sarah couldn't help but notice Papin's worried looks in her direction.

"Tell you what. How would you two like to sleep in a warm tent tonight with a fire right in the center of it?"

Papin's thin shoulders began to shake under her wet jumper. She looked at Sarah with trust and expectation. "Don't tease us."

"In my country, Indians make teepees with a hole in the top so they could have their campfires inside and I think we can fashion something like that using our blankets and this old widow-maker."

The dead tree she indicated was easily fifteen feet tall and caught in its fall by two smaller trees beneath it. By stretching their blankets and securing them to the adjacent saplings near the widow-maker, Sarah was sure she could fashion a rudimentary tented lean-to. She grabbed her knife and began stripping one of the saplings nearest her of its branches.

"Do you really think so, Sarah?" Papin asked, looking at the skinny trees that surrounded them.

"My brothers and I used to make them all the time up in north Georgia," Sarah said. "I don't remember ever doing it in a thunderstorm, but the principle is the same. Evvie, you just sit tight. Papin, go stand over there with the ponies and make sure none of them gets an idea to bolt out of here."

Papin nodded and moved out from the meager shelter of the trees to stand with the horses. Sarah could hear her soft voice under the sound of the rain as she talked to the animals.

She worked quickly to pull together the tree fort by stretching their blankets on the sapling notches and leaving a large gap in the top for the smoke to come out. As soon as she could she ushered Evvie inside and settled her down next to one of the saddles. She opened her shirt and dumped out the armful of twigs and kindling she'd collected when she built the tent, and handed Evvie the flint and the knife.

"Th—there's no tinder," Evvie said, her hands shaking with the cold.

"I know. Sit tight." Sarah went out to where Papin stood with the quivering horses. "Papin, you got any money?"

"Money?"

"Yes, as in bills?"

Papin lifted her sweater away from her waistband and pulled out a slim wallet, which she handed to Sarah. "Why do you need money?"

"I don't, specifically," Sarah said, pulling out several bills and handing the wallet back to her. "I'll call you when the fire's going."

She hurried back to the tent and knelt next to Evvie and began crumpling up the pound notes. "Not really good for much else," she said as Evvie struck a spark off the flint and caught the paper money. Sarah quickly tucked it under the kindling and the fire grew.

"Oh, thank you, Sarah," Evvie said, her voice quivering. She held her hands out to the little campfire and watched the smoke escape up and out the top of the tent. "I don't think I could have endured a whole night wet and cold."

"I think we need to get you dry somehow, Evvie," Sarah said, eyeing her critically.

Papin entered the tent. "Blimey, I'm freezing."

Sarah disappeared outside and returned with a long stick in her hands. "Get as close to the fire as you can, Evvie, and slip off your cardie."

"I don't think I can bear to."

"Okay, never mind." Sarah shrugged off her own thin jacket and stuck it on one of the sticks. She handed it to Papin. "Over the fire, not in it. I'll be back in a sec."

A mighty crack of thunder coincided with her squeezing back out of the small-tented enclosure. Papin squeaked at the sound of the crash and dropped Sarah's jacket into the fire, nearly extinguishing it. Hurriedly, she pulled it out and began blowing on the embers again to bring the fire back to life.

Sarah trotted over to where the ponies were hobbled. She was tempted to unhobble them. If they got spooked enough they could really hurt themselves trying to flee. On the other hand, tying them up would be even more dangerous. She pulled the saddle off her horse—the only one who had yet to be untacked —and carried it back to the tent.

Standing a few feet outside, she could see the smoke coming out of the top in an orderly slim line. She could make out the shapes of Evvie and Papin inside and felt a rush of gratitude that she had been able to provide some kind of shelter against the terrible night. She parked her saddle in the opening of the tent and pulled out her backpack from where she'd tied it to the saddle.

"Check the jacket, Papin. It won't be dry but it'll be better than what she's got on. Evvie, take off your cardie."

"Oh, God, it's so cold," Evvie said through chattering teeth as she peeled her wet sweater off and handed it to Papin. She pulled on the jacket and Sarah had the satisfaction of hearing her friend groan with ecstasy. "Ohhhhh! Sooooo warm!"

"Good. And here's dinner." Sarah handed Evvie a chunk of bread.

Papin was arranging Evvie's sweater on the stick and her eyes were large. "Where did you get that?"

"I put it in my bag yesterday and then thought we'd already eaten it. I've never been so glad to be forgetful in my life. Here's yours." She handed another large piece of bread to Papin, who held it in her free hand and looked at Evvie and then back at Sarah. "Well, it's not the Dorchester," she said with a grin, "but it's not shite either."

"Remind me to needlepoint that on a pillow when we get home," Sarah said, taking a bite out of her own bread. "Might just be our new family motto."

It was another night that Sarah knew she didn't have to worry about someone sneaking up on them. No one in his or her right mind would be out on a night like tonight.

"Tell us about your David," Evvie said to Sarah, though Sarah'd been sure everyone had dozed off. Soft snores came from where Papin was curled up by the fire.

"I'm really not in the mood, Evvie."

"I know you miss him terribly."

"Same as you and your Mark. It's just easier not to think of him, and what happened, when I'm trying to be strong and do what's necessary."

"I understand. Well, can you tell me about this Donovan chap, then? The one who'll be taking us all in?"

Sarah listened for a moment to the sounds of the rain as it continued to bear down on the little tent and the surrounding trees. Twice she'd gotten up to check on the horses and had to re-dry her wet t-shirt before putting it back on. "Mike is like this ultimate paternalistic leader. He likes to be in charge and he's good at it so people pretty much let him lead the way."

"My. An Alpha male."

Sarah grinned at Evvie. "What's that mean?"

"Oh, I've read my share of romance books, Miz Scarlett. I know the sounds of a stubborn but natural-born leader."

"I guess so. I mean, before The Crisis he was probably this way, too. He thinks everyone should just fall in line and do it his way. He's not a bully. He just has his own way of seeing things and pretty much encourages you to see things that way, too."

"You like him."

"Everybody likes him."

"Oh, sure because *that's* what I meant."

Sarah wagged a finger at her. "There's nothing between me and Mike. I like him. And he's exactly what the community needs—a strong leader who's willing to work hard to make the group safe."

"He's like a papa that takes care of everyone," Papin said sleepily.

"Exactly. I guarantee you both will love him."

"Do *you* love him?" Papin asked.

"Alright, enough of that. Why don't we all go to sleep? It's going to be a long day tomorrow."

"Can't you tell us a little something about the new world you're bringing us to?"

"I thought I just did."

"Well, how about your son? What's John like?"

Sarah hesitated and looked into the fire. It occurred to her that she had been working very hard *not* to think of John, not to picture his face, not to remember his voice. It was just too painful while they were still so far apart. And because as soon as she saw him she knew the reunion would be bittersweet.

David.

Sarah pushed the accompanying image out of her head. The picture of David slumped on the ground, his hands lifeless in his lap, his dear head turned away, never to look at her or smile or…

"Sarah?"

She shook herself out of the mood and threw a small stick onto the fire. "John is like most twelve-year-old American boys: he loves his iPad and video games, plays soccer at school and is addicted to Netflix."

There was a pause and then Evvie said, "Except, of course, he doesn't do any of those things any more."

Sarah felt a wave of exhaustion crash down over her. Evvie was right, of course. John was no longer that little boy who had climbed into his airplane seat a year ago full of questions and concerns about keeping all his electronics charged.

He was somebody different now.

"Well, he's safe," Sarah said. "And right now, from where I'm sitting, that's the only thing that really matters."

"How do you know?" Papin asked.

Evvie patted the girl's hand. "To a mother, the world would smell different, feel different without him in it. You'd know. When I think of my Mark, there's something about the thinking of him that makes me feel…that he's not in the world anymore."

"Oh, Evvie…"

"It's true. I know Mark isn't coming for me. I know he's not trying to find me because I can feel that he's gone."

Papin picked up Evvie's hand and smoothed her own small one on top of it. "When I was eight, some men came and set me mum and me dad on fire," she said. "Killed me little brother, too. So I can't ever play games of wondering, you know? I can't ever *not* see them gone. Or how. When I close my eyes— *every time I close my eyes*—I see them leaving me."

"Holy God, Papin. How?"

"Me mum shoved me in a closet in the caravan when she saw them coming. I heard 'em screaming, so I snuck out to see. Afterward, the men wanted to steal the caravan but it didn't work. So they just left. And never found me."

"Papin, I am so sorry for your terrible loss. But…this was before The Crisis? These men killed your family *before* the lights went out?"

Papin nodded. "One of the men accused my father of cheating him. I was too young and too scared to really understand what he was saying. He might have been right. My papa probably did cheat him."

"Those men were monsters and should have been arrested and put in cages."

"I know."

"And you've been on your own ever since?"

"No, there are families in the Kale. I was taken in and raised with my cousins. We were all one family."

"When did you leave to strike out on your own?"

"Well, actually, the night I met you, Sarah."

Sarah opened her mouth as if to speak, but just looked at Papin in confusion.

"I could tell from the minute I saw you," Papin said. "You know gypsies have the gift of second sight, aye? Well, I just knew."

"Knew what?"

"That you were a mother looking for her child."

Tears sprang to Sarah's eyes. Of course Papin's radar would be very sensitive to *that*. Whether it could have been seen so clearly by anybody other than a motherless child was doubtful. "Well, I am definitely that," Sarah said softly.

"What happened to your extended family?" Evvie asked.

"They left."

"*Left?* Moved away and didn't tell you?"

"No, they told me. I guess most *gadjikane* think all gypsies are whores, but my family couldn't accept me doing this."

"Selling your body for food," Sarah said.

"That's right." She looked at Sarah with eyes filled with such sadness and pain that Sarah quickly moved to take her into her arms. There would be time to hear the whole terrible story, to bear the unbearable agony of the child's broken heart. Later.

"Never again, Papin," Sarah whispered. "I'm your family now." She reached out an arm to include Evvie in the hug. "*We* are your family now, by God, and nobody will leave anybody ever again. I promise."

Sarah felt Papin's thin body sag as she released the tension that had been holding her so securely together. Her arms tightened around Sarah's neck. "Thank you," she whispered, sounding for the first time like the little girl she really was.

An hour later, Papin and Evvie were both asleep, the girl once more in the arms of the elder, who clung to her just as fiercely in her need. Sarah stepped out of the tent to relieve herself and to check again on the animals. They were calmer now that the storm seemed to have moved on and Sarah was grateful that it looked like they'd have transportation in the morning.

That had never been a sure thing while the storm lashed them. She plucked downed twigs and branches from where the horses stood and checked to see that the falling limbs hadn't hit them. While they could use a bag of oats about now, Sarah knew there was enough grass in the pasture to keep them going. And the travel, while relentless, wasn't arduous.

It helped to be out in the night air, listening to the nickering and murmurs from the three horses. It helped to put her hand out on a sturdy flank and feel the reassuring strength of the beasts. She remembered, as a horse-crazy teenager in a northern suburb of Atlanta where she grew up, turning to her own horse many times in the midst of some silly teen angst.

She knew now what she knew then, that there were few more comforting friends than a kindhearted horse that you loved.

She thought of her horse, Dan, back at the cottage and how she had been so afraid of him when she and David and John first came to Ireland. In her adult life, Sarah had suffered from a fear of horses after a nasty fall had ended her young career as a hunter-jumper.

When she thought of Dan, so big and so fearless, and how she had allowed him to renew her strength and carry her through so much in the last year, she felt a sudden longing for the beast that nearly rivaled, for a moment, her need to see John again. She hadn't ridden Dan in months, what with one thing or another. There hadn't really been a need. Her life was comfortably centered around her husband and her child and trying to make a home for them in the new world order.

She tugged on the mane of Papin's pony and smiled sadly. This little guy had surely been the mount of some little rich girl, she thought. He was probably used to hot mash and fresh flakes of hay and his own little stall, cleaned and tidied on a daily basis, with his name in a plaque on the stall door, and ribbons in his mane. And now he was the new best friend of an orphaned gypsy girl who had seen more horror in her thirteen years than many urban police do in a career.

David.

The name and the image crept into her thoughts like a silent thief. This is why she refused to stop and reflect, to observe and to think. When she slowed down, the image of him came back to her and the unthinkable grief began to regroup to tear her down and weaken her. And she couldn't stop yet. She couldn't give in to the sadness. Not yet. She turned away from the horses to head back to the tent, noting that the rain had finally stopped.

It was at that moment that the surrounding world of peaceful pastures and sloping Welsh fields was pierced with an abrupt and ungodly wail.

Chapter Twenty-five

Later, given that she had lost everything and the world was disintegrating in front of her very eyes, Sarah would realize that she, of all people, should have been prepared for the world to change in one drastic and terrible moment.

She ran back to the tent to see Papin shaking Evvie and whimpering. "Wake up, Granny! Wake up!"

Oh, God, no.

Sarah ripped back the tent flap and went to Evvie.

"Sarah, make her wake up! She don't look good at all."

Sarah put her fingers against Evvie's throat to catch the pulse—the pulse that would never be caught again.

She looks so peaceful, Sarah thought. *Her brow free of creases, the lines of her mouth relaxed…she's with her Mark now.*

"Sarah, please…" Papin still gripped Evvie's sweater in her attempt to awaken her.

Sarah sighed and put a hand on Papin's arm. "Come away, Papin," she said. "Evvie's gone."

"Noooooo!" Papin looked at Sarah with horror and then back at Evvie. "She can't be! I need her!"

It struck Sarah as she fought to put away her feelings that it seemed that for a very long time now every instinct to mourn or grieve was trumped by a greater need to address an immediate threat. She pushed back the sadness, the incapacitating sadness, and closed her eyes to the sight of her dear friend lying by the campfire in her last sleep. She pulled Papin into her arms.

"She was old, Papin. She was tired. She's with God now."

"I want her to be with *me*," Papin sobbed.

"I know, sweetie. I know." Sarah pulled back and made Papin look her in the eye. "Today's ride would have been terrible for her. She was exhausted—"

"We could've rested! We shouldn't have been riding so hard. We could've camped here for awhile…"

Sarah winced. The girl was right. It was *Sarah* who had set the pace and insisted they move as quickly as they had. It was Sarah who had pushed Evvie beyond her endurance.

"She picked the wrong person to travel with," Sarah said. "It's because I have bad people chasing me that she died. We couldn't travel normally on the road with everyone else. It's because of me."

Papin shook her head and eased back in Sarah's arms, her shoulders limp with resignation. "Don't say that," she said. "You're all I have now."

The day's ride was harder than Sarah could ever have imagined. It began by dismantling the teepee and fashioning a litter that could then be dragged behind Evvie's horse. A litter with Evvie's body on it. Sarah had intended to take Evvie's sweater but Papin wouldn't hear of it. *"She was always so cold!"* In the end, they wrapped the body in remnant blankets and dragged it behind the horse until they found the river they'd come upon the day before.

The idea of dumping poor Evvie's body in the fast-moving river was the least terrible idea in a long list of terrible ideas. Considering Papin's history, Sarah wouldn't even mention the possibility of fire, but they had no means by which to bury the body. They couldn't get it up in the trees and they couldn't just leave it. It made Sarah sick, too, to be standing on the riverbank and considering slipping her sweet friend into its unwelcoming waters.

But what else was there to do?

Papin had not stopped weeping since she had discovered Evvie unresponsive. Sarah glanced at her now as she held her hands to her face, her shoulders shaking, and worried she might not recover from this.

Oh, Evvie, Sarah thought, her own heart fractured in a thousand places at the loss of the dear old soul. She knelt next to the litter and touched Evvie's hands, placed together over her chest. "Pray with me, Papin," she said without looking up. Papin's sniffles answered her.

"Lord God, please look upon your servant, Evvie, who was a loving, caring soul to everyone she touched." Papin's weeping increased.

"And please bring her to yourself and give her the comfort and care that she rarely found in this world. And Lord, please help Papin and myself to have the courage we need to finish this journey safely and get back to our family. In Your name we pray, and in Your name we commend the spirit of our dear friend, Evvie."

Sarah stood and unfastened the belt she'd tied to the back of the horse's saddle to connect to the litter of branches and blankets. She knelt quickly and kissed Evvie on the cheek. "I'll see you again one day, Evvie," she whispered. Then she stood with the end of the litter in her hands and tipped the body into the river as Papin's cries rose higher and higher on the wind.

They reached the outskirts of the ferry town of Fishguard by nightfall. Sarah knew Papin was distraught during the long day's ride, but she couldn't believe stopping was going to help her. When they saw the flickering lights of the town in the distance, Sarah stopped and dismounted.

The plan was simple, but that didn't mean a hundred things couldn't go wrong with it. Neither of them had eaten all day—or felt like it—but Sarah worried that their hunger would weaken them.

She led Evvie's horse and Papin to an empty feed shed in the nearest pasture to the town. It had long since stopped being used as any place to store grain or hay, although by the looks of it travelers had used it as a place to bunk down against the wind and the cold at night. Sarah loosened the girth on her saddle. She checked to make sure that all saddlebags were empty and that any grain or crumb of food had either been transferred to her backpack or eaten on the spot. She put Declan's tin cup and her flint, wrapped in the two thin blankets they had, in her backpack.

She handed the knife to Papin, who accepted it listlessly. "We can wait 'til morning if you'd rather," Sarah said.

Papin shook her head.

"Okay. Let's run through it."

Papin sighed, then seemed to force herself to sit up straight and shake off her dispiritedness. "I go to the ferry master," she said. "I find out when's the next crossing and will he take two horses for two tickets."

"Good. What else?"

Papin frowned. "I look around to see if there's anything suspicious like. If so, I say I only want one ticket. Why is that, Sarah? Why do I buy only one if we're both going?"

Sarah put her hand on Papin's knee from where she stood on the ground next to her on her pony. "If you see someone looking at everyone going on the boat, they might ask the ferry master how many tickets you bought."

"Oh, right. If I say two, then he knows someone else is hiding in the shadows. You."

"Exactly. And then?"

"If he'll sell me the tickets, I come back here making sure first nobody sees me."

"Good girl. It's light enough by the moon, but you'll have to be careful of anyone who might want to drag you from your horses."

"I know. I have the knife."

"Can you use it?"

"If I have to."

Sarah wouldn't send her at night if possible, but the chances of slipping by Angie's people—who almost certainly were somewhere near—would be greater under cloak of darkness. It wasn't just thieves and miscreants who chose to slink about in the dark, she thought bitterly. Tonight, the darkness was her friend—and Papin's.

"All right, sweetie," she said, her voice soft and full of pain to have to send her on this mission tonight of all nights. "Go now and come back to me safely." She patted Papin's leg.

"Sarah?"

Sarah looked up questioningly.

"Is it okay if I call you Mum, do you think?"

Sarah put her arms around Papin's waist as she sat on the little pony and squeezed her hard. She felt Papin lay her head on her shoulder for a moment. "I would be honored if you would, cherub," Sarah said to her. She looked into Papin's eyes, her own shining with unshed tears. "You're my girl, now. I adopt you in the name of everything holy and good and right. You are my daughter."

Papin smiled and nodded, her face relaxed for the first time since Evvie died. "Okay, good," she said, then took a long breath. "I'll be back in tick." She turned her pony toward the road.

Sarah watched her go, leading the two horses behind her until she was gone from sight, then knelt in the feed shed and cried until she thought her heart would break.

As usual, Sarah thought as she squinted through the slats of the feed shed, *it's the ones left behind to wait that have it the roughest.* She had no way to estimate time and could only guess that Papin had been gone at least three hours. If sunset was seven o'clock, she reasoned, then it was close to nine now.

Even in the chill of the night, her hands were sweaty. She should have given her the gun. She should have trailed along behind at a safe distance. She should never have let her go.

By the time she heard the faint clip-clop sounds of a lone horse coming across the pasture, Sarah was seconds away from walking into town to find Papin. Seeing her come across the field, the light of the moon illuminating her path, was one of the happiest sights so far in Sarah's life.

She ran to meet her. "Thank God, you're back! What happened? Did you get the tickets? Did anyone stop you?" She could see the sheer exhaustion in Papin's face and felt a stab of guilt for being the reason for it. She helped Papin dismount and then unsaddled and hobbled the pony in the pasture of dried grass.

When she turned back to the shed, Papin was lying against the far wall, sound asleep. Sarah sat down next to her and gently pulled her into her arms, settling against the wall herself. Just holding her after so many hours of wondering and worry felt like an exquisite luxury. As she tightened her arms around the girl, she felt a large lump inside Papin's jersey that, upon exploration, turned out to be, miracles of all miracles, a fully roasted capon.

Papin slept the full night through, never once budging from Sarah's side. Twice Sarah got up to check on the pony and to listen for any noises but the night was peaceful.

In the morning, both fully rested, Sarah and Papin ate the capon and readied themselves for whatever the day would bring.

"I got the tickets," Papin said, pulling out two crudely marked pieces of paper that Sarah studied and confirmed were probably what people were using for tickets in the post-Crisis world. "He wanted to take little Sparky, too," she said, nodding toward her pony in the pasture, "but I said no. Problem is, we can't bring him across unless we get a ticket for him, too."

"Trust me, Sparky will be fine. There's no end of people who would be only to happy to give him a good home."

"Or eat him."

"He's too valuable for that," Sarah said, although truthfully, as small as he was, he *was* probably more valuable as food than a pack animal, and nobody larger than a child could comfortably ride him. "Did you see anybody?"

Papin nodded. "That bloke was there. The one who asked about you in Carmarthen."

Sarah's stomach lurched to hear the words although she had been expecting them.

"He stood right at the entrance to people getting on the boat and looked in the face of every woman stepping foot across the threshold."

Shit. "Just the one?"

"There was another guy who came over and gave him a sandwich. But it was only the one guy checking all the people going onboard. How're you gonna get on the boat? Even *with* a ticket?"

"I don't know."

"You could let me distract him."

Sarah frowned at her. "Distract him how?"

"You know how."

"No way."

"I can do it and then follow right behind you."

"I said, no."

"But Sarah, what other choice do we have? How else you gonna get on that boat?"

"I don't know, but there has to be another way."

"Look, it doesn't mean anything to me. It's just my body." Papin sat up earnestly and put aside the half eaten piece of poultry she had in her grip. "I go someplace in my head far away while they're doing it to me."

"Papin, nobody is ever doing anything to you again where you have to *go somewhere in your head* to escape it, do you hear me? We'll figure this out."

"How about if I distract him without doing the dirty?"

"What are you talking about?"

"I can distract him into wanting me and then I can make myself throw up. If I throw up at just the right moment, trust me, he won't want nothing to do with me."

Sarah frowned. "Won't he be highly irritated with you?"

"Is a beating better than letting him poke me?"

"Dear God, what a question," Sarah said, rubbing her face with both hands. "I don't know. Not a beating where you lose your hearing or a couple of teeth or…"

"It won't be like that," Papin insisted. "He'll slap me a couple of times and then he'll want to see the back of me real quick like, what with me reeking of puke."

Sarah looked away. How many more times would she risk Papin's safety for the sake of getting them both back to Donovan's Lot and John?

"Please, Mum," Papin said, touching Sarah's hand shyly. "It's just playacting and I promise I won't get hurt. This time tomorrow, we'll both be safe on the other side in Ireland."

Seeing Jeff again, especially in the full light of day, threatened to bring up Sarah's breakfast of stolen roast capon. In a flash, she was back in her own pasture under a bright October sun, watching her husband bleed to death while this man stood over him. Just watching him from behind the thin hedge of laurel where she and Papin both crouched made her want to pull the gun from her jeans and empty every round into his murdering, filthy heart. When she thought of his hands on Papin, it was all she could do not to call off the whole thing.

She was shaken from her thoughts by a quick kiss on the cheek from Papin.

"If I can't make it on your same boat," Papin said in a whisper, "I'll be along directly so just wait for me."

"You've got your ticket?" Sarah felt like an anxious mother asking if her child remembered to bring her lunchbox to school.

"I do. Wish me luck and I'll see you as soon as I can."

"I love you, Papin," Sarah said. "Be safe and don't take any chances."

"Love you too, Mum," Papin said, and then she was gone.

Desperate times, Sarah thought rubbing her arms in agitation as she watched Papin stroll straight up to Jeff, a provocative saunter in her little hips. She saw him zero in on her before she even crossed the streets. If he had been a cartoon, he would have licked his lips, she thought with disgust. Papin began to converse with him. From her position, she could see Jeff's expression but not Papin's. And his expression was X-rated.

She saw Jeff's glance flick back to the ferry entrance as two plump Indian women and a man trundled onto the gangplank. But his attention was brought instantly back to the little gypsy girl in front of him as Sarah saw Papin pull apart her blouse, exposing her breasts to him. His reaction was immediate. He left his post and went straight for her, his right hand already fumbling with his belt buckle.

If Papin, who he had now scooped up in his arms and was straddling his waist with her legs, hadn't whispered a different plan into his ear, Sarah was sure Jeff would have taken her right there in the street. Without even a backward glance at the ferry gangplank, Jeff, his hand firmly on Papin's bottom, turned and trotted with her into a nearby storefront.

Praying she wouldn't vomit, Sarah bolted from behind the hedge and headed for the gangplank.

Susan Kiernan-Lewis

Chapter Twenty-six

Sarah walked purposely to the gangplank, not running, not looking over her shoulder. It took all her strength not to look to see if she were being watched by anyone other than Jeff. Two older men stood in front of her at the ferry threshold, their tickets in their hands. When it was her turn to board, the ferry master never even looked at her face, just took the ticket and waved her onto the boat. Even then, she didn't dare turn around, fearing it would be a public announcement of her attempted stealth.

She slunk to the bow of the boat as it pointed toward Ireland across the St. George's Channel and sat on one of the wooden benches that lined the ferry. In the middle of the boat were several horse carts, and even a few bicycles, as well as several large tarp covered platforms of food and provisions.

Papin had said there were only two crossings today, weather permitting. They deliberately planned on Sarah making the first one. That way, if Papin missed the boat she could still cross and reunite with Sarah before nightfall.

For a change, Sarah was grateful for the harsh breeze that tore through the little cargo of horses, food and people. It meant she wouldn't look out of place with the blanket pulled over her head like a hood. She knew she hadn't been the first one onboard, but she was still surprised and dismayed to feel the boat lurch away from the dock so soon after she sat down. Again, she forced herself not to look for Papin in the group of passengers. Likely she would have to take the second crossing after all.

Her stomach roiled with a mixture of dread and exhilaration as she watched the dock on the Welsh shore become increasingly smaller the further the boat moved into the channel. Papin had said the trip would take three hours if the weather wasn't an issue. Sarah glanced at the sky. Grey clouds, but nothing that looked threatening. The second ferry should be on schedule for later that afternoon.

With the United Kingdom receding over her shoulder, Sarah felt the tension in her shoulders relax. She looked ahead and tried unsuccessfully to catch a glimpse of the Irish coast. It was 36 days after the attack. As much as she tried to focus on how far she'd come and how she close she was to John, Sarah couldn't ignore the lump of unease that squirmed in her gut. She couldn't stop wondering if Papin had been able to deflect Jeff—the same man responsible for David's murder! If she had any doubts about whether he could kill Papin without remorse, she only had to remember the sound of his raucous laughter as her husband bled to death at her feet.

Had she just been so desperate to get across the channel that she was willing to sacrifice the girl? How could she have believed so readily Papin's foolish plan for distracting the monster?

Sarah stood up restlessly and felt the sweat trickle down her back in spite of the chill air. She gripped the railing and, for one mad moment, thought about jumping into the water and swimming back to Wales. A woman standing near her watched her with suspicious eyes and pulled her young daughter away, as if Sarah might contaminate her somehow. Sarah pulled her blanket hood down more to shield her face.

A wave pounded the front of the ferry and Sarah felt her stomach leap up into her throat, carrying her meager breakfast with it. She turned her head and vomited over the side of the railing. She heard a shriek of dismay and guessed she'd probably sprayed the couple behind her. She wanted to apologize—even if it was just a chagrinned look—except the next wave launched another bout of roiling seasickness. She pushed her face into the wind and tried to concentrate on the horizon or the clouds, but her stomach wasn't to be fooled. It heaved its contents again moments after the next sharp movement of the ferry cresting the rough sea. The vomit was underfoot now and Sarah fought to stay upright in the slick mess.

She inched her way further apart from the closest group of people—the elderly black couple, who'd caught the first onslaught of her sickness—and wedged herself between a stack of secured wooden crates and a barrel of what smelled like dead fish. Cramped in this space with no need to hold herself upright, she let the nausea wash over her in a relentless series of contractions.

Later, she would be glad for the few moments of peace from worry and anxiety that the experience gave her. In an hour, she was weak and empty, cold and wet, but the sea had smoothed out and her nausea abated. It was then that she had time to torture herself with thoughts of all the people she had let down and lost.

David.

John.

Evvie.

Papin.

She took each person and addressed her wrongs to them, one by one. She itemized how she had failed them and how her failure had cost them. With the exception of John and Papin— whom she wasn't absolutely sure were even alive—the price of loving Sarah had been their very lives.

She was travelling back to Ireland again. The last time she had come to this country, she was with her husband and their young son. John had morphed away from that sweet, naïve boy in a matter of days of their arriving in Ireland

As for David, he had survived just a little over the first year.

As sick as she still felt, she forced herself to remember Evvie's twinkling eyes, her sorrow at her betrayal by her daughter, her playfulness with Papin.

Papin. So much in need of a mother, so full of loss and disappointment. With every surge over every wave, the ferry took Sarah further and further away from her. A sacrifice Papin could bring herself to make…because she loved Sarah.

They all loved me. Every tragic one of them loved the wrong person when they decided to love me. Sarah covered her face with her hands, smelling the vomit on her sleeves as she did. *And all I've got left now is prayer and hope that I haven't lost the children, that I haven't lost Papin or John.*

The rest of the trip passed. For an hour or longer, Sarah realized she had been seeing the coast of Ireland ahead coming steadily nearer without really seeing it. It occurred to her that Angie might have people on this end waiting to catch her. She touched the gun in her pocket. It was not possible to believe that she had come this far, lost so much, only to be stopped now.

She set her jaw resolutely and stood into the wind to face the shoreline as it grew larger. She knew she didn't want to be the first or the last one off the boat—just in case.

Should she slip into the water? It didn't look that deep and it would help her avoid any unwanted welcome party on the other end. On the other hand, she didn't know what submerging guns did to their efficacy, but she didn't feel good about taking the chance of rendering her one weapon useless.

When they reached the other side, the ferry slammed into the tire-lined cement pier with a sickening thud that sent many of the passengers sliding into one another. There didn't seem to be an orderly process for disembarking, which suited Sarah. For her purposes, chaos and confusion could only be her ally. She dove into the middle of the exiting crowd, her hood pulled over her head, and prayed there was no one to care.

It seemed a fairly pathetic plan against attack, but in the end, it didn't matter. No one accosted her, no one even looked at her as she dropped onto the bulkhead at Rosslare Harbour and quickly melted into the crowd of travelers and villagers milling about the wide cement pier that serviced the channel.

Her hand on her gun and her head down, Sarah moved into the heart of an active farmer's market that separated the harbor from the little village of Boreen that supported it.

Now that she was on firm ground again, her empty stomach made itself known. She had no money and no food. She walked past tables of roasted meats, cheeses and wine—there were even iced bottles of cola filling a large wooden drum.

She couldn't imagine how they had survived this long with no replenishment or distribution or bottling plants. Surely, they were an unimaginable luxury at this point in The Crisis. There were, nonetheless, she noticed, several people lining up to buy a soft drink with whatever they had in the way of payment.

Tempted to steal a bun from the bakery table, Sarah wasn't sure she wouldn't be severely punished, possibly killed, for the crime. *You just never knew these days.* She kept moving through the market, heading for the pastures on the other side of the small village—really only a short line of houses and a store on one side of the street—where she would wait until the second ferry was due in. That would be several hours from now. She smelled the aroma of fresh baked bread and wished she could get something for Papin when she arrived. *She'll be hungry.*

Pray God she isn't hurt. Sarah pushed images out of her head of Jeff beating Papin for her ruse. Jeff strangling Papin with his filthy, murdering hands…

She began to trot through the village, partially to chase the images away, partially to remove herself from the painful temptation of the food she could not have. She reached the end of the village lane and turned inland, hopping over a disintegrating stonewall that might have been there since the time of the Normans. The more she moved up the hill into the fields, the better view she had of the harbor and the channel. Unfortunately, she couldn't see Wales no matter how high she climbed, just endless water that stretched seemingly to infinity.

Wales, and Papin, were a long way away.

Sarah sat in the pasture and looked down at the harbor. From here she would be able to see the ferry as it left again. She would see it when it came back with Papin onboard. She watched as the clouds rolled in and the sky darkened. She watched as the ferry master lashed the ferry to the dock and disappeared into his pier house to wait out the storm. Sarah found a stand of trees and huddled under them, watching the lightning flick through the branches while the thunder bellowed.

When the storm abated, she ran to the pasture's edge to see that the ferry still sat, the light now too dim to chance another crossing today...no matter who had paid for a passing.

The disappointment when she realized she wouldn't see Papin today, that she would have to spend a night apart from her —still not knowing if the child was safe—brought Sarah to her knees. She slumped in the pasture and stared at the sight of the ferry, locked down and immobile for the night.

Chapter Twenty-seven

"You'll *do* something about that little *hoor*, Mike Donovan, or I'll scratch her eyes out and feed 'em to the hogs!"

"I'll handle it, Anna."

"I'll not be eased by smarm, mind! *Do* something or I will! My Davie can't seem to stay away from that *sleeveen* and I've a mind to throw in a pair of bollocks to sweeten the deal with yon pigs!"

God's teeth, I'll kill that fecking Caitlin!

"She'll not be bothering your Davie any more, Anna. I promise you. What you do with your husband's bollocks is entirely up to you."

"Are ya being funny, Mike? Only maybe you've developed a sense of humor on your travels that don't translate here." Anna stood with her hands on her hips, the very picture of the irate wife.

"Not at all, Anna," he said soothingly. "I'll take care of it, you can be sure."

The woman snorted and stomped out of the cottage he used as an office. Fiona sat in a corner of the room, her feet up on a chair. She shook her head at him.

"Don't you have work to do?" he asked, irritated. "Is this what went on while I was gone? A bunch of layabouts and no work?"

"Oh, I'm pretty sure you don't want to go *there*, brother dear," Fiona said, getting slowly to her feet. "I told you Caitlin was becoming a handful."

"Screwing the other women's husbands in camp?" He shook his head in bafflement. "Is she just bored or barking? Or both?"

"I don't know, but it was well beyond Gavin's ability to handle, that's for sure."

"Fine, Fi. I get it. I'm back now. I'll handle it."

"How? Are you going to put stocks in the center of camp? I hear that worked well in America in the seventeen hundreds. Oh, wait, no it didn't. How about stripping her and shaving her head? Although I have to say, our Caitlin is just perverse enough to enjoy the attention."

"Good God, was she always like this?"

"You mean when Ellen was alive?" Fiona softened her tone when she mentioned the name of Mike's dead wife. "I don't know. Might be we just didn't see it then."

"Well, whatever, can you send her in to me? Do you know where she is?" Mike ran a frustrated hand through his hair and pushed aside the stack of maps on his desk. He had been trying to sort out where the existing pits and snares were located around the perimeter of camp to decide if more needed to be dug.

Gavin had earlier helpfully pointed out that there weren't enough men in the camp to man the ones they already had.

"And John, too? If you should happen to see him."

Fiona stopped as she was moving toward the door. "I'll try."

Mike glanced up in time to catch the sympathetic look she gave him. His homecoming had been everything he had expected it would be.

It hadn't been pretty.

John was one of the very first people to watch him ride into camp, and the look on his face when he saw Mike was one that Mike would take with him to his grave. If he'd had it all to do over again, he would've told Aideen *sorry-for-your-troubles* and gone on to Wales without a second thought. Although Mike knew he couldn't have.

But to see the look of stark betrayal on John's face was as damaging a wound as if John had accused him of killing his father.

While he shared much of his adventures that first night and what news he had with the camp, John continued to avoid him. Whatever had existed between them before—as friends or even avuncular camaraderie—was gone, likely forever.

Mike would always be, in John's eyes, the grownup he'd had to depend on because he was too young to go after and rescue his mother himself.

And Mike had failed. Failed him. Failed his mother.

And the killer of it was that John needed him. He needed a father and he needed everything that Mike wanted very much to give him.

But he'd have none of it.

"Right," he said as Fiona turned away. "Just Caitlin, then."

***

Sarah waited for two days. Two days of ferries arriving and leaving again. Two days of people coming from and going to Wales.

And no sign of Papin.

Sarah sat hunched on the perimeter of the pasture looking down at the harbor as she had done for two full days.

Why didn't Papin come? All the answers to that question were immediate and unwelcome. She had been prevented. She was dead.

Sarah couldn't stay much longer. There was no more dangerous spot for her than at this ferry crossing. But she couldn't leave either. She stood now and turned away from the harbor and looked across the pasture westward. Fewer than fifty miles in that direction—two days of walking if she hurried—was Donovan's Lot, *and John*. If Papin had come when they had planned, Sarah would be home by now. Her stomach lurched in frustration.

As the light receded from the sky, marking another day wasted, Sarah found she could wait no longer. Papin wasn't coming, for whatever reason. It was time for Sarah to move ahead.

As soon as it was morning, she would return to town and do whatever she had to do to get back across that fucking channel.

Chapter Twenty-eight

Angie stood by the window and stared out at the channel. "Well, at least we know she's back in Ireland."

Jeff came up behind her and put his hands on her waist. "It wasn't my fault, Angie," he said. "It was the gypsy skank who tricked me."

Angie turned her head to see the girl lying—unconscious or dead, she wasn't sure which—on the bed. "It *was* your fault. You let the Yank slip by. You and your dick."

"I love it when you talk to me like that."

"You'll love it less when Denny's picking your teeth out of the seawall when he hears."

"Why does he have to hear?"

Angie turned to him in frustration. She pointed to the man standing next to the bed. "Dump the body in the channel or a ditch. Report back in thirty minutes. We're on the next ferry." He nodded and, tossing the girl over his shoulder, left the room.

"He has to hear because otherwise he's going to blame me."

Jeff grinned and reached around to cup her bottom with one hand. "Don't you know yet, Ange, that he's going to blame you anyway?"

He was right and she knew it. The minute the little gypsy girl told them—bleeding and weeping so she was barely understandable—that Sarah had made it onto the boat, Angie knew that she would pay for the cock-up. She pushed Jeff's hands away and turned back to the window.

How many times had she wondered if Jeff and the rest of them would follow her if something happened to Denny? It would be so easy. She was one of the last people he'd ever expect it to come from.

Jeff's hands were back on her waist and this time Angie didn't repulse him. Would Jeff follow her? Would the rest of them? Did they only mind her now because of Denny? Her mind unwillingly brought up the image of a darling little girl with bouncing dark curls, blue eyes sparkling. Hadn't she been told hundreds of times, maybe thousands, that Dana could be a child model?

Jeff hands were back on her arse again. Yes, they followed her now. But even in just the few months since The Crisis she had seen how the roles of men and women had been reshaped and hammered back into place the way they'd been for centuries. The stronger sex either protected or abused his strength, and the weaker sex either bartered her sex for safety or had it taken by force.

And thinking for one moment that any of these men would follow her or accept her as their leader if she didn't have the long shadow of that lunatic behind her was as crazy as thinking little Dana would finally get her chance with the child modeling agencies.

The door burst open behind them and both she and Jeff jumped at the sound.

Denny's bodyguard was a large black man named Eli. He grinned at the way he'd startled the two, but Angie wasn't fooled by his smile. As the closest person to Denny, Eli had his own demons to fight.

"Oy! Denny!" he yelled over his shoulder. "They're in here."

Angie felt Jeff's hands drop from her body. She couldn't blame him. She would've done the same. When Denny walked into the small hotel room with the harbor view, he looked around the room at the bloody bedclothes where the girl had been tortured for what she knew, the two standing by the window, and the chair and desk that anchored the center of the room and he pulled out his Glock and pointed it at Angie. Jeff stepped away.

"Give me one reason why I shouldn't blow your fucking head off right now, Angie."

As ready as she always tried to be for this moment, Angie felt the blood leave her face and the tips of her fingers began to tingle. "I know exactly where she's going," she said hoarsely.

"Jeff?"

"Yeah?"

"You remember where this compound is?"

"Of course."

"Wanna try a little harder, Angie?"

"I want her as bad as you do, Denny. I'll walk through fire to get her. I'll be the vanguard going into the camp because, being a woman, they won't suspect me. And besides, Sarah thinks I'm her friend." That part was a lie but she had nothing to lose at this point by trying everything.

Denny lowered his gun an inch. "She trusts you? I thought she knew you were with us."

"She does, but she thinks I'm a mother like her and that I'm doing this for my child."

Nothing like the truth to really ring true, Angie thought bitterly. A full moment ticked by when nobody moved and nobody spoke until Denny finally tucked his gun into the waistband of his jeans.

"How did she get this far?"

"She picked up some friends along the way."

"Friends?"

"They've been taken care of."

Denny nodded. "So she's made it all the way back to Ireland. Anyone see her get off the boat on the other side?"

Angie felt her skin crawl again. She hadn't posted anyone on the other side. There hadn't seemed to be a point. "We know where she's going and we know she's on foot. It seemed a better use of our resources to just go to the settlement she's heading for.

We'll either intercept her on the road or take the camp—with her and the boy—if she makes it back before us."

"You got any information about this camp? How well defended it is?"

"I sent Aidan there last week to scout it out. He'll give us a full report as soon as we arrive."

"I want the whole community wiped off the map."

"Of course."

"And the Yank taken alive. *And* her boy."

Angie nodded.

Denny looked at the three faces staring at him as if he hadn't just held them at gunpoint for the last five minutes. "What are we waiting for? Let's ride."

***

Dear Lord, was it possible he was even sexier now than before? His month away had clearly chiseled him lean while keeping him big —just how Caitlin liked her men. And he was as grumpy as ever, too. She walked to his desk and sat on the edge of it. She knew her skirt was riding up just high enough. If he made even the smallest effort, he'd get a little treat.

"Are you listening to me, Caitlin?"

She leaned toward him, knowing she was about to fall out of her top and grinned when she saw his eyes go to her breasts. "I am, Mike," she said. "Every word."

"Get off my desk."

"It's not my fault the men like me." She hadn't moved but his eyes were on hers now.

"I see it different. We'll now have rules that I didn't think necessary to outline because I just assumed everyone would know how to act."

"Rules?" she said, forming the word and feeling like a naughty schoolgirl with him. She knew she affected him. She could see it. If she leaned over a little bit more she bet she would see it in his pants, too.

"Like how to dress. This, for example, isn't appropriate." He waved a hand at her outfit. "Get the feck off my desk, Caitlin, before I scrape you off."

Yeah, baby. Get physical with me. I love it. But she slid off the desk and sat in the chair opposite him. She crossed her legs, doing her best to flash him in the process.

"Rule number one," he said, glowering at her in what she considered his best angry daddy impersonation. "No relations with the other women's menfolk. Rule number two, only pants. I don't see any reason for anyone to wear a dress, but especially not you. That's not the kind of life we have here."

"I can't wear a skirt?"

"That's right. No skirts, no dresses and your top buttoned all the way up unless you're taking a bath. Like I said, Caitlin, I hate to have to spell it out to you but clearly I do."

"And if I don't agree?" She positively tingled at the thought that he was about to stand up, take her across his knee and reinforce his demands to her. After which, of course, he would knock his papers on the floor and take her hard right here, with the door open and all the world to see. She waited for him and smiled, biting her bottom lip in anticipation.

"Break any of these rules even once and you're gone. I'll have old Jerry take you to Limerick. I know you've got cousins there. Play by my rules, Caitlin, or get out."

"You don't mean that."

"Try me."

"You would throw me out? Your wife's sister?"

"I see it more as you *deciding* to leave since, if you abide my rules, you could stay."

"And if I think your rules are bollocks?"

"You're welcome to find someplace else more to your liking."

A dull pain erupted in her chest as the humiliation of what he was saying ignited in her brain. Her cheeks blazed hot and she turned so he couldn't see his effect on her.

"You'll be sorry you did this, Mike Donovan," she said heatedly. "You'll be dead sorry you did this."

She turned and ran out the door, stopping only to pick up the glass vase that she knew he had given Ellen years ago, and smashed it against the open door to the cottage.

***

40 Days after the attack.

Sarah watched the ferryman stroll out onto the pier. He still had a plastic coffee mug from one of the boutique coffee chains that she and David had been so addicted to back in Jacksonville. Watching the little ferryman sipping from it now seemed one of the most incredibly surreal moments of her life. Likely, it wasn't coffee he was sipping in any case.

From her surveillance of the harbor over the last two days, she knew that the ferry managed two round trips a day when weather wasn't too bad. Powered by steam with ancient paddles at the stern, the ferry looked like the antique it probably was. It certainly wasn't large enough to handle cars, and just barely sufficed for carrying people and their livestock from the UK to Ireland and back again. Whoever had been in a position to resurrect and re-outfit the old paddle steamer was becoming very rich, Sarah mused.

It was always the same, in every country and in every age: the inventive and the opportunistic jumped at the new windows of chance that life—and hardship—opened for them. And profited.

An image of Denny came to mind. Whatever his background was, whoever he had been before the lights went out, he had ruthlessly taken advantage of the situation. In a world without laws, he was free to grow and prosper without cost to himself.

A small pocket of people stood at the gate leading onto the ferry. Sarah could see the tickets clutched in their hands from where she stood, over fifty yards away.

Her plan was simple. She would try and see if there was any way she might be able to sneak on board unnoticed, either by waiting until the boat launched and then slipping into the water to grab its towlines and hugging the bow for the trip, or by taking advantage of any natural distraction at the boarding area to join the crowd that would soon be gathering to board.

If she failed with the first ferry crossing, she would go to the ferryman's shack on the pier—there were two drivers that spelled each other. She would offer whatever service he required to get her passage on the final ferry of the day.

Her stomach roiled at the thought and she fought not to touch the gun snug in the waistband of her jeans as antidote to it. It was a revolting almost unthinkable thought, but if it was her best shot at the crossing, then so be it. At her age, five minutes of allowing a stranger access to her body wouldn't define her view of who she was or taint her memories of her sex life with David. It would just be one more necessary thing she had to do in a depraved and sinister world-gone-mad.

She'd survive.

She thought seriously about hijacking the damn boat instead, but she was already taking a major risk just remaining in the area with Angie's thugs on the loose. She couldn't imagine what the odds might be of her surviving an attempt to cross while holding a gun to the ferry driver's head.

She prayed she would be able to slip onboard unseen.

She watched the crowd of passengers grow at the end of the pier. Before long, she could see the ferryman standing at the gangway and beginning to accept tickets and ushering the people onto the boat. She moved onto the pier and walked down the long cement runway to where the steamboat was parked. It was lightly raining and the clouds were gray and threatening, but Sarah had seen them travel in much worse weather and she knew the trip would go. The chill wind bit into her thin sweater and she hurried to join the crowd now becoming more insistent on boarding and finding shelter from the rain.

It was when she reached the end of the small disorderly queue that it happened.

A child squealed and burst from the group. Sarah watched the little girl run careening along the edge of the pier. Her mother screamed and the crowd stopped moving onto the boat long enough to witness whatever might happen. Sarah's spotted the ferryman, as interested in the drama unfolding as anyone, as he moved around the crowd to get a better look.

She wouldn't waste the gift. She moved silently, unobtrusively, onto the gangplank and onto the boat. Behind her she heard shouting, but the voices were directed away from her. She ran to the bow of the boat, invisible to any just standing at the entrance and scanning the passengers. She sat on the far side of the largest bulwark. Her heart was pounding in her ears as, within seconds, a couple sauntered over to her, clearly having just been allowed on by the ferryman.

"I'd give her a blistering, were she mine," the man said, as he shoved his hands in his pocket.

"She's just a baby."

"Baby or not."

As diversions went, Sarah thought, it hadn't been much. But it had been enough. She was onboard. She smiled at the couple and pretended to dig into her backpack to hide her face. No point in giving anybody anything to remember, she thought.

Was she safe? She shivered inside her sweater and felt the rain splash against her jeans, which weren't under the protective arc of the heavy bulwark. The rest of the boarding seemed to take forever. Sarah glanced at the sky and prayed it wouldn't rain any harder. To make her way onboard just to have to turn back...

She noticed the couple next to her was still holding their tickets in their hands. She felt the color drop from her face. Peering around the bulwark, she saw the ferryman standing in the center aisle. He was doing a head count.

Shit! She looked under the bench to see if there was a place she could squeeze under but it was solid. She knew the couple on the bench next to her was watching her with some concern. Short of slipping over the side of the boat, there was no place she could go if the ferryman stepped around the bulwark to complete his count. She looked at the railing. *Do it! There's no time to think about it!* She bit her lip and stood up...

"Oy! You there! Did I get your ticket?"

Sarah jerked her head around to see the ferryman standing twenty feet away staring at her. He was clearly in the middle of his head count because he still held the fingers of his hand up to his face.

"Of course," Sarah said. Her accent sounded fake even to her.

He approached, his posture aggressive and brash with his intention. "Let's see it then."

"You took it, didn't you?" Sarah said. She looked at the couple next to her but they seemed to edge away from her, as if afraid to be infected by her.

"You're a feckin' stowaway, you are!" the man bellowed, reaching out to grab Sarah by the shoulders.

She twisted away, stepping on the foot of the man next to her. Without thinking of what she was doing, she pulled the gun out of her jeans and aimed it at the ferryman.

He stopped and held up his hands, his eyes gone from her face to the gun. "Oy, Danny! Get out 'ere! Got a feckin' stowaway with a feckin' gun!"

Sarah stumbled against someone else, her eyes darting to the opening to the gangplank—the opening which the ferryman was standing directly in front of.

"Move out of my way," she said, flicking the gun barrel at him to indicate she wanted him to move.

"Jaysus, Joseph and Mary, it's a feckin' Yank!" the ferryman said.

Sarah could hear the murmuring of the crowd become louder.

And the man didn't move.

There was no way she was going to get off this boat short of shooting him and stepping over his body on her way out.

And she knew she couldn't do that.

"I don't want to hurt you," she said, sick with regret for having ever pulled the gun.

"Goddam Americans are the reason we're in this fix!" someone yelled. Sarah heard a rumble of agreement and she could tell the people on the ferry were crowding in closer to get a look at her. "Grab 'er gun! She can't shoot all of us!"

The second Sarah glanced away from the ferryman to see who had spoken, he lunged at her. With a deep grunt, he hit full in the chest and batted the gun away. The air in her lungs whooshed out of her as she hit the railing of the boat, the sound of the gun skittering across the plank flooring ricocheting in her ears. She sank slowly to her knees as the nightmare turned to blessed blackness.

Chapter Twenty-nine

Fiona threw back the covers and sat up straight in bed, her heart pounding in building alarm, her body poised for flight. The bedroom was quiet except for her breath, coming in loud, rasping pants.

Are we being attacked?

And then she heard it again, louder. A long moan of anguish that slipped under the door to her room like a snake.

The lad was having another nightmare.

Fiona's feet hit the cold wooden floor as she grabbed up her robe at the end of the bed. They could probably both use a cup of tea first. It might take awhile to get him back to sleep.

She hurried across the cottage sitting area, the fireplace long gone cold, to the other bedroom. It was freezing in his room.

"John, lad?" She moved to his bed and knelt. She could see his face was wet with sweat. *He'd been in hell a good while before the horror of it finally woke him to cry out.*

"She needs me, Fi," he said, his eyes still closed. "I can tell she does."

Well, that's a safe bet, Fiona thought sadly. *Wherever the poor woman is she's likely to need a lot of things.*

"*Whisht,* John," she said soothingly, straightening his covers. "It's just a dream, *leanbha.*'"

"It felt so real," he whimpered.

"They always do. I'll make us a cup of tea, aye? Unless you think you can go back to sleep?"

He shook his head.

"Didn't think so." She stood up to leave.

"Fi, does it mean nothing that I can feel her alive somewhere in the world?"

A breath caught in Fi's throat and she returned to kneel by his bed again. Tonight the lad would break her heart in every way that it could be broken. "I'm sure it means something," she said.

"And with Mr. Donovan home, I'm just to hope she finds her way back home on her own?"

The lad used to call her brother *Uncle Mike*. Should she tell him that Mike might go out looking for her again someday? Mike already talked about doing just that. Would it only be getting the boy's hopes up?

"Your mother's a resourceful woman," she said, finally.

"I know. Mr. Donovan used to call her a female John Wayne."

"Aye, he did, I remember." She watched a tear escape his eye and trail down his cheek. *Did everything have to feel like a knife to the heart these days?* She squeezed his hand. "I'll get us that tea, *leanbha*."

***

Sarah heard them talking before she opened her eyes. Men's rough voices. She could tell she was no longer on the boat and that she had been placed on something a little more comfortable than a wooden floor. It was a pallet of some kind, probably straw. Her head hurt terribly and as much as she dreaded making anyone aware of the fact that she was conscious, she couldn't help it. She turned her head and retched up bile and water.

"Aw, feck me, she's puking all over the floor! Get a bucket, ya eejit! I told ya I wouldn't put her there."

Sarah wiped her mouth and opened her eyes. She was lying on the floor of what clearly used to be a convenience store of some kind. Long stripped of its shelves, the place looked naked and menacing. Two men stood over her. One of them had her gun.

"Oy! Awake are ya? Tried to feckin' sneak on the ferry, didn't ya? Ya bastard Yank." The man squatted near her. He was slightly balding. He wore a pair of glasses with the frames taped. He looked exactly like someone she would expect to see in an H&R Block Tax office, or perhaps a manager of a corporate office. Maybe that's who he had been.

In another life.

She looked from him to the other man, who returned her look with a sneer of disgust on his face. She could see it wasn't the ferryman. This man was older and much, much angrier.

"Water," Sarah said, her voice a rasping croak.

The bald man barked out a rude laugh. "Jaysus! She's asking for water. You don't at all understand your situation, do you, luv? Not at all."

As soon as he spoke the words, it was as if another level of volume turned up in Sarah's head and she was suddenly able to hear the sounds of people shouting outside. Her eyes glanced in the direction of the door, flanked by two large windows.

"That's right, luv. There's a lot of people ain't too happy with you right now. There's a lot who've lost loved ones, not to mention their homes, their feckin' jobs…"

Sarah was pretty sure the bald guy was talking about himself.

"I…I didn't do this," she said. She knew it was a mistake before the words were out of her mouth. These people didn't want to believe she wasn't responsible. They were angry.

They *needed* someone to be responsible.

"What? Are you Canadian, then? Is that what you're going to tell me?"

"That's right. I'm Canadian."

He turned from her and spoke to the man behind him. "Get Brian in here. He's got cousins in Winnipeg. We'll just do a little Q and A, eh?"

Shit. Sarah didn't know anything about Canada except they had Mounties, and she wasn't even sure they still did. "It sounds like you've made up your mind about me. Why are you holding me?"

"We're holding you, because you tried to steal passage on the Blue Lady, which is a very serious crime during these times. But don't worry," the man said standing up and towering over Sarah, "we're gonna try ya proper-like. With a jury of yer peers and a judge and everything." He leaned over and smiled at her in what looked like a genuine sign of affection. "And then we're gonna kill you."

Sarah felt the blood drain from her face. The expression on the men's faces was like nothing she had seen before. *Possession.* They were both clearly in the grip of a belief so profound and so unshakable that nothing she said would dissuade them. They wanted to kill her and unless she could find a way to escape, they would.

She wouldn't waste any more words. She needed to look around, take stock in her surroundings and find a way, find some way out.

"Oy! American bitch! What's the capital of Canada?"

Sarah looked at the newcomer, Brian. The one with the nail ready to drive into her coffin. He was middle age and flabby, as if he might have been chubby before The Crisis but now did not have that luxury.

Sarah stared at him. *Nova Scotia? Toronto?* Her shoulders sagged in defeat. What did it matter? Even if she'd been able to rattle off the entire Canadian parliamentary charter by heart, it wouldn't help. She could see that by the mad glint in their eyes.

And she had no idea anyway of what the sodding capital was.

She shrugged. "I'm pretty sure it's Go-Fuck-Yourself. Am I right?"

At first Brian just looked at her as if trying to decipher her answer.

Finally, the bald guy pushed past him. "Right. She's American. Nobody else'd be so bloody arrogant about not knowing the capital of a neighborin' country. Makes me sick." He grabbed Sarah by her sweater and jerked her to her feet. Her head spun and she grabbed at the store counter to steady herself.

"Alright, Miss America, your accommodations await. Dinner'll be in directly. That's a joke, by the way."

Sarah's knees gave out on her and for a moment she wondered if they hadn't drugged her. She looked wildly around the store to see if there wasn't something she could use as a weapon. She could see the people now on the other side of the window.

Where had they all come from? Were they just waiting for some likely candidate to come along so they could all vent their frustrations?

Brian moved ahead of her and pulled open the heavy door to the walk-in freezer. "Don't worry, thanks to you lot the electricity's turned off. You'll still freeze your tits off, though."

"I can't…there's no air in there," Sarah said, panic leaping into her throat. *I can't go in that freezer.*

"There's just enough," the bald guy said, giving her a shove that sent her falling head-first into the cold storage. Without another word, he shut the door behind her and she heard the lock slam down.

***

Her cell was roughly twenty feet by ten. What little she knew about freezers, she assumed the ceiling, walls, floor and door were at least four inches thick, probably with some kind of insulation, but covered in sheets of impermeable steel. It was totally dark. She was able to feel empty shelves in the freezer but nothing else. After her initial ten minutes of frantic groping, her heart pounding in panic, she settled on the floor and drew herself into a tight ball, gripping her knees with her hands.

So here she was, she thought, shivering violently. Everyone she ever loved in her life was either dead, missing or all alone in the world. And unless a miracle happened, she would die before the week was out.

Is this really the end? Is this how it all ends? If she had left Papin, if she had just walked on to Balinagh and Donovan's Lot, she would be with friends tonight, her boy in her arms. But she couldn't stop the thought that reminded her that she had to go back for Papin, even if it meant the death of her. She succumbed completely to the full brunt of that knowledge as the tears came. Hearing her hopeless sobs reverberate off the walls of steel—the gasping cries of a person who's lost everything and everyone—drove her deeper into despair.

She must have slept at some point, cold or not, because when the door opened blinding her with the dim light from the store interior, it felt like only minutes since she'd been entombed. Weak from lack of food and gasping for air, Sarah sat hunched against the wall as her captors shoved a tray of bread and cheese across the floor to her. She saw an uncapped bottle of cola and looked at it with as much stunned amazement as if it had been a seven-tiered wedding cake.

"Eat, Yank," the man said. Sarah looked up, but he was backlit against the glare of the store windows and she couldn't see his face. She crawled to the tray and reached for the cola first. It was flat and warm but also sweet. Her stomach lurched with nausea at the first sip but she forced herself to keep it down. Her eyes filled with unwanted memories of a childhood of cold sodas in the summer.

"We had the trial last night," the man said. She recognized the voice as the bald man's. "Sorry to have to tell ya, but you were found guilty."

His words just felt like water pinging off a tin roof. Their meaning meant nothing to her. This mob would do what it wanted and words and entreaties or even proof, if she'd anything like that to show them, would not stop them from their endgame. She tore a piece of bread in half and stuffed it in her mouth. It tasted of mold.

"We'll have it all read out to you good and proper later today. Didn't want you to be so weak with hunger you didn't know what was happening."

She finished chewing and took a last sip of cola to wash it down. "What is your name?"

That seemed to startle him. He even took a step backward. "Not that you need to know," he said, "but it's Edgar MacIntyre."

Sarah nodded. "Who were you before The Crisis?"

"Who was I? *Who was I?*"

She could see he was clenching his fists in frustration. He glanced over his shoulder and Sarah wondered if they were alone in the store. She didn't hear anybody else. Even the noises from the mob outside were gone, and she wondered if they'd left to go back to their cold little cottages to curse the Yanks and blame the woman they held in their local Jiffy-Market for all their miseries and discomforts.

"I was the manager of an auto parts distribution plant, if you want to know," he said, biting off every word. "That's who."

Sarah ate the last piece of bread and slumped back against the cold steel wall of her prison. "So you were somebody important," she said in a soft voice.

"Bloody right, I was." He hesitated for a moment, as if he would say more, then turned and stomped out of her sight, leaving the door open and the tray on the floor.

Sarah waited. She knew he hadn't left the store and wondered if he left the door open because he was afraid she'd asphyxiate before they had a chance to properly murder her.

She stood up and inched toward the open door.

"I can see you, Yank, so don't get any bright ideas."

Edgar's voice carried to her from the shop interior. Two more steps and she stood in the doorway, her knees shaking and wobbling, her hands clutching the hinges of the freezer door. The relative warmth of the shop tickled her face and she took another step towards it.

"That's far enough."

"I'm freezing in there."

"You're uncomfortable is all." Edgar appeared from around the corner. He was holding a ceramic mug with steam coming off the top. Things weren't so terrible he wasn't able to make himself a cup of tea, Sarah thought as she saw him.

She knew talking wouldn't help. Just seeing the cold dead look in his eyes told her that. He sipped his hot drink and watched her over the top of his mug.

But she couldn't help it.

"Is it fair to blame me for something my country might have done?"

"*Might* have done? See, that's kind of you Yanks all in a few words, ya know? *Might have done?*"

"Well, it wasn't me, personally. I am a wife and mother. I...I have a young son who needs—"

"Not interested, Yank," Edgar said, scowling over his steaming mug. "If I was you I'd breathe while I could. We got a schoolteacher in town says thirty minutes of oxygen, like, and then you can go back in 'til we're ready for you." He laughed harshly. "So breathe while you still can."

Sarah tried to imagine if he had always been an evil, heartless man or if there had been a reasonable mind somewhere down deep at one time. It didn't matter. This was who he was now and she could see only brute force could possibly save her. She leaned against the doorjamb as her knees began to give way.

Force was the very last thing she possessed now.

She hated herself for mentioning John to this man. Hated her appeal using his precious name and the fact that it was disdained. She hated reminding herself out loud that John was just a boy who needed his mother. Her heart squeezed as an image of him came to mind.

She looked around the store interior. It looked like any convenience store in the States, except for the lack of goods on the shelves. The floor had debris and broken furniture scattered about, so this was probably one of the first places looted when the lights went out.

She could see any number of items scattered in the rubble that might be used as a weapon. But she could also see her own gun stuck in Edgar's front waistband. In the end, nothing she could get her hands on—if that was even possible given her weakened state and the fact that he wasn't taking his eyes off her —would help her against a handgun.

"Don't move any closer," he said. "You can get all the air you want from right there."

"It's freezing in there."

"Should I care about your comfort when you're the reason my Amy is gone?"

Of course. In a world with no laws and no recourse for the wicked deeds or bad luck for the tragedies that came after The Crisis, he and many others would need someone to atone.

"Your wife?"

"Shut yer gob. Don't even say her name. *Yes*, my wife. In chemo for six months before you feckers dropped the bomb on us and then dead not a month later after the docs all said she'd beat it. You bastards."

Sarah knew it was useless to mention that it wasn't the *Americans* who had bombed them. In the end, it didn't matter. It was US actions in the Middle East that prompted retaliation to their allies, leaving as just a small part of the result a woman who should have lived but who had died instead.

"It's not just me," Edgar said. "Every man and woman out there," he jerked his head to indicate the crowd that was once more gathering outside the window, "has lost someone because of you feckers. Time you learned that you bastards can't act like you own the whole world."

And killing me will, of course, achieve that in your fevered, festering little mind, Sarah thought hopelessly.

"Back inside," Edgar said, abruptly, slamming his mug down on the counter nearest him. "It may not make much of a dent in what your people do next, but we have damn little left to lose anyway. Inside," he snarled.

Sarah staggered backward into the freezer as he slammed the heavy door in her face. With the darkness and the relentless cold came a sudden silence, too. Then, with just the amplified sounds of her terrified breaths coming in ragged pants, she slid to a seated position with her back against the cold steel wall to wait.

Edgar was wrong. They didn't come for her later that day. She had been allowed to breathe and eat three more times before they finally came for her. By then, she was ready to have it be done.

Every time Edgar opened the door, she wondered if this was the day. When, after the third day, the door opened and three men stood in the opening, she knew it was time. The daily food had given her enough strength to survive, and when she wasn't praying or trying to sleep to hurry the time, she spent the long hours in the cold room pacing and moving. It kept her warmer and her limbs from locking up.

She was standing when they finally came for her.

"Oy! Ready for us are you?" The man, Brian, stepped into the room and grabbed her by the elbow to pull her out. "Blimey, it's cold in there. Well done, Ed. Well feckin' done."

The warmth of the shop interior washed over her as she stepped out of the freezer, the light blinding her. She stumbled as they pushed her toward the door, one man holding each elbow. She was grateful that they hadn't bound her. She could see it was raining outside and the thought came to her: *Ireland is green because Ireland is wet.* Had it really been only fifteen months when she had first said those words? So full of excitement with David and John to start their vacation in Ireland.

Brian let go of her long enough to open the shop door and she was ushered out onto the street. She felt the rain on her face, and saw the mob of people crowded outside the shop. Their faces were angry and full of hate. One woman held a rosary and her face was shut into a grimace. Sarah didn't think she was praying for her.

Before she had a chance to fully take in the scene, she heard a shout and then felt a terrible punch on her chest. She staggered against the assault and her knees buckled but Edgar pulled her back from the ground. "Oy!" he shouted to the crowd. "Not yet! We'll do this proper, I said!"

Sarah saw the rock on the ground at her feet. Her ribs screamed with every breath she took.

Dear God, they're going to stone me to death. She turned to Edgar, who still had her gun in his belt. She'd assumed they would shoot her, or, at the very worst, hang her. When she looked at the crowd—getting louder and more unmanageable by the minute— she could see that all of them, every single one of them, was gripping a rock or brick in his or her hands.

Even the children.

She twisted her arm out of Edgar's grip and pushed away from him, but he quickly recaptured her and dragged her forward, forcing the crowd to part as he moved. Brian and two other men moved in front of them to prevent the mob from taking her before time. Sarah saw their faces close up and they were cursing her, some were screaming, several spat on her. One woman reached out and tried to slap her, catching only her ear but making it ring painfully.

Edgar hauled her forward to where, just a week before, the little outdoor market had stood—and probably would again by the weekend. There was a clearing and a small wooden platform that, before The Crisis, had likely served as a place where live bands would play on a summer's evening.

Sarah stared at it as she approached. This would be the place where she left this world.

When Edgar reached the clearing he drew out his gun and shot it into the air, forcing the crowd into an immediate silence. "Oy! I need to read the crimes and the verdict before we get to it. I need silence."

The crowd ringed the staging area. Sarah saw some of the men were tossing their rocks menacingly in their hands. Many carried burlap bags bulging with more rocks. Her terror edged up into her throat and her hands clutched spasmodically at her chest, as if she could somehow ease her labored breathing. *How long would this take? How long would it take before it was all over?*

"The convicted accused stands before you, good people of Boreen," Edgar said loudly. "She has confessed to being responsible for the terrible destruction of our lives, our loved ones, and our country."

Sarah saw many in the mob nodding. Loud shouts of assent punctuated the midmorning air.

"She has shown no remorse—which is typical, aye?"

The crowd roared its agreement. A child threw her stone. It landed at Sarah's feet but it seemed to galvanize the crowd even further.

"And so she will suffer the righteous retribution of our laws. Our *Irish* laws, by God!" He turned to Sarah and pulled out his gun. Sarah found herself praying he would just shoot her.

"Yank, ya have been condemned to death by the good people of Boreen, County Wexford, Ireland, most of whom have suffered untold misery and the death of loved ones and family members because of you and your country. If you try to flee while justice is being served, I'll shoot you in the legs. Do you have anything to say?"

Sarah turned to the crowd, her face white with fear and anger. The crowd quieted to hear her words. She took a deep breath, one of the last ones on this Earth she would be allowed to take, and said loudly and clearly...

"God bless America, you jealous bastards."

Chapter Thirty

The first stone caught her square in the stomach and she doubled over when it hit, gasping as the air escaped in a sharp burst of pain. Within seconds, a fusillade of rocks and bricks flew through the air. She cradled her head with her arms and turned away, feeling the impact of the barrage on her back and legs. Amazingly, most of the rocks hit near her or around her. If she had been praying for a quick death, she could see that was not to be.

The noise of the crowd had increased to a level of pandemonium that reminded Sarah of a college football stadium of screaming fans. Only in this case, they were calling for her blood.

In the pause before the crowd gathered up more rocks for a second onslaught, Sarah turned to look out toward the sea. It wasn't much, she thought as she focused on the horizon and the white caps dancing across the surface, but it wasn't the worst thing she could see in this life. The sound of another gunshot in the air made her snap her head around.

Had Edgar mistaken her step toward the sea as an escape attempt? A rock whistled through the air and caught her viciously in the mouth. She cried out and brought her hands up to her face. A tooth was loose and blood seeped out past her lips.

Another gunshot and a single piercing scream sliced into the air around her.

Something was happening. She looked wildly around, her eyes darting everywhere at once. She saw Edgar pointing his gun at someone in the crowd. He was speaking. She could see his lips move but seemed to have gone deaf. She put a hand to the side of her head and pulled away fingers coated with blood. The crowd was moving aside, parting, and still Edgar aimed his weapon at them.

Was he helping her? Did that make sense?

And then she saw him. Saw what they were looking at. Saw what Edgar was pointing his gun at.

Mike.

On his horse, his rifle stock tucked against this side and pointed at Edgar and coming closer.

Coming for her.

Sarah clapped her hands to her mouth and then knelt and scooped up the largest of the rocks that had hit her. If the last thing she did was disarm the bastard before he could shoot Mike…

She flung the rock at Edgar's head, drilling him in the cheek as directly as a line drive off a baseball bat. The gun fell from his fingers as he staggered against the blow and she could see his cheek open up in a wide gaping smile of blood and sinew. She snatched up the fallen gun from the ground in front of him and turned to the crowd, who had now dropped their rocks and were backing up as if one entity.

Before she could think of what to do next, Mike's horse was pressing in on her. He never took his eyes off the crowd but reached down with one arm, and when she clasped his hand, pulled her up onto the back of his horse as if she'd weighed no more than a child. She clutched him around the waist with one arm while holding the gun out with the other hand.

The good people of Boreen, clearly concerned that their victim might be feeling vindictive, turned and bolted back to their cottages and huts. Sarah felt her hearing return the moment Mike spurred his mount to a clattering canter down main street, the men, women and children scattering before them. She jammed the gun into the back waistband of her jeans and wrapped her arms around Mike, leaning her cheek against his strong, broad back.

They rode without speaking for nearly an hour in a solid rain before Mike stopped. He pulled up next to a stand of ash trees and walked his horse down into the shallow ditch and up the other side to the pasture beyond. He dismounted and gently pulled Sarah out of the saddle. She cried out when he did and hated herself for doing it.

For the last hour, she had been happier than she knew she had any right to be. She didn't deserve to be so joyous. Not with David dead and Papin lost for good. With every stride closer to Donovan's Lot, and John, she rejoiced in her life given back to her, and in the warmth and strength she took from seeing Mike again.

"Let's take a look at you, girl," he said, holding the reins in one hand and tilting her face to him.

"Thank you." Sarah felt the tears gather in her eyes and then streak down her face. "Thank you for not giving up on me. Thank you and thank God. I can't believe I'm alive."

"Nor me, lass." He shook his head and Sarah thought he'd aged since she saw him last, just five weeks ago. His eyes were full of worry and the tension she felt in his grip on her arm tightened.

"How did you know to come? How could you have known?" Sarah couldn't stop crying and she didn't care to try. She had been strong for so long and it felt so good to just weep.

"I heard a rumor about an American woman being held on the coast. I didn't know for sure if it was you but I had to see."

Sarah leaned into him and let him put his arms around her. Her broken ribs made every breath a spasm of fiery pain, but it was nulled out by the comfort and strength in his arms. "I never thought I'd see anybody I loved again," she said.

She thought she felt him start at that but he relaxed again. "Young John is fine and safe," he assured her. "And waiting for you, although he doesn't know it. I left camp yesterday only saying I had something I had to do. Didn't want to get the lad's hopes up. Are you hungry, Sarah?"

Sniffling, she nodded and wiped her face with the back of her hand. "How far away are we?"

Mike went to retrieve a small packet from his saddlebags. He led her to a downed tree and settled her on it while he tied his horse's reins to a branch. "It'll be too dark to travel much longer today," he said. "One more night, Sarah." He handed her a piece of cheese tucked into a slice of fresh bread.

She took the bread and began crying again. His kindness, the lack of bugs or mold in the food, and the miracle that she would see John in the morning was all too much.

Mike sat next to her on the log and put his arm around her, being careful of her ribs. "It's alright, Sarah. It's all over now. We've got you."

After she'd eaten, they rode for another hour before Mike stopped to make camp. He had no concern that the village mob would decide to pursue them, but Mike knew the more distance they created between them and the coast the easier Sarah would feel. Seeing her that morning, standing there, facing the crowd and believing she would die, was the most gut-wrenching moment in his life.

The bald wanker with the gun was lucky Mike didn't just shoot him straight-out.

He made a small campfire and hobbled the horse before bringing out more food. Sarah, looking bedraggled and drugged —although she didn't act it—sat on one of his bedroll blankets in front of the fire and faced west, toward her boy. They'd been lucky. It had rained on and off most of the day but the night looked to be clear, if cold. The first thing he'd done after their midday stop was to wrap her in his jacket, which had brought about another bout of tears.

A constantly crying Sarah was not a Sarah he knew, and it mildly unsettled him. He had seen her in life and death situations before where she never shed a tear. He tried to imagine what she must have experienced in the interim five weeks, but vowed he wouldn't ask.

When she was ready.

He handed her another cheese sandwich and a canteen of whisky and sat down close to her. As much as he needed to see her and touch her, he was grateful that she seemed to want that too. He didn't mistake it for anything other than what it was: the gratitude of an abused woman—and a new widow—reacting to the kindness of a friend. But it allowed him to touch her, to hold her, and he didn't think, after the loss of her, if he could've borne an insistence that they treat each other any less intimately.

She took a long draught of the whisky and made a face.

"Drink," he said. "It'll do you good."

"The Irishman's perennial cry."

That's good. It meant she was coming back to herself.

"Speaking of nationalities, did you *want* them to kill you, Sarah? I mean, was there possibly a time when saluting your stars and stripes might have been a little *less* inopportune?"

Sarah grinned and his heart soared to see it. "It wouldn't have mattered. Nothing short of me bursting into flames would've stopped them. In fact, now that I think of it, they probably were waiting for me to burst into flames."

"Well, there's bad feeling just now about the Yanks, no mistake. All the more reason..." He stopped.

She looked at him. "All the more reason, what?"

He shrugged. "That I'll be minding you from now on."

"I have a feeling you don't mean that in the way I'm used to hearing it."

"I mean protecting you," he said firmly.

She took another long drink from the canteen and shivered as it went down. She handed it back to him. "Works for me," she said, in another example of a Sarah he had never seen before.

That night, he placed their bedrolls next to each other with his nearest the fire so he could keep it going through the night. When he lay down, he was astounded that she lay down so close to him; it was almost like they were man and wife. He reminded himself that she craved the safety and security of human touch right now. She might even be imagining Mike was her David holding her.

As the moon flitted behind the lacy web of tree branches, dipping the campsite in and out of pale light, they lay silently together but Mike knew she was still awake.

"Mike?"

"Mmm?"

"I thought about giving my body for a boat ticket."

He felt an irrational bolt of jealousy and anger at what she must have had to endure since he saw her last but forced himself to keep his tone mild. "We're all thinking of doing crazy things to survive. It's the times, Sarah."

"I was a hair's breadth away from it."

"You would do what you need to do to survive, to see your lad again."

"Mike, we have to find Papin."

He sat up to give the fire a poke and reenergize it. She had briefly filled him in on the little gypsy whore that had travelled with her for a bit. "You know that's impossible, don't you?"

Sarah sat up too and inched closer to the fire. And him. "Mike, no."

"Have you asked yourself, Sarah, why she didn't come to you? Deep down, you must know."

"I told her I wouldn't leave her," Sarah said, beginning to cry again. "I told her I was her family."

"I'm sorry, darlin' I truly am." Mike pulled her into his arms, feeling her yield to him, her head tucked against his chest as she cried. "But your lad is waiting for you and he needs you, too."

"I know. But how can I live not knowing what happened to her?"

"You'll live. You'll have to, for John's sake."

If not my own.

*****

The helicopter appeared as the tiniest spec in the sky. John said when he first saw it—and he made it clear that he had been the first—he thought it was a seabird a long way off course.

How this could happen when Mike had gone off just the day before Fiona could well believe, because that was the kind of luck she had. She handed the handsome American co-pilot another cup of tea and wondered if he was really old enough to fly the helicopter. He was dressed in a US Air Force uniform and introduced himself as Captain Jim Rader.

Like every American she had ever met, he was confident and friendly. She figured the military component must have tempered the other typical American inclination to talk too much. The captain was unfailingly polite but also all business.

He'd landed in the pasture adjacent to Donovan's Lot not an hour earlier, with a crew of three and a small family of American ex-pats who, like the Woodsons, had been on holiday in Ireland when The Crisis happened. She had no idea what their circumstances were or how they managed to stay alive and in one piece. They refused to get off the aircraft even to stretch their legs when the helicopter landed.

Captain Rader's machine was bigger than anything Fiona had ever seen up close. John and Gavin and most of the other boys in the camp had crawled all over it and still hadn't had their fill. She shook her head.

John.

Dear God in holy heaven. Was it herself that was supposed to make this call?

"Thanks for the tea, ma'am," the young captain said, standing. "But we really need to be going. I've got another stop today before I deliver my cargo."

"So it won't be yourself that takes John back to the States?"

"No, ma'am. My orders are to collect the Woodson family and bring 'em to Limerick. They'll leave for the States from there." He looked over his shoulder as John entered the cottage.

"That is one cool bird," John said as he sat down next to Fiona. She noticed his eyes were brighter than she'd seen since Sarah was taken and his father slain. *Boys and their toys.*

"Would you like to ride on it, young John?" she asked him as she patted his knee.

He frowned, his eyes darting to the pilot. "Are you giving rides?"

The pilot reached into his jacket and pulled out an envelope. "Nearly forgot this," he said, handing it to Fiona. "It's a copy of my orders, so you know I'm not kidnapping him. And…" he nodded at John, "…a letter from his folks in Florida."

"Grandma and Grandpa?" John jumped up and reached for the letter. "They're alive? They're okay? Fi, let me see the letter."

"It's not addressed to you," Fiona said, glancing at the letter with Sarah's name marked clearly on it.

"I'm to bring the family with me to Limerick," the pilot said. "Don't know if we'll be coming back this way." He shrugged. "Don't expect so."

"So is the US back on its feet then?" Fiona asked. She gave John a strict look to be interpreted: *settle down.* He was standing, looking like he was about to burst with questions and excitement.

"Yes, ma'am. We never got hit, really. So we're dropping food and supplies and gathering up all our nationals who were stranded around the world when the thing happened."

"My dad died," John said, his voice wavering. "He's not here to leave with us."

"Yeah, sorry, sport. That's what Miss Donovan was telling me. That's rough."

"And my mom's gone missing." John looked at Fiona, as if to ask if she was reading the situation any differently than he was.

"Yeah, sorry about that, too. But my orders are to take you with me, son."

"Take me? Back to the States?"

"That's right."

"But what about my mom?" John looked from the captain to Fiona.

Fiona stood and walked to the door of the cottage. "Could you give us a moment, please, Captain Rader?" she said, smiling at him.

"I need to be leaving, ma'am."

"Yes, I know. We won't be a tick."

When he nodded and exited the cottage, John sat down hard in one of the kitchen chairs. "I'm not leaving without Mom."

Fiona sat next to him and picked up his hand. "John, this is the moment we've all prayed for."

"Maybe you have. I haven't prayed for this."

"Your grandparents are distraught with worry for all of you —"

"I'm not leaving without my mom!"

Fiona could see his eyes filling with tears and she would curse Mike for the rest of her days that he had left and forced her to deal with this situation instead of him.

"John, I'm not saying your mam's dead and gone…" John jumped to his feet and Fiona grabbed his arm to keep him in the room, "…but *wherever* she is, I do know she would want you to get on that helicopter. And if she *is* gone, and please God I hope that's not true, I know she would want you with your grandparents. You can see that, can't you?"

John covered his face with his hands. "I can't leave her," he said, his voice muffled by his hands and his tears.

"You're not, darling," Fiona said as she pulled him into her arms and kissed his bent head. "You're just going on ahead. It's what she'd want."

The co-pilot rapped on the cottage door and stuck his head inside. "Let's go, John," he said. "Someday you might be able to come back and visit. But we gotta go *now*."

Fiona squeezed him tightly in her arms, then gave him a push toward the pilot. She watched as he walked to the waiting helicopter, its rotors wind-milling the air above him. Gavin ran out and threw an arm around John's shoulders and she saw their heads close together as they said goodbye.

When the captain opened the helicopter door, John hesitated, turned and looked back at the camp, then climbed onboard.

Fiona watched as the aircraft lifted off and then became smaller and smaller in the sky before it disappeared from view. She walked back to the kitchen table, her eye falling on the letter to Sarah.

The minute John agreed to get on that helicopter, she knew was the minute he had finally faced the fact that his mother was probably dead.

And for that, Fiona wept for him.

Chapter Thirty-one

Angie pulled the blanket over her nakedness. The snores pummeling her from the other side of the bed assured her that Jeff still slept. She watched his unmoving form and a wave of nausea settled in her stomach.

I sure hope it's because of what I've become, she thought. *And not another feckin' baby.* She stood up and pulled on her pants and sweatshirt and moved to the window. Jeff had nailed a blanket up to it last night at her insistence.

So fucking chivalrous.

It wasn't her first time with Jeff, and the way he had hounded her over the last month she always knew in the back of her mind it wouldn't be the last. But she wasn't fool enough to think it meant anything.

As if she even wanted it to mean something.

"Oy, Jeff," she said. "Denny'll be here soon. Get your arse up." She turned to the window and peeled a flap back on the blanket. They'd arrived in Ballinagh two days before. It wasn't much of a town as those things go, Angie thought. Maybe it was before The Crisis. Now it was just a street with abandoned storefronts, several of which she and the rest of Denny's crew had commandeered for their headquarters.

It had been a hard two days. Denny wasn't used to waiting. Angie wasn't crazy about it, herself. But it was still the smartest course of action. Even crazy Denny understood that.

Because the bitch hadn't come back yet.

"Angie, luv, come back to bed. I want ta show ya something."

He wasn't really a bad sort, she thought, glancing at the now moving form in the bed. He didn't push her. He didn't take, he asked. He always had her back and he listened to her. Living this kind of life, he was as good an ally as any.

And allies were essential if you were going to survive. Before she could stop herself, Angie caught an image in her mind of her little girl. She was usually so good at stopping the pictures before they fully formed. Little Dana, her dark curls bouncing as she tossed her head. *If the child gets a chance to grow up, she'll be a real little flirt someday.*

It was up to Angie to make sure she got that chance.

The sounds of the aircraft in the distance were indecipherable at first. It had been so long since Angie had heard any kind of motor that her brain couldn't seem to make sense of it. But the louder and more distinct the noise became, the more obvious it was that a helicopter was approaching. She strained to catch a glimpse of it through the window and realized she was hesitant to rush out into the street as she could see some of the other men were doing.

Why is that, Angie? Afraid the world has suddenly righted itself and it's time for your comeuppance?

She shook the voice out of her head and bolted for the door.

There was a fucking helicopter flying overhead. And one thing she knew, that wasn't good news for any of them.

***

45 Days after the attack.

Six weeks since her world had imploded and left her reeling. Six weeks of rough travel and living in fear and being hunted. Six weeks and now her trial was nearly over. They would arrive back at Donovan's Lot today.

If Sarah had had it her way, she would have galloped the horse the last three miles. The thought that her journey was finally at and end, and her boy was nearly in her arms, was all that ran through her mind for the last several hours of the ride. Now that she could allow herself to freely think of him, to remember his face, his voice, she also reminded herself that John had had to deal with his father's death and his mother's disappearance all by himself.

"Well, we did our best, Sarah," Mike said. "We've none of us let the boy alone for too very long."

"No, I know, Mike."

"Especially Fiona, ya ken. She loves the boy as her own. You know that."

"And he's been okay? I mean, considering?"

"He's been sad, Sarah, there's no denying that, of course. But he's kept busy and he's fine. He's cared for and loved. You'd expect nothing less of us, surely?"

Sarah hugged him tightly from where she sat behind him in the saddle, not caring what he must think of her. Just the thought that she would have her child back in her arms again was all that mattered now. "Can't we at least trot?"

Mike laughed. "Have you ever put a horse into a trot riding double? It'll rattle your teeth."

In the end, Sarah rested her face against his strong, broad back and enjoyed the rocking walking gait of the big bay. The sun broke through the clouds and she closed her eyes to better feel the warmth against her cheeks. Mike had taken his jacket back against the November air, but she was well wrapped in the woolen blankets that they'd bedded down with.

She decided there was plenty of time to tell him about Denny and Angie and what may or may not be coming down on them.

Surely the Lord above would give her a respite, a few moments without having to fight for her life, to just hold and keep her child once more?

"Nearly there, Sarah," Mike said, his voice warm and close.

"I need down," she said. "I need to go faster on foot."

"Your ribs—"

"I don't care, Mike. I don't care." She swung her leg behind the saddle and slid down the length of the horse until her feet hit the ground, jarring her broken ribs in a punch that made her gasp.

"Sarah?"

"I'm fine," she said, turning in the direction of the camp. It hurt too much at first to jog, but she could still make faster time on foot by cutting through the south end of the perimeter pastures. By the time she reached the camp's main entrance, she was running and never even felt her ribs.

"John! John!" she called as soon as she entered camp. A few boys about his age were sitting by the center campfire whittling on sticks and they looked up in surprise when she ran up to them. "Have you guys seen John Woodson?" They shook their heads.

Sarah turned toward the main cottage on the perimeter of the center of camp. It hadn't been ready the last time she saw it, but now smoke came from the chimney. She ran up the steps of the porch and burst through the door without knocking.

"Fiona!"

Fiona turned from the cook stove, a pan of biscuits in her gloved hands, and stared at Sarah as if she'd risen from the dead. "Oh my God, Sarah."

"Fiona, where is he? I'm back! Oh my God, it's so good to see you. Put that thing down so I can hug you!"

Fiona thumped the pan down on the table in front of her and a hand flew to her mouth in horror.

Sarah stopped abruptly. Fiona's expression literally took her breath away. A moment passed between them. Then Sarah spoke warily. "Where is he, Fi? Where's John?"

"Oh, Sarah, may God forgive me. He's gone."

Later, Mike knew, she'd listen to reason. Later she'd realize all the reasons, all the perfectly logical reasons, and maybe someday she'd even come to believe she'd have done the same.

But not today.

When Mike came riding into camp a few minutes behind Sarah, he was not prepared for the frenzy of destruction and hysteria that greeted him. Sarah was in the middle of the camp, literally attempting to climb into the main cook fire, with Fiona hanging on her like they were of one flesh. Stunned but finally spurred into action when Sarah grabbed the hot tongs and pots over the fire with her bare hands and began flinging them around the camp, he leapt from his horse to tackle her before she hurt herself or anybody else.

What in the name of God could have happened in the five minutes they'd been apart?

He held her on the ground while she struggled and screamed, her hysteria more terrible than what he could imagine any insane asylum could produce.

It had to be about John. That was the only thing that made sense.

Now he heard Fiona crying too, and apologizing like it was *her* who'd gone berserk and tried to wreck the camp and fling herself into the fire!

"Forgive me, Sarah! I'm so sorry! I would die rather than... oh, please God, strike me dead now. I am so, so sorry! I didn't know!"

Mike knew that to the day they laid him in his coffin, he would hear Sarah's heart-wrenching sobs as she called for her boy, gone as surely and completely for her this day as if he'd died in his sleep.

"What the feck happened?" he said to Fiona. "Pull yourself together, Fi, and talk to me!"

"The Yanks came for him," she said, sobbing into her hands and watching Sarah roll spasmodically in Mike's grasp. "They came in a military helicopter and said they were here for the Woodsons and they was to take him."

"When? When did this happen?"

Fiona shook her head as if she wouldn't answer.

"*Today*, Da," Gavin said. He stood on the edge of the cook fire and used a long stick to put some of the embers and stones Sarah kicked away back into place. "Just this morning."

The wail that came from Sarah then was the sound of a mother's heart broken, never to be whole again in this life.

Mike held her close as she cried herself to exhaustion. Then he picked her up and carried her into Fiona's cottage, her weight limp in his arms. Out of the corner of his eye he saw Gavin take his horse and head toward the stables. Fiona ran into the cottage and began pulling out first aid ointments and bandages. Behind them, the people in the community who had gathered began to slowly shuffle back to their homes, tents and huts.

Mike set Sarah down on the couch in the living room.

"I can't bear it," Sarah said, her voice so small, Mike almost didn't hear her. He sat next to her and gingerly picked up both her hands. The palms and fingers were bright red and already badly blistered. He had nothing cold to ease the pain.

Fiona knelt in front of Sarah and took her hands from Mike. She covered the palms with a light coating of the greasy unguent and then wrapped both hands in clean bandages.

All the while, Sarah looked straight ahead as if in a trance, as if her anguish had rendered her dead in every way but a functioning body.

Now was not the time for more questions.

Nor for finding fault. Because if it was, then Mike of all people knew that if he'd just *told* someone where he was going—instead of opting for the pleasure of the big surprise for young John—that the boy would still be here.

That night, Sarah slept in Fiona's bed, drugged numbed by grief and a stubborn insistence on her mind's part not to feel or think.

Weary from his trip and the emotion of their terrible homecoming, Mike walked out onto the porch after Sarah fell sleep. Fiona joined him and handed him a cigarette that she lighted off her own.

"Where'd you get these?"

She stared out onto the peaceful center of camp—the fire banked, the spilled pots back in place over the iron tripods, dinner long since over.

"It's my fault," he said.

"Why didn't you tell someone where you were going?"

Mike took a long drag off the cigarette and realized a part of him didn't expect to ever feel as sad as he had this last month now that Sarah was back. At least, he hadn't expected to quite so soon.

"I didn't want to get anyone's hopes up."

"Well, mission accomplished."

"I don't think I've ever felt as bad in me whole life, Fi, as I did today when I saw Sarah....so...so..."

"Unhinged."

"By God, how do things get so bollocks-up?"

She put a hand on her brother's arm. "By all of us insisting on going around being human, I suppose," she said kindly.

***

Denny sat opposite Angie, Jeff and Aidan, a chipped and broken kitchen table between them. The place, like nearly every other store in Ballinagh, had been looted and stripped of anything of value. Angie thought the place must have served as the village pub at one point. Because wooden furniture was seen nowadays as an important fuel resource, it was surprising to find the table intact.

They had brought their own food and whisky with them. At one point, Angie looked around the broken interior of the bar and imagined how it must have been before: a warm interior, music playing, probably savory cottage pie sold by the slice. She glanced at the cold cheese sandwich on the table in front of her.

"Why would they do that?" Denny asked, snapping Angie back to the conversation.

"Sounds like the US is still flying and eating hot food and watching TV," Angie said, shrugging.

"While the rest of us are back in the feckin' Stone Age," Aidan said, sourly. "Thanks to them."

Angie watched Denny's reaction. Since he had been in prison serving a life sentence when the lights went out—effectively freeing every lowlife and scumbag behind bars—she would be very surprised if he affected to long for the good old days before The Crisis. He merely grunted.

"But why would they take the kid? That's just crazy."

Angie felt tired. Thanks to Jeff, she had gotten very little sleep the night before. And she had desperately needed sleep.

"It's just the Americans raking in their own, gathering everyone together," she said. "I don't know."

"But to send a helicopter for a kid?"

Denny had been irate, to the say the least, when he'd been informed a few hours after the copter sighting that the incident had resulted in the removal of one of the major reasons he was even on this crusade to Ireland.

And Angie knew he was well aware that *she* was the reason they'd waited. She watched him carefully now. As irrational as he famously was, it was impossible to believe he would forgive her for that.

"So what's the plan, Angie?" Denny's words were slightly slurred, alerting her to the fact that he'd already been drinking heavily today. The good news about that, she thought, was that it took the edge off his temper.

The bad news was that he would either be completely useless in another few hours…or completely mental.

"If she doesn't come back soon, we go ahead and take the camp and just wait for her to stroll in."

"If we'd done that yesterday, we'd have the kid," Denny said, narrowing his eyes at her.

Angie looked away from Denny's glare. *If I deny it, it'll trigger a rage. If I agree, he'll just shoot me where I sit.*

"Well," Jeff said, "except that when the US Calvary came flying in with their big-ass helicopter this morning, they'd see what we'd done and strafe us before we could hightail it back into the bushes."

Denny looked at Jeff as if he'd started speaking Urdu. "Good point," he said finally. He looked at Angie. "Well done."

Angie fought the impulse to look at Jeff. She knew he was smirking. He would expect to be rewarded later.

He deserved whatever he had in mind.

"Your girlfriend got any more juicy tidbits, Aidan?" Denny said, turning to the big man to his left. "Anything we can use?"

Aidan pulled himself up into a straighter position in the chair. He'd risen in the ranks and value in Denny's eyes thanks to the good fortune of meeting a woman in town who was not only agreeable to his lecherous attentions, but who happened to have detailed knowledge about Sarah's little outlier community.

"She told me we'll have to block the escape routes that lead to the caves. I got a map she drew for me of where they are."

"Will we need to use men for that? Because we can't afford to post sentries."

"Nah, she says we can pull the trees down around the exits and nobody'll be able to get through."

"What kind of trees can be pulled down, you daft eejit?" Jeff said.

"They're a part of a system of traps that Donovan and his lot put together. Like catapults and such."

Denny grinned. "So let me get this straight. We'll be able to block their secret escape routes *and* destroy their ability to make an offensive strike at the same time?"

Aidan, clearly delighting in the approval of his master, nodded. "Yeah."

"Excellent."

"She's gonna show me the exact locations of the perimeter tree snares. So we can wreck 'em before time."

"I have to say, Aidan. You've put your dick to good use in this case." Denny looked around the table, inviting appreciation for his wit. Angie, Jeff and Aidan laughed on cue.

A loud knock at the door made Angie jump.

"Whoa, Ange," Jeff said, putting a heavy hand on her neck. "You gotta learn to relax."

Angie shrugged off his hand and got up to answer the door. One of the other men, Danny, stood on the other side of it, scratching his crotch. "Aidan's slag is here," he said.

"Send her in, and bring more wood to burn in the hearth. It's freezing in there." She returned to the room. "Your girlfriend's on her way, Aidan. I need you to take her off straightaway to find and dismantle those snares around the camp."

"Well, maybe not *straightaway*." Aidan sniggered and high-fived Jeff.

The door opened behind her and the young woman entered. She wore a ridiculously short skirt and a low-cut blouse. She went straight to Aidan, who pulled her onto his lap. "Hey, baby, I missed you," he murmured into her neck.

Angie saw that Denny seemed to be looking at the two as if not totally sure what he was seeing. She wondered how much he'd already had to drink. She cleared her throat. "Oy, Aidan, take Barbie and go check out the snares. *Now*." The girl giggled and grabbed for Aidan's belt buckle.

Angie raised her voice. "Aidan? Did you hear me?"

Aidan stood up with the girl in his arms, flashing the table with the fact that she wasn't wearing any underwear. She squealed and wrapped her arms around his neck.

"Oh! Before we go, Aidan," she said, "I probably should mention the thing I discovered before coming here."

Angie spoke sharply. "You have news about the camp?"

"You could say that."

Angie couldn't believe how patient Denny was being with this little bitch. It was like he was hypnotized by the cow. She sighed in frustration but tried to temper her words when she spoke. "Yes? And that would be?"

Caitlin looked up into Aidan's face. "I thought you'd want to know as soon as possible." She turned to look at Denny, her eyes flashing with malice. "She's back."

Susan Kiernan-Lewis

Chapter Thirty-two

"I'll take you to Limerick first thing in the morning. That's where Fi said the pilot was headed. If it's some kind of American military landing stage, we'll get you on the next plane to the States. That can't have been the only one. I promise you, Sarah, we'll get you back to your boy."

Sarah nodded. It had just been a shock. It wasn't forever. She would see John again. She knew that. She believed that.

He wasn't dead.

She rode next to Mike on her horse, Dan. It had been so long since she'd been on his back that it surprised her to feel so immediately comfortable once she was seated on him again. It's true, she thought patting Dan's neck, there's something so good for the inside of a person to be on the outside of a horse. *That and a good plan was all anyone needed in this world.*

A plan to reunite with loved ones.

In the quiet moments of the night when Mike and Fiona—so worried about her, so attentive!—thought she was asleep, it occurred to her that what life was really all about was getting back home again. In fact, life was just an endless series of leaving and finding your way home. Nothing else really mattered. She glanced at Mike as they rode the dusty lane down what used to be the main drag in this part of Ireland, but was now just a very serviceable bridle path.

He felt yesterday's tragedy so keenly, it was almost as if he'd lost his own son. That's because he loves me.

The thought didn't shock her when it came, but the ease with which she accepted it, so soon after losing David, made her stomach clench.

She had insisted they go back to her cottage the very next morning after arriving back in camp. She knew Mike didn't think it was a good idea, but he also didn't feel he could deny her much after what she'd lost.

Don't say it like that. Not even in your head. You haven't lost him. You'll get him back.

"Look, about the people who kidnapped me..."

"There's plenty of time to talk about that, Sarah."

"I know, and I think this is one of those times. They are coming after me, Mike. They were waiting for me at the channel crossing and, trust me, they haven't given up. It wouldn't take much for them to find out I was heading back to Donovan's Lot."

"We'll deal with them if they come."

"They're ruthless killers, Mike. Worse than Finn's gang." Soon after The Crisis happened, she and Mike and David had fought a gypsy sociopath bent on destroying or ruling the Irish countryside.

"That's hard to believe."

"Well, maybe just as bad then."

"Why in the world would they follow you all the way back to Ireland?"

"I...it's a long story."

"We have time right now, as you've just pointed out."

"Okay, fine. I...I escaped with my life from these bastards, and in the process...I killed a man."

"Jesus, Joseph and Mary!" Mike pulled up his horse and stared at her. "How in the name of God did you do that?"

"Really, Mike?" Sarah looked at him, her eyes flashing. "Are you surprised that I was driven to that? Okay, let's see. Well, first I temporarily disabled him with a knee to the groin, then I grabbed the knife I found in his boot and I slit his throat with it." She realized she was crying and that Mike was looking at her with horror, but she found she couldn't stop talking. "Oh, did I mention I was naked at the time? Because that's a really important part of the story..."

"Sarah, shirrup, stop! Stop!"

Sarah dropped her reins and covered her face with her hands. Within seconds she felt herself being pulled out of the saddle and crushed into Mike's arms.

"Stop, stop," he murmured into her hair as she wept. "My poor girl, my poor, brave girl. I can't imagine what you've been through."

Sarah knew he felt helpless to comfort her, but the strength of his arms supported her and soothed her. She felt a tiny part of the revulsion of the experience begin to wane and the comfort of being loved and protected once more began to grow inside her, blotting out the rest. She pulled away from him. "I'm sorry, Mike."

"Don't be sorry. You've every right to have a good cry. In fact, to be half mad considering what you've endured." He shook his head and began to pull her even closer but she stopped him.

"I'm okay. Or at least I will be. It didn't kill me. I'm still standing."

"You're a tough one, Sarah Woodson," Mike said, touching her hair.

She pulled away and smiled to soften the rejection. "I'm okay, Mike. I'm ready to go on."

"If you're sure."

"I just want you to realize that they're evil, evil people and I'm afraid I've probably led them straight to Donovan's Lot."

"Pshht! We're ready for them," Mike said, as she turned to face her horse. She bent her knee and he boosted her easily onto Dan's back. "As you know, we run drills constantly on clearing the camp and we're not without offensive resources. We won't be taken by surprise. You're not to worry, Sarah. Not anymore."

She gathered up her reins and smiled down on him. "That's like saying I should hold off breathing for a while."

"Well, at least let me do the worrying for a little bit, eh?" He mounted his horse, but when she moved forward she noticed he stood unmoving in the middle of the road.

"Why are you stopped?" she asked.

He looked like he wasn't sure of how to phrase his words, and his hesitancy was starting to annoy her.

"Stop treating me like I'm going to break in two, Mike Donovan," she said, hoping her voice had some of her old spirit back and that he could hear it.

"It's a hard thing you're doing today, Sarah. I don't want to make it harder."

"Just tell me."

"We buried him in the east pasture," Mike said, pointing off the road. "There's a gate yonder a bit where we can access it."

Sarah's eyes followed where he pointed. "Why not near the cottage?" she asked quietly.

He cleared his throat, clearly still pained to talk about it. "It was John's preference. He said his da loved to watch the sun pop up behind the cairns of a morning."

Sarah nodded and forced herself to swallow past the large lump that was forming in her throat. John had made the decision. He'd had to deal with so much all alone. "Take me there, then," she said, hearing the anguish in her voice.

***

Angie spotted the first sentry perched high in a tree about a half-kilometer from the compound. She was tempted to point him out to Denny for whatever brownie points that might earn her, but she knew he'd just open fire on the kid and they needed him to alert the others. Besides, there'd be plenty of time to shine her star with him.

After they got Sarah.

When the kid began to noisily descend the tree, Angie was amazed that nobody else in her group could hear him. She had stationed Jimmy, Aidan and Damian at the escape exits to usher the fleeing masses back into camp. By the time tree-boy got back to raise the alarm, all he would effectively have done was round everyone up for Denny in one neat, terrified little parcel.

Angie nudged her horse to ride up to Denny. "This is the entrance."

"Doesn't look like much."

"Jeff's tied strips of white sheets to mark where the traps and pits are."

"I see that. How many men did Aidan say there were?"

"About twenty. Five more that us."

"Except we have automatic rifles."

"And they'll have to deal with their women and children," Angie reminded him. "When they're not allowed to run to safety, the men will lay down pretty quick."

"That's what I'm counting on," Denny said.

Angie twisted around in her saddle to face the men behind her. "Anybody in camp tries to use their gun, kill 'em. Anybody tries to run, kill 'em. Keep yer eyes out for the Yank. Any questions?"

A few laughs and a rude comment or two filtered back to her.

Denny nodded. "Let's do this," he said, urging his horse forward.

The camp sentry had done his job, Angie saw when they entered the camp. The campfire was untended, the center of the camp and all the huts and cottages ringing it were empty. She posted six men to stand equal distance from each other around the camp's perimeter and then dismounted, handing the reins of her horse to one of the new men. He was young and she hadn't learned his name yet. She gave orders for him to collect everyone's mounts and have them ready but off to the side.

Denny stood in the middle of the camp and looked around. "What a dump." He looked at Angie. "Where is everyone?"

How many times had they discussed this? It was all she could do not to roll her eyes...something that would definitely get her killed.

"Just wait," she said.

The minutes crept by and Angie was starting to envision how she would murder that idiot whore, Caitlin—and Aidan, too for good measure—if the information they'd been given was bad, when she heard them coming. They came from two different sides of the camp, women, children, and men.

When Angie saw them, she could see that some of the Irishmen were bleeding, obviously the result of unwise resistance against a stronger force. Some of the children were crying, but for the most part the group was surprisingly silent.

As the community stumbled back into camp, Denny ran up to them, hungrily scanning faces in the crowd.

Looking for her.

Angie's gut pinched again when she saw the children. They were afraid but not terrified. They trusted that the adults would not let real harm happen to them, she thought. How could they have lived this long in the new world since and still believe that?

She watched Denny walk up to a young girl—no older than Dana—and put a gun to her head. Her mother shrieked and grabbed the girl's arm to pull her away. The bodyguard, Eli, lunged at the mother, and a man from the crowd charged him. Angie saw Denny point his gun skyward and pull the trigger. Everyone froze, then a woman came from the middle of the crowd to stand in front of Denny. She put her hands on the sobbing girl and, looking into Denny's crazed eyes, said, "I'll be taking the *bairn's* place if you'll allow it."

Angie watched Denny hesitate. He didn't like ideas that weren't his own, she knew, but the girl was attractive in a strongly Irish kind of way, curly hair, green eyes and freckles. And she had a good body. That counted for a lot in Denny's mind. And if he had a brain cell in his skull he could see that attacking the child was going to get them mobbed, automatic weapons or no.

He released the girl and she ran screeching to her mother. Eli relinquished his grip on the woman.

Denny put his gun away in a show of accommodation and reasonableness that Angie knew was the lead-up to something much worse.

With a broad smile etching slowly across his face, he pulled out a short-handled dagger and pointed it at the young woman.

"Thank you for your suggestion, luv," he said. "Now, I'll be needing you to tell me where the Yank bitch is since I'm not able to see her and I know she's back. You have until the count of three, after which I'll slit yer feckin throat and start on the kiddies as originally planned."

Susan Kiernan-Lewis

Chapter Thirty-three

Sarah knelt in the grass by David's grave. It was a simple mound with a cross. The words, *David Woodson, Loving Husband and Father,* were carved on the wooden cross.

"John wanted to put the dates on himself," Mike said softly from where he stood behind her.

She touched the grass that edged the grave. The last time she had seen David was in this pasture. It was nearly impossible to believe that he now lay under this sod, the very sod where they'd grazed their goats and horses all summer long.

She wasn't sure what she thought she'd feel when she saw David's grave. Closure of some kind, she supposed. Instead, she felt nothing. It just didn't feel real to her that her animated, handsome husband was here. Not when the sky was so blue, the birds still sang and the trout still jumped in the pond.

David was here, but she'd never touch him again. She'd never hear his voice again. She stood up abruptly and dusted the dirt from her jeans.

A wave of irrational anger pierced her. She felt like she wanted to punch something. *Hard.*

"You all right, Sarah?"

"As good as I can be," she said, staring at the simple cross.

"I'll get the dates on it straightaway."

She shook her head. Poor Mike. So helpless in the face of her agony. Flailing around desperately to come up with *something* that would somehow make a difference or make it all better. She looked at the grave and all she could think was, *David gone, Evvie gone, Papin gone, John gone.*

273

Why am I still here? What possible reason or purpose could that be?

"You all right, Sarah?"

She turned to him and nodded. "Let's go on back. I don't know what I was expecting to see."

"Would you feel better if he were in the kirkyard? We could do that."

"No. John's right. This is as good a place as any for his earthly body to rest."

"I'm just so sorry, Sarah."

"I know. Thanks."

A shout off in the distance made Mike turn in that direction. Sarah could see a figure running toward them across the pasture. It was the most direct route from Donovan's Lot but was rarely used because there was no road.

"It's Gavin," Mike said. He was moving toward the boy before Sarah even registered his words. She grabbed the reins of both horses and led them after Mike. When she reached the two, Gavin was gasping for breath. There was a gash on his forehead and his eyes looked wild. Frightened.

"Slow down, son. What's happened?"

"Da, they took the camp! They came from all sides and when we…it was all I could do…I hated to run but…Da, we have to hurry!"

"Gavin, lad, take a breath. Who's come? What's happened?"

Sarah stood, holding both horses, trying to fight down the panic that was rising up in her throat.

"It's them, Mike," she said. "It's Denny's gang. They've come for me."

"Are the women and children safely out at least?"

"They tried but was herded back into the center of camp. The blighters knew about the escape routes. Someone told 'em where they were."

Mike cursed. "How many of them are there?"

Gavin shook his head and looked back over his shoulder. "I guess, ten? Maybe more. They were on horseback. And they're armed, Da. They had automatic weapons."

Mike strode to his bay and pulled out his rifle. He checked the cartridges and handed it to Gavin. "Go to the tree overlooking the wash pond and climb to the top like we practiced."

Gavin took the gun, but before he could move away Mike grabbed him by the shoulder. "Wait for my signal. Don't just start shooting or they'll pick you off like a sitting duck."

"Right."

"Take Mrs. Woodson's horse. We'll double up. Now hurry!"

Sarah handed her reins to Gavin and watched him vault onto Dan's back and swivel him into a gallop back toward the community. She turned to Mike. "What are we going to do?"

"Do you remember exactly where David put the landmines by the goat pond?"

"I think so."

"Take me to them." He mounted his big bay and held out his hand to pull her up behind him on the saddle.

They cantered across the pasture with Sarah holding to Mike's waist. Out of the corner of her eye she could see the white cross that marked David's grave. The same people who put him there were back to kill more people she cared about. Somewhere deep inside her, a low, slow fury began to build.

She pointed to the southeast corner of the pond and Mike rode to it. She slid to the ground and ran to the spot where she had last seen the ordinances. She splashed into the soggy lip of the pond and pulled back the rushes. Mike jumped down to search too. She felt every precious second tick by, knowing those monsters were terrorizing the people at the community, the children, Fiona…

She felt a wave of relief that John wasn't there.

"Son of a bitch," Mike said in frustration and looked at her. She knew he desperately wanted a different answer but she didn't have one for him. She looked at the pond bank, willing herself to see them where they should be. But it was no use.

The landmines were gone.

***

They rode as close as they dared before Mike let his horse roam free and then walked the rest of the way to the camp. Mike touched her on the shoulder when they got close and held a finger to his lips.

She knew. The bastards would have sentries posted. As soon as Denny discovered she wasn't in the camp, he'd be waiting for her to make her entrance. She nodded and kept walking. When they were still far enough away not to be able to pick up sounds, Mike stopped. He brought his hands together and gave a birdcall.

Sarah frowned and looked around.

"Gavin?" she whispered.

He looked at her in frustration and what she thought looked very much like burgeoning fear. The sight of it made her stomach roil. "He should be here," he said in a low voice.

She scanned the treetops but could see nothing. "Could he have mistaken which tree you wanted him in?"

"No. He's trained in this tree for six months."

"Mike, we can't wait. Trust me, they're hurting people. We need to go." Sarah gave the trees one last look, hoping to catch sight of the boy, and then walked toward the camp. Mike hurried next to her until they could hear voices from the camp, then he tugged on her sleeve to indicate they should crouch in the bushes.

On her hands and knees, Sarah crept up to the camp until Denny's voice, the words still indistinct, seemed to be the only thing in her ears. Its loud nasal tone rang in the quiet of the early afternoon. When she got close enough to see him, she stopped. Mike bumped into her from behind and she put a hand out to tell him to stay down.

In the center of the camp, Denny stood next to a woman who he held wrapped in his arms. Sarah's eyes swept the crowd that lined the camp center. She was close enough to see the terror on their faces. The men had protective arms around their women and children. Even the camp dogs were quiet. Or had been slain.

Sarah stifled a gasp when Denny turned in her direction.

The woman he held was Fiona. One hand was entangled in her hair. The other held a large double-edged dagger to her bared throat.

Susan Kiernan-Lewis

Chapter Thirty-four

Sarah was on her feet and moving toward the center of camp before Mike fully processed what he was seeing. He jerked out an arm to pull her back but it was too late. He got to his feet, his hand on his hunting knife—the only weapon he had—and followed her.

"Stop it!" Sarah screamed as she entered the camp. "Leave her alone!"

A man came out of the bushes and grabbed Mike by the shoulders. With a grunt, he slammed Mike against a tree trunk. He was easily two inches shorter but Mike held up his hands in surrender. The man seized his knife then punched him in the stomach. Fighting for breath with a rasping groan, Mike folded up and sank to his knees, explosions of pain thrumming out from his core.

"Get up, ya bastard," the man snarled, delivering a vicious kick to Mike's midsection. "I can shoot ya here just as easy."

Mike forced himself to his feet, looking up in time to see Denny fling Fiona away and lunge for Sarah. Suddenly, a monstrous roar of noise bombarded the camp, hurling a cannonade of excruciating echo and sharp debris. A shower of rock and dirt pummeled the group as the thunderous salvo of sound strafed the camp.

A hut across the camp center collapsed and the jagged sounds of terrified screams mixed with the din of the aftershocks reverberating in the air.

Mike slammed his fist into the man's jaw, following it with a bone-crunching uppercut to the bastard's chin. The thug went down with a grunt and didn't get back up. Mike snatched up the man's gun and dashed toward the camp center, pushing past fleeing women and children.

Were the wankers bombing them?

He walked to the center of the camp—his arm outstretched pointing the gun at Denny. Fiona sat on the ground, stunned by the impact of the explosion. Mike breeched the outer ring of the camp's interior and saw Sarah struggling between two men who held her.

"You've got one minute to clear out," he bellowed to Denny, who pivoted around to face him. He was disconcertingly confident, Mike thought, for having a gun pointed at his head.

"Really? And how about *you've* got one minute to *live*," Denny retorted, a malicious grin stretching across his face.

Mike made a quick assessment of the situation. Sarah captured, most of the camp, including the men, fled into the woods—at least a dozen fatigue-clad hoodlums, including one woman, running unchecked, knocking over cook pots and ransacking the tents and huts.

He heard the ominous sounds of multiple guns cocking and chambering their rounds—and all of them pointed at him.

"Drop it, matey," Denny said. He jerked his head to indicate Fiona on the ground. "I'm afraid I won't give your sister my best performance with you holding a gun on me."

Mike pulled the trigger at the same moment a terrible pressure imploded at the back of his head. Seconds later, he realized he had blacked out and was being dragged facedown in the dirt. All his senses were engulfed by an embracing, crushing pain in his head. He felt rivulets of blood streaming down his face as he fought to come fully conscious.

He could hear Sarah's voice—hysterically pitched and shrieking—and Fiona's screams. His stomach clenched in a nauseating whirl of motion as strong hands heaved him over onto his back and wrenched him into a sitting position against the porch.

"Oy, Jason! Denny wants him awake."

The man, Jason, backhanded him hard across the mouth. "Oy! Wake up, ye bogger."

The woman held a gun to Mike's head. "Come on now, Buck, open those pretty blues. I know you're not gonna want to miss this."

When he tried to move, the pain became a fusillade of agonizing spasms that migrated from the back of his head to the front. The intensified pitch of Fiona's screams cleared his double vision back into single focus. He tried to get up and felt the gun barrel pressed against his cheek.

"Settle down, big fella," the woman said. "Your turn's coming. Woulda shot ya before now, but Denny wants everyone alive for the show."

Mike could see both Fiona and Sarah on their knees, holding each other by the main campfire. The maniac, Denny, was walking in front of them, waving his gun. Although Mike couldn't hear what he was saying, from his body language, it was clear he was gearing up for something. Sarah's back was to Mike, but Fiona's face was visible over her shoulder. Her eyes were squeezed shut and her lips moving in prayer.

Mike surged to his feet with a roar, knocking the woman backward onto the porch steps in the process. He nearly made it as far as the camp center before Denny whirled around and brought his pistol up to take aim. Mike knew there was no way he would reach him before the bugger pulled the trigger.

He tucked his head and charged.

***

The sound of Angie's scream jerked Sarah out of her cocoon of hopeless inevitability and she twisted around to see Mike, his head bloodied, his eyes unfocused, staggering toward her and Fiona while Denny drew a bead on him.

Sarah closed her eyes, burying her face in Fiona's neck. When she heard the gunshot, she forced herself to look back at the body—Mike's body—on the ground. But what she saw instead didn't make sense.

Mike was still coming.

Had Denny missed? At that range? Had his gun misfired?

Denny, screaming in rage and pain, turned away from Mike's advance. Sarah saw Denny's face contorted in agony as he reached for the handle of the knife protruding from his left thigh where somebody had thrown it.

Mike hit him from behind, knocking the gun from his grip. Sarah pulled free of Fiona and scrambled to her feet as Mike lifted Denny in the air and heaved him onto the campfire.

She had to get that gun.

Denny crawled out of the fire, slapping at the embers on his pant legs and bellowing bloody retribution, his eyes searching the ground for his weapon. When Sarah saw it, lying in the dirt not two steps from where she stood, she lunged for it. But before she could reach it, a tall man wearing rags and rings in his dreadlocks appeared as if from nowhere and scooped it up in one fluid movement. He hefted the weapon in his hand and gave Sarah a large, toothy grin. She staggered backwards in shock.

"Declan!"

Declan turned and shouted to six men who were with him. Together they swarmed the camp, wielding clubs, hammers and hatchets. Sarah ran to Fiona and Mike, who watched the gypsies in stark amazement.

"It's the gypsies!" Sarah said. "The ones I met on the road!"

Mike nodded to indicate he understood, then picked up a large piece of firewood and entered the fray. "Go to the woods!" he shouted.

Sarah grabbed Fiona's hand and ran to the edge of the camp, where she stopped and grabbed up a knife that was on the ground. "You go on, Fi," she said. "Tell the men to come back and help."

"You come with me."

"Just go!" Sarah gave her a hard push and ran back to the camp.

The scene at the center of camp was bedlam. If it weren't for the gypsies looking like a band of rioting homeless people, Sarah wouldn't have been able to tell the good guys apart from the thugs. Even with the gypsies' help, she knew that short-handled knives and pieces of firewood were no match against automatic weapons.

Taken by surprise as the invaders had been, no shots had yet been fired. But that wouldn't last forever.

If they didn't get those automatic weapons away from them soon...

She looked wildly around to see Mike in the melee, or Denny. And she looked for one other. She searched for the one man she knew she had been looking for from the moment she stepped back into camp—the man called Jeff.

When she finally caught a glimpse of him in the same ugly black trainers and filthy jeans he had been wearing in their last encounter, he was standing—gun in hand, talking animatedly to Angie. Sarah's stomach clenched and a vision of that afternoon in the pasture came rushing back to her. She remembered his laughing eyes as he regarded her terror. She remembered how he tricked her into dropping her gun.

And she remembered what happened next.

Without even knowing she was doing it, Sarah moved toward him. Two other gang members joined Angie and Jeff, and Sarah watched as Angie pointed to the camp exit that led to the grain storage area where the community kept their food and seed supply.

So it was true. They know every point of entry to the camp, and every weakness.

Jeff nodded and then, with the two other men, ran in the direction Angie had pointed.

Sarah couldn't let them do whatever they intended on doing.

She couldn't let David's killer get away.

Sarah skirted the worst of the hand-to-hand fighting by jumping on porch fronts and over collapsed tents to reach the exit where the men had gone. Most of the men from Donovan's Lot, and even some of the women, had returned to help fight. It wouldn't matter, though, if they couldn't disarm Denny's thugs before they started shooting.

The exit Jeff and his group slipped through was just a gap between two large tents, but before Sarah could reach it the thunderous rumble of a second explosion erupted, knocking her off her feet. This time, large stones and rocks flew through the air. Sarah crawled behind one of the short stonewalls that lined a section of the camp's perimeter and covered her head with her arms.

A gypsy fighter lay stunned next to a jagged boulder, a thin line of blood creeping down his face. When she saw the smoking rubble strewn around the camp—the fighters momentarily dazed or running for cover—she realized that the explosion must have come from somewhere near the cairn.

As Sarah stood up, she saw the bloody stump of a leg with the foot still attached lying inches from where she had crouched.

The foot was still wearing a black trainer.

The sound of the explosion seemed to come seconds after Mike felt the ground jerk away beneath his feet. He released the man he'd been grappling with and the body fell limply to the ground like a discarded rag doll, Mike's knife embedded in his ribs.

Mike jerked the knife out and lurched to his feet. Two of the camp tents by the main fire had been flattened and their canvas was now flapping wildly. He tried to find Sarah but all he could see were the small groups of grappling men.

And then he saw Denny. His leg was crudely tied with a piece of shirtsleeve that was already sodden red and he was attempting to pick himself up from the last blast.

Mike watched in disbelief as Denny aimed his gun at a scrum of men wrestling on the ground near the fire and fired into the midst of them. Someone howled and the other three jerked away and separated.

The psycho had shot his own man.

Mike grabbed up the automatic rifle from the man whose neck he had just broken and tossed it to the big gypsy, Declan, as he ran past. "Find Sarah!" he yelled. Declan nodded and reversed course, running through the growing smoke that was starting to envelop the camp and quickly disappeared.

"Correy!" Mike bellowed as he crossed the camp toward him. "Drop your gun, arsehole and call your men off." He watched Denny face him, his face creased with rage and frustration.

"You sorry Irish bastard!" Denny shrieked. "I'll have her and then my men will have her—"

Mike reached him and backhanded him before Denny could get his gun aimed, knocking it out of his hand. Denny lunged at him, grasping Mike's head in his hands and smashing his own hard into his forehead. Mike crumpled to his knees, his eyesight gone to black, his head a blinding monument of agony. He reached, unseeing, for Denny's face as he went down, trying to pull the bastard down with him.

"I'll gut you like the fish you smell like, you country shite," Denny snarled, panting. Mike felt Denny's fingers working to pry Mike's knife from his hand. When that happened, it would be all over.

Blindly, Mike released the knife, then grasped Denny's head between his hands—and wrenched.

A woman's strangled scream jerked Sarah's attention away from the piece of bloody leg. Angie stood not twenty feet from her, staring at the wreckage the bomb had created. Behind her, three of Denny's men stood with their automatic rifles to their shoulders. They were aiming into the crowd of gypsy fighters.

Angie shifted her gaze from the smoking rocks and body parts to Sarah. They locked eyes. Sarah saw the ugly stub of a gun appear in Angie's hand.

Angie took aim and Sarah dove for cover.

She heard the shot but felt no impact. She tried to protect her head with her arms, but heard no other shot fired. Sarah peeked out from under her arms in time to see Angie drop to her knees, her hands clutching a gaping wound in her stomach. Gore poured from the wound, pumping the bloody life force from her body.

When Sarah snapped her head around to see where the shot had come from, she saw Declan standing behind her, the rifle he'd shot Angie with still to his shoulder. He adjusted his stance and aimed his rifle at the three gunmen standing behind Angie.

Sarah knew she and Declan didn't stand a chance against them. She closed her eyes, took a breath and held it, waiting.

Finally, when nothing happened, she opened her eyes to see Denny's men, one by one, lowering their weapons. One even dropped his in the dirt.

She turned to Declan. His face was streaked with blood and one eye was closed. There was an open gash on the side of his head and the hand that gripped the gun was caked with dirt and blood. "What's happening?" she asked hoarsely. "Are they giving up?"

The big gypsy glanced away and Sarah followed his direction to see Denny, walking with difficulty between Mike and one of Declan's gypsy brothers. As they approached, Sarah could see that Denny wasn't walking at all. Nor would he ever again.

Mike heaved Denny's body on the ground. Denny's neck flopped at an unnatural angle. As Sarah turned away, her stomach roiling, she saw Denny's men move in to look at the body of their fallen leader.

"Head of the snake," Declan muttered. "They're not going to fight on if he's not here to make 'em."

Declan stepped over Denny's body and held his hand out to Mike. "Met your Sarah on the road. Said if I was ever in Ireland,

I needed to come look up Mike Donovan. Didn't expect to have to work for my supper, though."

Mike grinned and clasped the gypsy's hand before Sarah launched herself into Declan's arms. "Thank you, Declan," she said, tears streaming down her dirt-streaked face. "Thank God for you."

***

Sarah knelt by Angie. She could see there was nothing they had in the way of first aid that was going to make any difference but she couldn't let her die alone. She eased Angie's head onto her lap.

Around them, the camp was noisy with people righting carts, and bandaging wounds. The laughter that floated over the noise told Sarah that none of their own had been seriously hurt. She could see Mike and Declan, shoulder to shoulder, as they labored to put the camp back to order.

Denny's men had melted into the woods.

"I always wondered if they'd fight on without Denny," Angie said, grimacing against the bleeding wound in her middle that she clutched with both hands. "If I'd only killed the bastard myself. I had plenty of opportunities. I can't believe it's going down like this." She coughed and cried out. Sarah didn't speak. She hoped it was enough that she was here. She wasn't sure she had the stomach to offer anything more.

"You were right, Yank." Angie's eyes fluttered and finally closed. "I have a little girl. Named Dana."

Sarah scanned the camp. It was still smoking in spots from where the cairn had exploded.

Angie coughed again. "I was just trying to give her a chance to grow up, same as you and your lad."

"Angie, I..." Sarah stopped talking when she realized Angie had had the last word. She touched the woman's no longer tortured brow. "Sleep now, Angie," she said. "It's over."

***

Mike sat on the top porch step and surveyed the cleanup while Fiona wrapped a clean bandage around his head. It still hurt like bloody blazes, but his eyesight had at least returned to normal and he could only hope the pain—if it was just a concussion—would soon abate.

"You sure you're okay, Fi?"

"Sure, why wouldn't I be?"

"Okay, very funny. Just trying to be brotherly."

"Well, at least you can feel a little less guilty about young John not being anywhere near all of this."

"That thought did run through my mind," he admitted, "in my ever-ongoing quest to think on the bright side of things while people are trying to kill me and mine."

"Speaking of which, you seen Caitlin recently?"

He winced as she tied the knot to secure the bandage. "I'll deal with it, Fi."

"You know it had to be her told them all our secrets."

"I said I'd deal with it."

"Well, you'd best get ready to do it because here she comes as bold as chalk, *and* with one of 'em!"

Mike looked up to see Caitlin walking down the center path of the camp, hanging on the arm of a large man with an ugly cut across his forehead. It was the man who'd attacked him in the woods.

She must have been waiting in the woods until the battle was over, Mike thought as she and the English wanker stood in front of him.

"I'll be needing Fiona to tend to the injuries that your *bowsies* gave me Aidan. He'll be staying with me in me tent."

Had the daft bitch gone mental? Maybe Fi was right and she really was insane.

Mike stood up, feeling the sky sway just a bit. "Take this piece of shite and piss off, Caitlin. You're not welcome here. Be glad I don't dip you in tar first."

Her mouth fell open in astonishment. "You can't throw me out! I'm your kin!"

"You're nothing to me. Now bugger off. Don't make me lay hands on you."

Aidan snarled at him. "I'd like to see you try, you big Irish bastard."

Before Mike could respond, Sarah, who he'd last seen sitting with the woman Declan had shot, stepped forward. She must have come over as soon as she saw Caitlin return to camp.

"A word, Mike," Sarah said turning to stare at Caitlin and Aidan. "Do we have laws in Donovan's Lot?"

He frowned. "Aye. We do."

Sarah pointed to Aidan. "This man aided in the murder of my husband, David Woodson."

Aidan dropped Caitlin's arm. "She lies!"

Sarah stepped up to him and put her face into his. "I *saw* you."

Mike jumped down from the porch and pulled Sarah back as he bellowed out, "Jimmy! Patrick!"

Aidan whirled and ran four steps before two men standing nearby tackled him.

"Tie him up," Mike said. "Throw him in the granary. I'll deal with him later."

Caitlin flew at Mike, her fists pounding his chest until he pushed her away and she fell in the dirt. "You can't do this!" she cried as Aidan was dragged away cursing and fighting.

"I can. And you've got two minutes to leave on your own steam, Caitlin. After that I'll lock you up so you can answer for your hand in today's events."

Caitlin looked at him, disbelieving, then climbed to her feet. She gave Sarah a look of loathing.

"Sixty seconds," Mike said.

"I'll see you in Hell, Mike Donovan! You and your Yankee whore!"

Sarah watched until Caitlin disappeared into the woods and then she turned to Mike. "What will you do with him?"

"There's no traveling magistrate to hear the case, Sarah, if that's what you're asking," he said wearily. "I'm the law here. He

289

abetted in David's murder." He sat down heavily on the porch, as if standing were suddenly too taxing, and looked into her face, his expression stern and unrelenting. "So he dies."

Suddenly, Fiona jumped down from the porch. "It's Gavin!" she called. "He's safe, Mike. Thank the Lord."

Mike looked up to see the miraculous sight of his only child loping into the center of camp on Sarah's horse, beaming and looking very much like he had something to do with today's victory. A wave of relief cascaded over him. Now he could relax. Now he could finally rest.

Fiona ran up to Gavin when he dismounted and he picked her up and swung her in a wide arc. She squealed.

"We did it, Auntie!" he said. "I just wished I coulda seen the expressions on those bastards' faces."

Fiona laughed. "Was that *you* made all those explosions and saved our lives you big gobshite?"

Gavin walked over to where Mike and Sarah waited on the porch steps, both of them smiling to see him unharmed and well. "You know," he said, grinning, "much as I'd love to take the credit, I reckon that mostly it was all John." He looked at Sarah and grinned even more broadly.

Mike watched as Sarah looked at Gavin and then, her hand covering her mouth to stifle a gasp. Immediately over Gavin's shoulder, jogging up the main center of camp, was twelve-year-old John Woodson, grinning from ear to ear.

Chapter Thirty-five

Sarah knew that no matter how long she lived she would never get her fill of looking at him. She gazed at her son as he sat at the dinner table, laughing and shoving with Mike's boy, Gavin, and she knew she hadn't stopped smiling since the moment she had seen him trot down the center aisle of camp, his face filthy, his hair wild around his head, straight for her. For the time it took for her to see him coming toward her—unharmed and jubilant —and then feel him in her arms again, Sarah knew she would never ask for more in this lifetime.

Like most miracles, how it all came about was as thrilling a story of luck and happenstance combined with the stubbornness of the human spirit as there could ever be.

"When the pilot told me they had news of a VIP they needed to stop for in Limerick, I could see by the way he was looking at me that if I wanted to wander off from a bathroom break when we stopped they wouldn't look too hard for me." John bit into his third sandwich as he told his tale.

Sarah kept one hand on his arm the whole time, as if to confirm to herself that he was really there, flesh and blood.

"Who was the VIP?' Gavin asked.

Fiona slapped him playfully on the back of the head. "What does it matter? Let him tell the story!"

"Oh, no, Aunt, Fi," John said. "That's the cool part." He looked at his mother. "It was Prince William. He was on a fishing trip in Ireland and was in a hurry to get back to London."

"Mercy," Fiona said. "You gave your seat up for the future King of England? Well done, lad!"

"Yeah, well, I would've given it up for a French poodle if it meant I could get back home."

"So you walked all the way from Limerick?" Declan asked. He sat beside Mike as the two smoked and sipped whiskey. Sarah was delighted, but not surprised, to see the obvious beginning of a strong friendship.

John shook his head. "The pilot put me down nearer to Adare. It's only twenty miles or so and the weather was fine."

"You just slipped away?" Mike was shaking his head, either at the simplicity of it all or the grotesque priorities of the pilot choosing a celebrity over the young American who had been his first responsibility.

"Yeah, and when I got nearly to camp I ran into Gavin who told me what was happening."

Mike looked at his son. "Is that why you weren't where you were supposed to be?" he asked pointedly.

"Sorry, Da," Gavin said, and there was something about the way he answered that told Sarah that Gavin had grown up since she'd last seen him. "It's true I wasn't where you told me to be, but I reckon I was exactly where I was *supposed* to be."

"What riddle is this?" Mike growled.

"It's on account of me, sir," John said, looking at Mike. "And I'm sorry for making Gav disobey you. But I had to."

"Go on."

"Well," John said, reaching for a small sugar cake from the plate Fiona extended to him. "I figured I knew better 'coz I had intel that you didn't."

Mike snorted but didn't respond.

"So *why* did you not want Gavin in the tree his da told him to be in?" Fiona asked.

John put the cake down and wiped his fingers on his sleeve. Sarah could see that, although he was still the same size since she last saw him, his eyes seemed to belong to a much older boy.

"Uncle Mike wanted him in a certain tree as a sniper, but I needed him in a different tree so he could detonate the land mines."

"You replanted the land mines after I told your father to dig them up and remove them?" Mike spoke evenly, but Sarah could tell there was no heat in his voice.

"Yes sir, I did," John said, meeting his eyes. "My dad was right about needing those mines to defend the community. You must've thought the same thing when you found out we were under attack, 'coz my mom said you went looking for them."

Sarah stole a glance at Mike. He didn't say anything.

"The weeks you were gone, Mom, I did a lot of thinking about a lot of things. I figured Dad was right about us needing the explosives, but Uncle Mike was right, too, about not wanting people to accidentally walk on 'em. I figured, since they could be detonated by any mechanism that could activate their blasting caps, we didn't have to use them as somebody stepping on 'em."

"A bullet would work," Gavin said.

"Right. So I buried 'em in the cairn where nobody goes and under the stonewall by the eastern pasture."

"And then forgot to tell anyone about it," Gavin said, elbowing John good-naturedly.

John grinned. "Yeah. I meant to tell Gav, but next thing I know I'm on a helicopter and nobody knows but me that the whole place is rigged to blow with two well-placed hits."

"How did you know when to time the explosions?" Declan asked.

John shrugged. "I didn't. The first one, we just let 'er rip. We didn't have a plan at all. The second time, though..." John stopped speaking and Sarah found herself holding her breath.

The second time, Sarah knew, John had seen the three men exit the camp and saw that they would walk right by the cairn where the explosive was planted.

What he *didn't* know, she thought as she watched him struggle with the thought of what he had done, was that he had given the signal that killed the man who murdered his father. She didn't know if she would ever tell him that.

"Well," Mike said, finishing off his whiskey. "I'd like to raise a toast to young John, here, and Declan and his family, without whose help in defending Donovan's Lot we'd none of us be here to give a toast."

Everyone seconded the toast and drank. Sarah's eyes stung with tears as she watched her son.

"And I'd also like to raise a glass to the memory of David Woodson," Mike said. Sarah picked up her glass again and felt the tears streak down her face. "Who was right, when I was wrong. And being right helped save us all on this day."

"Hear, hear," the room chorused as everyone drank.

Sarah saw Mike exchange a look with John over the cheers and conversation of the group. She saw Mike nod and John smile in response.

That night, as Sarah sat next to John on his bed in Fiona's cottage, she felt a warmth radiating throughout her body that left her tingling with joy. To touch him again, to watch his expressions, to hold him just by reaching out…she couldn't remember a time when she felt more grace than she felt right now. It had been a long day and they were both exhausted, but still she hesitated to leave him to go to her bed, even as weary as she was. And so she sat near him as he talked, his eyelids growing heavier and heavier.

"I knew you weren't dead, Mom. I mean, if you were dead, I know I'd have felt it." He yawned and rubbed his eyes. "I just knew you were somewhere in the world. You know what I mean?"

Sarah leaned over and kissed him, a vision of dear Evvie coming to mind and prompting an exhausted smile though her tears. "I do, sweetie," she said as she watched her boy fall into sleep before her eyes. "I know exactly what you mean."

Chapter Thirty-six

Dear Mom and Dad,

As I write this, I have in front of me a letter that was delivered to me from you a month ago. As far as I can tell, it was written a month before that. I can't tell you of the joy and relief I felt when I saw your handwriting again, Mom! Knowing that you and Dad are alive and well, and that Jacksonville was not even touched by this international incident has given me more strength and hope than I can say.

John and I are both fine and I tell you that straightaway because I have some devastatingly bad news and I need you to brace yourselves. A little over two months ago, the cottage where David and John and I lived was attacked by raiders and David was killed. Even writing the words I have to stop and have a good cry. Maybe it'll always be that way.

It's hard for me to believe, even two months later, that David didn't survive this ordeal of ours. It's especially painful when I see signs every day that John and I may be able to go home soon—and yet David won't be coming with us. I don't know whom else you might notify about David. His parents, as you know, are both gone and he had no siblings.

In the interim two months, many things have happened, and not all of them bad. After David was killed, I travelled to a small town somewhere in the Cotswolds. In the column of "not all bad," is the fact that I met many good people as I made my way back across the UK and Wales. One of them was a young gypsy girl who did everything she could to sacrifice her life so that I could get back to John in Ireland. She was more than just a brave, heroic girl, though. While we traveled together I found her funny, optimistic, affectionate and incredibly resilient. If I were to tell you what her childhood was like, you'd be amazed that she could even laugh, let alone be the plucky, lovely girl she was.

Sarah stared out the window, the tears gathering in her eyes once more at the thought of Papin. She forced herself to turn away from the sounds of the children's laughter out her window to concentrate on her letter.

Well, folks, the sun is starting to dip, which actually begins the busiest part of my day because it means dinner preparation. Sometimes I long for the days of a frozen peel-back carton and a microwave oven. Ha ha. Just kidding. What do I mean "sometimes?"

Anyway, love to you both. I can't tell you how relieved I was to get your letter and to know that all is well with you both at home. The helicopter the came for us last month gave me confidence that one day our trial here will be done and John and I will both be back home again.

In the meantime, please know that we are both well and we are happy.

Love,
Your daughter,
Sarah

PS - I forgot to mention, in case you were worried about where I'm living, that Mike Donovan, who runs the big community here, has moved me and John into a very sweet little cottage right in the middle of the community boundaries—in fact very near his own hut. So we are safe and snug amidst our friends and dear ones.

Until I see you again....

Sarah set her pen down and carefully folded the letter. She placed it inside the large wooden box that Mike had brought from the cottage she'd shared with David. The box had belonged to Deirdre.

Out the window, she could see John on his pony. He looked like he was giving riding lessons to some of the smaller children. It hadn't been that long ago—not quite a year—when he had climbed onto the back of a horse for the first time himself. She saw Mike join the group. He held a piece of a plough in his hands and she guessed he was on his way to the work shed with it.

Seeing him unexpectedly sent a tiny thrill through her that she had come to expect whenever she saw him. She didn't know what her life going forward in *Donovan's Lot* would be like, but she had a feeling it would always be strongly affected by the undeniable pull she felt in the big Irishman's direction.

While it had only been a week since she and Mike had made their way back to the camp, it had taken every ounce of self-restraint she had not to harangue him on a daily basis about going back to Wales to look for Papin.

Tonight was the night, she knew. After everything she had been through, the time for waiting was through. She straightened her back to physically steel her resolve.

A head popped up in the window outside Sarah's writing table making her jump, and then laugh when she realized it was John still sitting on his pony.

"Hey, Mom, Aunt Fi wants to know if we're eating communal tonight again. She's got a big lamb stew and I told her you baked today."

"Yes, sweetie, of course," Sarah said. "Go ahead and feed Star and put him up for the night. I'll be there directly."

"Uncle Mike's coming, too, Mom. He's gonna show me and Gav how to do that disappearing card trick thing."

***

Sarah was amazed that she could find such pleasure after so many weeks of horror. The days and weeks of living like an animal—ready to kill at any moment, ready to distrust any kind face or motive—had disappeared after just a few days of being back in the loving embrace of her friends and family. As she looked around the dinner table she thought that tonight was a perfect example of that.

Fiona was as bossy as ever, instructing where everyone should eat and whacking reaching hands with a ready wooden spoon, but there was a glint of humor in her eye.

And something more.

The gypsy, Declan, had taken to spending more and more time at her table. And in her front parlor. And trailing behind her as she went to bring in the goats…

At first glance, Sarah thought they were the ultimate mismatch. The fisherman's daughter and the gypsy. But listening to them interact had changed her mind. And looking at Fiona's face when she watched Declan helped change her mind, too. It was hard to argue that something was wrong when it created such a picture of happiness in the beaming face of your best friend.

Mike sat next to Sarah, as he always did. Sarah knew there was a change in their relationship—although it was, of course, unspoken and as yet not acted upon. Partly it was because David was out of the picture, and Sarah knew that. But it was also because of what the two of them had recently endured—for the sake of the other. Now that Sarah was safely back at camp with John she realized she had been trying to get back to Mike nearly as much.

Which did not change the fact that she had a serious bone to pick with him.

After supper, Sarah shooed everyone out of Fiona's kitchen—except Mike—and turned to the sink full of dirty dishes.

"I'll be thanking you for recruiting me for the wash up," he said drily, picking up a dishtowel. "I often wonder how I'll unwind after a hard day of mending fences, chasing goats around the pasture and breaking up fights in camp."

Sarah laughed but didn't speak.

He sighed and reached for a dish. "Let's have it, Sarah. I know you've got something to say."

"And you know what it is, too," Sarah said, plunging her hands into the cold soapy dishwater.

He sighed again. "I was hoping you'd let it alone by now."

"I have to know what happened to her."

"Some things are best not known."

"This isn't one of them." She turned to him, her hands dripping on the floor. "I can't leave John again and he won't let me go alone."

"And I won't let you go, period."

"Oh, so is this Donovan's Lot the Dictatorship now?"

"My God, woman, it never ends with you, does it? We're all finally back in one piece and you're ready to go dig up more trouble."

"That's just it, Mike. I'm *not* in one piece until I find out what happened to her."

"Even if what you find out is...is..."

"Yes. Even then."

"Da, let me go," Gavin coming from the other room where he'd obviously been listening. "I can be to the coast and back in three days. Me and Benjy are dying to stretch our legs a bit."

Mike hesitated just long enough. "God, the pair of ya, will be the death of me," he said looking at Sarah and Gavin together. "But the answer's still no. It's too dangerous and I'll not have it. Everyone stays put where I can keep an eye on 'em. And that's me last word on the subject."

Sarah nodded sadly and turned back to the dishes. "I understand, Mike," she said quietly. "I don't want to be any more trouble than I already have been. I'm sorry."

"Ahhh, stop that, now," Mike said throwing the dishtowel over his shoulder. "Bugger me if I can't get comfortable for five fecking minutes without someone wanting me to step in front of a bullet or put me hand up a cow's arse."

"Well, I'm not sure about that last bit," Sarah said, fighting to keep the amusement and hope out of her voice, "but I mean, you just said *I* can't do it. So..."

"Yes, fine," Mike said. He looked at Gavin who seemed to be literally jumping up and down at the prospect. "We'll go. We'll go. Tomorrow at first light." He tossed down the dishtowel onto the counter. "I assume this means I'm at least released from KP duty?"

Sarah dried her hands and slipped into his arms, resting her head against his broad chest. When she felt him pull her in closer with one large hand stroking her on her back, she forced herself to step away and turn back to the dishes. The warmth of emotion—and *desire*—that flooded through her body shocked her with its urgency.

More than that, she realized, blushing and breathless with guilt and longing, was the stunning realization that nothing in her life up to now had ever felt more right than the few seconds she had just experienced in his arms.

***

The ride to Boreen on well-rested horses with a full saddlebag full of food and water made all the difference in the world, Mike thought bemusedly. He glanced over at Gavin who appeared happy just to be out in the world, regardless of the weather, the reason or errand. Mike had warned him they would likely come back empty handed— or worse, with news that would not comfort anyone, but the lad seemed as focused on the adventure of it all than the outcome.

They arrived at Boreen by midday and boarded the ferry to Fishguard by late afternoon. Once cross the Channel, Mike gave Gavin the reins to both horses and told him to wait for him. Although clearly disappointed not to be joining his father as he searched the bars and brothels of Fishguard, Gavin wisely, did not openly complain.

There were several reasons why Mike hated this errand, not least of which was the fact that if he found out what happened to the gypsy and it was bad, Sarah would be stricken. And if he found out nothing, the stubborn lass would likely never give up the search.

What do they call that? Lose-lose?

In the first two hours in Fishguard combing the harbor bars, he bought four beers with money he did not have to throw away and questioned dozens of fishermen, tradesmen, travelers and anybody else who looked like they might know something.

Before he stumbled, fuzzy-headed and discouraged, to where Gavin sat with the horses to find a place for the night, he'd been told by no fewer than three people that they'd heard of a little gypsy girl who'd been killed two weeks earlier.

One said he heard she'd been strangled. One said stabbed. The other couldn't remember.

"Does that mean we know what happened to her?" Gavin asked, finishing off the last of their grub as Mike untacked the horses and brushed them down for the night.

"It's not proof enough," Mike said.

"Will you need to see the body?"

"I don't know what I'll need," Mike said truthfully. "I just know that hearsay isn't enough."

They slept the night in the stall next to their horses. The next morning, Mike told Gavin not to bothering tacking up. Just stay with the horses until Mike returned.

"Some adventure," Gavin said. "Here I am in Wales and I'm seeing the inside of a fecking stable."

Mike chose to ignore the grumbling. "I'll bring you back lunch," he said, checking his pockets to see how much coin he had left. Not much.

A light rap on the stall door startled them both and they looked at each other warily.

"Well, you *were* asking a lot of questions to a lot of people," Gavin whispered, shrugging.

"Come in," Mike said, pulling his rifle out of his saddle sheath.

The heavy stable door creaked open and a young boy poked his head through. "Oy, mister? You lookin' for the gypsy girl?"

Mike put the gun back and beckoned for the boy to enter. "What do you know about her?"

"You related to her or something?" the boy asked, still not completely entering the stable.

"Something like that. Can I give you an American dollar to hear what you know?" The money wasn't worth anything as far as buying beer but the contents of Sarah's billfold might be useful in other ways.

"Cor, really? A greenback? Can I see it?"

"If you can tell me where I can find the gypsy girl, you can have it."

The boy licked his lips and stepped into the stable. "She's at me auntie Mabel's place."

Mike held out the dollar to him but when the boy reached for it, Mike didn't let go. "Where is your auntie Mabel's place, if I may be so bold?"

The boy jerked his head to indicate it was outside the stable. "I'll lead ya," he said. "I'll take ya straight there. But ya gotta be quiet, like. The girls is all sleeping this early."

"The girls?"

"Blimey, Da," Gavin said. "He's taking ya to a whorehouse!"

Mike released the dollar to the boy who examined it closely and then folded it and stuck it in his pocket.

"So she's alive?"

The boy stopped and frowned. "I'm not sure," he said. "She was pretty smashed up when they dumped her at me Auntie Mabel's. But I think she was alive last time I saw her."

"When was that?" Mike pulled on his jacket.

"A week ago?"

Mike's stomach muscles clenched, but he nodded to the boy. "Take me there, son," he said. "And hurry."

If you want to see what happens next to Sarah, John and Mike, check out *Heading Home*, Book 3 in the Irish End Game Series.

ABOUT THE AUTHOR

Susan Kiernan-Lewis lives in Florida and writes mysteries and romantic suspense. Like many authors, Susan depends on the reviews and word of mouth referrals of her readers. If you enjoyed *Going Gone*, please consider leaving a review saying so on Amazon.com, Barnesandnoble.com or Goodreads.com.

Check out Susan's blog at susankiernanlewis.com and feel free to contact her at sanmarcopress@me.com.

AUTHOR'S NOTES:

For anyone who's Welsh or looks at a map, you may notice that I moved *Merlins Bridge* from south of *Haverfordwest* to north of it, around where *Spittal* is located. Sorry for any confusion, but I couldn't give up the wonderful name of *Merlins Bridge* and it was a necessary plot point that Sarah travel to a ferry crossing by way of it.

Susan Kiernan-Lewis

Going Gone

32039772R00190

Made in the USA
San Bernardino, CA
10 April 2019